Truly,
Madly,
Amy

BOOKS BY KERRY WILKINSON

Truly, Madly, Amy

KERRY WILKINSON

bookouture

Published by Bookouture in 2022

An imprint of Storyfire Ltd.
Carmelite House
50 Victoria Embankment
London EC4Y 0DZ

www.bookouture.com

ISBN: 978-1-80314-273-9
eBook ISBN: 978-1-80314-272-2

1

PARACHUTE

I was hoping the parachute didn't spring open when I first met Amy Ashworth.

It was heavier than I thought, packed tight into an oversized rucksack. The sort of thing people wear when they've spent too much money in an outdoors shop. They end up taking gentle, flat walks through the woods, weighed down by more gear than they'd need if they were trekking across the Arctic.

Or, more obviously, the type of thing someone wears before jumping out of a plane.

I lugged the bag down from the shelf and almost dropped it when the tent flap opened and in walked a girl. I didn't know her name then but it was easy enough to recognise her as one of the counsellors. Everyone our age at Camp Sycamore was a counsellor of some sort and, on that first day, that first morning, she was as bemused and wide-eyed as the rest of us. Our matching white camp T-shirts, with the green tree logo, were all clean at the start, free from the mud and sweat that would come soon enough.

The girl flipped her long black hair away from her face and

blinked out of the sun into the gloomy interior of the supply tent.

'That looks heavy,' she said.

I heaved the parachute bag up onto a table and it thundered down with a *whump* that echoed around the small space.

'It's not too bad,' I replied, gasping, which made her laugh right away.

I've wondered in the years since if that's where it began. You hear people talk about losing themselves in someone else's eyes, or smell, or touch – but it was that laugh. That, once I'd heard it, there was no going back.

'You sound like my dad,' she said, before slipping into a mock man's voice. *'Oh, it's not the weight, it's the shape. It's not heavy, just awkward.'* Back into her own voice. 'Then he puts his back out and that's it for the next month.'

The enclosed space inside the tent had rows of shelves pressed to the edges, with boxes, bags and cans rammed up against one another. The shelves ran the entire way around and, with the table as well, there wasn't much room for a person, let alone two.

She scanned the shelves for a moment, craning around me, and then chewed the corner of her mouth.

'Bandages...' she said, before focusing in on me. Her accent reminded me a bit of the women who sit outside the tea shops in town. The ones who hold their teacup handles between thumb and index finger, with their little fingers sticking out. There was a hint of their poshness to her but something else, too. As if she was never more than a word or two away from laughing, or making a joke.

'If you were a bandage, where would you be?' she added.

'Medical bay?'

The girl nodded along. 'That's where I've just come from. No bandages there.'

'Wouldn't that be the best place for them?'

'You'd think so. If you want cotton wool, they have loads of it. Bandages? Not one.'

She picked up a box from the shelf, took off the lid, looked inside, then put it back.

'What happened?' I asked.

The girl waved an arm in the vague direction of the field beyond the tent. 'Camper tripped over a tent peg.'

'That is the problem with tents,' I replied. 'Lots of ropes. Lots of pegs.'

'Yeah...' She nodded along and checked another box, then another, before letting out a long *hrmmmm*.

'Is she hurt?' I asked.

'Twisted ankle. It'll probably be OK.'

'Is that the nursing degree telling you that?'

She laughed again, more of a snort this time. 'Bandages...'

The girl opened another box and so I joined in. We went along the shelves together opening and closing various containers until, eventually, she let out a gentle 'A-ha!' as she held up a box containing bandages. She put it on the table, next to the bagged parachute and then lifted a few out, checking underneath to see what else was in the box. As it turned out, there were more bandages.

'I think I should probably take these to the medical bay,' she said.

'That's where I'd be if I were a bandage.'

We nodded at each other in agreement and then she took a half-step backwards before stopping and turning back to me.

'Are you one of the famous assistant counsellors?' she asked.

'I'm not so sure about the "famous" part – but I am an assistant counsellor.'

More nodding, mainly her this time. She pouted her lip out a little, head slightly tilted. 'Are you the only one? It feels like you're going to be very busy if you are.'

It was my turn to vaguely waft a hand. For me, it was in the direction of the field beyond the field. Lots of fields. 'There's Luke too. A Volvo's stuck in the car park and he's helping push the guy out.'

'Are you both sort of... caretakers?'

I thought back to school and the grubby guy in the grubby dungarees doing grubby jobs. The one with the really thick glasses who we all assumed – almost certainly unfairly – was a paedo. 'I wouldn't say "caretaker",' I replied. 'More... an assistant.'

'The more you say "assistant", the more I hear "caretaker".'

'Not a caretaker.'

The girl laughed again, the third time, and I was definitely counting by then. She picked up the box of bandages again and then moved backwards towards the tent flap. 'Gotta go,' she said. 'Girl with a bad ankle and all that.'

'Look out for those tent pegs.'

There was a swish of material, a momentary shower of sunlight and warmth, and then she was gone. I think I stood for a moment, watching the space she'd temporarily occupied. Wondering why I was suddenly confident enough to talk to her when that wasn't how I felt. It had all come out without me having to consider any of it.

When my friends and I were together, we spent all our time working on those endless in-jokes in an attempt to get even the smallest laugh. It came almost without thought, but that was them and this was something else.

The moment must have lasted longer than I thought because, as I made another attempt at lifting the parachute, the tent flap swished again, the sunlight and warmth showered in once more, and the girl was back. She flicked the strand of dark hair away from her face again.

'You look like you need a hand,' she said. 'I know you gave it the whole "*not heavy just awkward*"-thing – but you're not fooling anyone.'

'Actually, I think *you* said that.'

She stopped, chewed the corner of her lip. Thought. 'Hmm. Maybe you're right. Anyway, I've dropped off the bandages, a crisis has been averted, so now I'm back.'

The girl reached for the bag and then pulled her hand anyway.

'What's inside?' she asked, with a smidge of suspicion.

'A parachute.'

More chewing. 'What are you doing with a parachute?'

'I was thinking of jumping off the gorge.'

She nodded along. 'I don't think it'll have time to open before you hit the ground.'

'It's a big gorge.'

'True... but I'm more worried about any potential cleaning up after the jump. If I help you move the parachute, am I responsible for it in any way afterwards?'

'I don't think so.'

'Good.'

She reached for the parachute again, tried to lift it with one hand and then puffed out a big breath.

'That is definitely heavy and *not* awkward.'

'I never said otherwise.'

She clasped one strap and I took the other. Together we waddled like a pair of constipated penguins, huffing and puffing out of the tent. We grumbled our way across the grass and into the middle of the girls' field, where we dropped it.

The supply tent had been cool but the sun was singeing outside. Sweat oozed down my back, dribbling into the gap at the top of my underwear. I hoped she wouldn't notice, then realised she'd have no reason to look.

She took a couple of deep breaths and then stretched high and rolled her neck in a circle. My shoulders ached and I squeezed my thumbs into the balls, pressing and grinding, trying to get some life back into them. We each let out long breaths and then focused back on one another.

'What now?' she asked.

'Don't you have an injured girl to be looking after?'

My new companion grimaced slightly and we stared together across the field towards the mass of bigger tents on the other side of the campsite. We were close to the girls' bunks, where there were six tents in a row, all made of thick cream canvas, on top of a wooden platform a few centimetres off the ground.

It was similar on the far side of the campsite, where six boys' bunks were in a line. Separating them was the larger main field, plus the mess hall and a series of smaller tents including the staff lounge, the medical bay, the supply tent and a couple of others.

'You're my alibi,' she said, looking towards the large group of girls who were running around a part of the girls' field past the bunks.

'Alibi from what?'

'The campers are hyper because their parents have left. The girls are playing a massive game of tag. That's how someone fell over the tent peg.'

From the other end of the field, the screams and screeches went up a few notches. It was surprising, or perhaps it wasn't, quite how loud fifty to sixty ten-, eleven- and twelve-year-old girls could be. Over on the boys' field, another fifty or sixty boys were playing football.

As things stood, the genders were yet to mix.

'Tag not your thing?' I asked.

'Is it anyone's thing? Who plays tag? It's not like it's in the Olympics.'

She had a point as she looked down to the bag and then back to me.

'What next?' she added.

'We unpack the parachute.'

'Why?'

I stretched again, feeling the heat of the day, even though it was still morning. If every day was like this, full of fetching and carrying, of setting up and pulling down, I wasn't sure I'd get through the six weeks.

'Luke said it's a day one getting-to-know-people game,' I replied. 'All the counsellors and kids grab a bit of the parachute and stand around the edge flapping it up and down. Then you all run underneath and shout your names.'

Even as I spoke, I didn't quite understand what I was on about. I hadn't wanted to tell Luke it made no sense.

She stared across towards the manic tag game. If the pace and energy of the girls was anything to go by, it was going to be a long six weeks for everyone.

'There's not a test afterwards, is there?' she asked. 'There is zero chance I'm going to remember any names after all that.'

There was a sigh, or perhaps just a breath because of the heat, and then I realised she was looking at me.

'Let's start with yours,' she added.

'My what?'

That got an eye roll. 'Your name.'

'Joe,' I replied. 'It's Joe.'

'Well, Joe,' she said. 'I'm Amy. Amy Ashworth.'

2

EGG

After spreading out the parachute with Amy, her alibi was gone. I felt a strange emptiness as I watched her sigh her way across to the girls to call them over for their name game. I almost called her back, trying to think of something else I could ask to keep the conversation going. When she was there, the words came easily; when she wasn't, I was left floundering.

It was only a moment until I remembered I had other work to do, so headed back towards the main staff lounge. The word 'lounge' was something of an exaggeration, given it was, essentially, a biggish tent that contained two battered sofas and a vending machine.

I was looking for Luke, wondering what the next job of the day would be, when George, the camp director, strode into the lounge. He was tall in personality as well as size. The sort of person who dominated a room but only if he wanted to.

George glanced around the lounge and then focused in on me. 'Have you seen Fiona?' he asked, talking about his wife, another of the directors.

'Not since first thing.'

He bobbed on one foot, weighing up his next move. It's a

strange feeling when you barely know a person, when you've hardly met – and yet, at the same time, it's as if you've *always* known them.

I'd got the job of assistant camp counsellor through my sister, Michelle. It was a little over a week before camp was due to start and she arrived home from the garage where she worked as a mechanic. I was in the kitchen, looking for something to eat when she said she had a summer job for me if I wanted it.

The 'if you want' wasn't much of an option.

I didn't want it, obviously. I was sixteen and hadn't long taken my GCSEs. Results were due after a couple of months and, until then, why would I want to give up my summer? Those were days that would be better spent with my friends, trying to get served under-age, or hanging around town, looking for something exciting that didn't cost too much.

'What job?' I asked, though I had little interest in my sister's answer.

'Camp Sycamore,' she replied – and I groaned. I'd assumed it would be something I didn't want to do but this was worse.

'I'm not working there,' I said.

Michelle took over from me, hunting through the cupboards and fridge, before pulling out a tray of eggs.

'Eggs on toast?' she offered.

'If you're making.'

'I've been at work all day. You should be cooking for me.'

'I can cook if you want...'

Michelle reached for the bread and took it out of the wrapper, examining the crust, looking for mould. 'Not after last time.'

She scrabbled around in one of the low cupboards and took out a frying pan, then checked over the eggs individually, looking for cracked shells.

'What's wrong with working at camp?' she asked.

'Have you *seen* the people who work there?'

Michelle opened the door to the living room and looked in on Mum, then asked if she wanted eggs on toast. The answer was apparently 'no', because she closed it quickly and turned back to me.

'It's not lame. A few of my friends went as campers when we were in year six or seven. They had a great time. I wish I'd gone.'

She caught me rolling my eyes, as she was meant to. She's six years older than me and those were the ages when I felt that gap more than any other. We both lived at home but she was working every day, while, until then, I was at school.

'Don't do that,' she said – and there was something sharper about her than normal. Not a simple brother–sister niggle but a stronger rebuke. It was so unexpected that it made me stop leaning on the counter and stand straighter.

Camp Sycamore was on a site on the edge of our town, sitting in a series of fields underneath the steepling gorge that towered over everything. It had been running for six or seven years, with campers arriving from all around the region. They were looked after by counsellors who were sixteen or seventeen – and, above them, there was some sort of director team that I didn't understand at the time.

My friends and I broadly ignored the whole thing, other than the occasions where we made fun of the counsellors who dared make their way down to our town for an evening out.

Michelle likely knew that, though it didn't stop her. 'I fixed a guy's car earlier,' she said. 'George-something. Got talking to him after and he's the main guy who runs the camp. One of his assistant counsellors has broken his leg playing football and he's had to drop out. George is looking for someone at short notice. I told him my brother's sixteen and not doing anything all summer and he said you could go up to the site a week Saturday. I think he wants to make sure you're the right sort of person. If you are, then the job's yours.'

She cracked a pair of eggs into the frying pan and then started playing with the dials of the hob.

'Why do you think I'm not doing anything all summer?'

She turned and looked to me with a single raised eyebrow, something that was hard to argue against.

'Fine,' I said. 'What sort of person is he after?'

'I dunno... the usual stuff. Conscientious, trustworthy, does what they're told, learns on their feet, all that.' A pause. 'Or is it *thinks* on their feet?'

'What does an assistant counsellor do?'

The contempt must have been obvious because she scowled at me. 'I'm sure you'll find out when you go for the interview.'

It was very matter-of-fact, as if I had no choice. In retrospect, I suppose I didn't.

'How much does it pay?' I asked.

Michelle faced the oven and didn't bother to turn. Her reply was almost lost among the spattering of the eggs.

'It's volunteering,' she said.

'For *free*?' There was definitely indignant disgust in my tone.

'Not free. There's an expenses allowance that you get every week. He said it's twenty-five or thirty quid.'

I stared at her back, wondering if this was some sort of joke. As if I was going to give up my entire summer for, at best, a hundred-and-eighty quid total.

'It's good for your CV,' she added.

It was all nonsense, of course – or so I thought at the time. An older kid had told me and my friends that nobody cared about GCSEs after they'd been done. He said he'd taken his Duke of Edinburgh Award folder and dumped it in the bin after not needing it in the years after he'd done his exams. '*They don't tell you any of that*,' he insisted. We believed him, of course, because it was what we wanted to hear. Or what some of us wanted to hear.

I scoffed at the idea of anything that was 'good for your CV' but it didn't feel as if I had much choice in the end. Michelle drove me to camp on that Saturday, I met George, and then two days later camp began and I was in that supply tent with Amy Ashworth. It was as if it all happened without me being a part of the decision-making. As if fate had taken over.

Perhaps it had.

Back in the staff lounge, two days after I first met him, George paused after asking about the whereabouts of his wife.

'How's the first day going?' he asked.

I avoided his stare, which was something I didn't realise I did until later in the summer. 'OK,' I replied.

'Are you getting on with Luke?'

'Yeah, he's off trying to get a stuck car off the field.'

George's forehead crinkled momentarily as this was seemingly the first he'd heard of it. It only occurred to me then that Luke had been gone for quite a while considering it was only one car.

'Luke's a veteran,' George said. 'Did three years as a camper and he was an assistant counsellor last year. He should be able to answer anything you want to know – but don't be afraid to come to Fee or me if you need anything. We're always around somewhere.' He patted his trousers and then pulled out a key from his back pocket. 'You're sixteen, aren't you?'

'Right.'

He muttered 'too young to drive' to himself and then asked how I got to camp that morning. I said I'd ridden my bike and that had him nodding as he reached to hand me the key.

'I left some batteries at my house,' he said. 'Everything's been so busy and it's been a rush to get all the stuff over here. Do you reckon you could cycle over and get them?'

I asked where he lived and he described an address in the hills on the other side of town. He asked if I knew it and I said that I did, without adding that my friends and I used to haul our bikes up to the top of the hill where his house sat and freewheel down.

'No rush,' he added, as I pocketed his house key. 'If Luke has things that need doing, then help him first.'

George smiled and I remember feeling something new. An undiscovered emotion, perhaps. Like going to bed on a cold night and pulling the warm covers up tight and tucking it under your chin. There was a kindness and security to which I wasn't used.

I suppose that's what made it all the worse when I came to betray him.

3

BATTERY

I didn't rush when cycling across town to George's house. Any time away from camp was time away from hard work that was apparently worth a fiver each day in 'expenses', whatever that meant.

The route took me past the garage where my sister worked – and she was standing in the yard at the side, talking to a customer before wiping her greasy hands on her overalls. The customer drove away as I slowed and stopped near the gate. Michelle had taken a few steps back towards the main part of the garage when she noticed me and shouted across.

'You've not quit already, have you?'

'No.'

She strode across the cracked tarmac, apparently not believing me. 'What are you doing then?'

'I'm going to George's house to pick up batteries.'

Michelle frowned, unsure if it was a lie. 'How was Mum when you got up?' she asked.

'The same.'

'Good day or bad?'

I thought about the question. It was so subjective at the

time. That line between good and bad was paper-thin. A wrong word here, a door closing too loudly there, and one answer could swing wildly and instantly to another.

'Not bad,' I said. 'She was still in bed when I left.'

Michelle puffed out a long breath. She stretched and wiped her forehead with her sleeve. It left a streak of black across her skin and, when I motioned towards it, she winced and swore under her breath.

'I'll check in on her at lunch,' she said.

There was something resigned about the way she said it, which we both felt. She must have picked up my expression because I didn't say anything before she continued.

'You've got to live your own life, Joe. Enjoy camp.'

'But—'

'It doesn't mean we forget her, or ignore her. It just means you've got an opportunity to do something with your summer. If you don't want to do A levels, or GNVQs, or whatever, that's fine. But you can't sit home, or in your mate's garage, all day. You need something.'

It was the sort of pep talk I didn't need and didn't want. The final two years of school had been a series of people telling us how important everything was. We either did well and were massive successes, or we did badly and were massive failures. There was nothing in the middle – and I always knew I was never going to be a massive success.

'Don't do that,' Michelle said. I had probably rolled my eyes again. Her voice was hard. Harsh. It was the same way she'd spoken to me in the kitchen when she'd somehow persuaded me to throw away my summer. 'You don't know what chances you might get,' she added. 'George is a good guy. He knows people and *they* know people. You don't realise until you're older that it's about who you know – and who *they* know.' She huffed in annoyance. 'I wish I'd tried harder,' she concluded.

'You're doing all right.'

She slipped her sleeve across her forehead a second time, realising what she'd done without me needing to say. There was another silent swear and she rubbed her skin hard with the heel of her palm. I looked past her, towards the main part of the garage, where a man in overalls had emerged. Beyond him was a calendar with a topless woman on the front that was easily viewable from the street.

'Shell!'

He called her name and Michelle turned, taking him in and then looking back to me. 'I've gotta get back,' she said quickly. 'I'll check on Mum at lunch and see you later.' Another glance towards the main garage. 'I need to talk to you then.'

'What about?'

'I don't have the time now.'

'Shell!'

She started walking backwards and then spun and broke into a jog back to work as she and the man disappeared back into the garage.

I waited for a moment, wondering if she might come back. When she didn't, I straddled the bike again and continued the journey towards George's house.

The hill up to where he lived was wide and open, which was great for the view but not for the shade on a warm July day. My T-shirt clung to my back and sweat dribbled into my eyes as I chugged halfway up before giving in and walking the rest of the way.

The top of the gorge might offer the best view of the town – but the best view of the gorge undoubtedly came from this area. I stopped and looked up as the towering wall of rock soared high, like a giant emerging from the earth. There were ants standing on the top, probably leaning over and taking photos of the majesty below. The gorge pretty much always made the top-ten list of things to see in Britain, though it was hard to know whether it was more stunning from the ground looking up, or the top looking down.

When I got to the top of the hill, I stopped and turned again, taking it all in. I know that a lot of people don't necessarily visit the things on their doorstep. I once met someone from Arizona who'd only been to the Grand Canyon once. When I mentioned it, he shrugged away the idea, as if it was some ditch at the bottom of his garden. I was never like that. The gorge always felt like something special to me – and I felt it more that summer than any time before or since.

After wasting those extra minutes, I continued on to George's house, which was detached and almost isolated at the end of a cul-de-sac. I'd expected something nice but it was more than I could have imagined. There was a huge bay window at the front, overlooking a patch of grass that was more like a bowling green. The wide garage had space for at least two cars and there was a path leading down the side of the house.

I thought about taking the path, nosing around to see how George and Fiona lived. I almost did, except Michelle's words about limited chances had stuck with me for some reason. My sister could be annoying with things like that.

I ended up unlocking his front door and edging nervously into the cool, dark hallway. George had said the batteries were on a table next to the phone – and they were impossible to miss. It's an odd thing to remember but, at home, we'd only ever had cheap pound-shop batteries that stopped working with minimal use. On the table was a box with at least a hundred black and gold Duracells inside.

For the second time that day, something was heavier than I thought. I put them in my rucksack and, after looping my shoulders through, I felt them hanging heavy at the base of my back.

I locked up the house and, even though I'd only been inside a couple of minutes, the heat hit hard. That was until I got on my bike and freewheeled back down the hill. The wind rushed and I let the pedals spin and, with the gorge looming in the distance, there was a sense of being alive. That perhaps it wouldn't be a summer wasted, after all.

Back at camp, George took a couple of batteries from the box, then told me to leave the rest in the supply tent. I offered him back his key but he waved it away, saying I should look after it and that there would be more errands to run over the coming weeks.

'How was the hill on your bike?' he asked.

'Better coming down.'

He laughed as he clung onto the batteries – and then said 'thank you' before disappearing off, seemingly still in search of his wife. It was his never-ending quest that summer and there were times when it felt as if Fiona only existed in a parallel dimension George could never find.

It was only later when I realised how unusual it was for someone to actually thank me for something I'd done. That sort of admission was almost a sign of weakness when it came to my friends and me. Not only that, I didn't do enough around the house to ever have Michelle or Mum thank me.

I was on my way out of the staff lounge, wondering what Luke was up to, when I bumped into someone who was on their way in. Our shoulders clunked into each other, not that hard, but enough to spin us each half around. We were both already apologising when he stopped himself mid-word and eyed me up.

Ian was a familiar face from school. We'd been in the same year through both primary and secondary school, even if not in the exact same classes. He stepped back and gave me the up-and-down, what-are-you-doing-here? stare. His eyes narrowed and his nose twitched as if he'd stepped in something grim. I started to mumble something that might have been a 'hi' or even a 'fancy seeing you here' – but I never got that far.

Instead of heading into the staff lounge, Ian turned and walked back the way he'd come. I didn't catch everything he said under his breath but I did get the final word, which was a spat and decisive 'off'.

4

UMBRELLA

Getting one Volvo out of the car park had turned into helping 'seven or eight' off when I next caught up with Luke. He was a year older than me, with the wispy beginnings of a sandy-coloured beard that I could only hope of growing. He was one of those kids that always looked older than they were. Seventeen going on twenty-one when it came to looks, if nothing else. Getting served underage was little challenge at that time but, for Luke, they wouldn't have even bothered raising an eyebrow before reaching for the pump handle.

I asked about the next job and he took a big breath before leading me off towards a stack of large patio-style umbrellas behind the mess hall.

'Reading hour,' he said. 'Best time of the day. All that screaming and running is about to stop because every camper is going to settle on the field and read. It happens every day.'

'What's that got to do with umbrellas?'

He flexed his muscles and then hoisted one of the umbrellas onto his shoulder. 'It's hot out there and we have to set out the umbrellas so they have shade.'

I copied him, lifting one of the brollies onto my own shoulders, and then followed him across the main field onto the boys' side. We dropped the umbrellas next to each other close to the bunks and then each dragged a metal stand out to the same space and inserted an umbrella.

Luke sheltered under one of the newly created shaded spots and brushed the sweat from his brow.

'There's six for each field,' he said. 'You've got to set them up every afternoon, then put them away after. Hardest job of the day – but it's worth it for the quiet.'

We waited for a moment, getting our breath as the campers on both fields raced around, howling at the tops of their voices. I tried to remember whether I had that much energy at the same age but it only took a moment to conclude that I probably did.

'Boys or girls?' Luke asked.

'Huh?'

'Six umbrellas on each side, so we might as well divide it up now. You do one side and I'll take the other.'

A few bunks away, close to the cluster of racing boys, I saw Ian coming out of the tent. He said something to the nearest other counsellor and they headed off towards the pack.

'Girls,' I said.

Luke laughed. 'You sure? I'm not swapping back.'

'I'm sure.'

'Fair enough. I did the girls last year and you've got to be careful over there. The lads want you to join in with football and whatever. Over there, you're getting your nails done before the summer's out.'

I laughed nervously, wondering if he was having me on.

'No joke,' he said as he gripped the umbrella pole. 'I'll help you with the first two but then you're on your own.'

We carried an umbrella each across to the girls' side and set them up – and then we separated.

I spent a long time after wondering if that snap decision changed everything. If I'd not run into Ian that morning, hadn't known he'd be supervising the boys, I'd have probably chosen the boys' side. I can't imagine any way in which things would have played out how they did.

I continued setting up the umbrellas and was putting the final one in place when another familiar face bounded across to me. Ian might have muttered his contempt under his breath but Gemma had no such desire to keep her thoughts to herself. She was another person with whom I'd grown up. We'd been in the same class through primary school and again through much of secondary. 'Friends' was a definite push but we knew each other better than I knew Ian.

'What are *you* doing here?' she asked – and the derision bled through far stronger than any surprise.

I was exhausted from the umbrellas and could have done with a moment to settle. I couldn't think of anything smart to say.

'What do you mean?' I replied.

'It's not like this is your thing, is it?' She held out her arms, indicating the campsite. 'I came here as a kid but you've never been.'

'I didn't know there was a requirement.'

'There's not – but we read books here. There are craft workshops. We wrote our own play and put it on last year. You can't pretend you're into any of that.'

Gemma was pointing a finger, though it didn't feel as if she was actually annoyed. More that sort of fake outrage to get a reaction. I think it was more of a challenge, that if I had an answer, then perhaps she'd opt not to give me a hard time.

'They were short,' I replied. 'Someone was supposed to be doing this job but he broke his leg. George said something to my sister about a job, so here I am.'

She examined me, eyes narrow, as if trying to figure out if this was some sort of lie. 'How *is* Michelle?' she asked, more carefully this time. 'Still at the garage?'

'It's been a year now.'

A nod. 'Dad reckons she knows what she's doing – and that comes from someone who spent a week bothering Mum about whether he should take his car in because he didn't want a girl to do the MOT.'

It took me a moment to realise what she was talking about. For me, Michelle being a mechanic was perfectly normal. The idea that it might be a 'man's job' had never occurred.

'Anyway,' Gemma continued, 'Mum asked if there were any *other* jobs that he didn't think women could do and he let it go after that.'

She looked me up and down again and the inquisitive frown returned. We'd been friends when we were first in primary school, back before boys and girls separated into their own tribes. We sat together for a few years when I was one of the cleverer kids. She won some sort of handwriting competition and I was second. It seemed ridiculous in that moment on the field, like a distant relic of a dream I'd had, as opposed to something that actually happened.

I was trying to think of something to say when two more counsellors appeared at Gemma's side. The trio of girls eyed me warily, though it was Amy who spoke. She poked a thumb towards the counsellor I didn't know.

'Can you tell Sarah I wasn't skiving off earlier.'

'She wasn't skiving off earlier,' I replied.

Sarah was having none of it. She exchanged a sceptical shake of the head with Gemma. 'She told you to say that.'

'We were unpacking the parachute,' I said.

Amy threw up both hands in a show of righteous indignation. 'See!'

The disbelieving shake of the heads had turned into the smirks of wind-up merchants.

'I *knew* you were pretending to be annoyed,' Amy said – and then she broke into a smile too.

Perhaps she hadn't smiled earlier in the day, or maybe I hadn't noticed. It changed the person she was, her greeny eyes twinkling with mischief in the shaded sun.

'Six weeks,' she said. 'I've got six weeks of this.'

Sarah put an arm around Amy's shoulders, which was playfully shaken off. 'Alcott-girls all the way!'

'No chance,' Gemma replied. 'Dahl-girls forever.'

I knew a little about the bunk names from the morning of setting up. The six bunks were named after children's authors. There was Roald Dahl, CS Lewis, AA Milne, Beatrix Potter, Enid Blyton – and the one of which I'd never heard: Louisa May Alcott. Each bunk had a girls' and boys' version, with a pair of counsellors assigned to anything from eight to ten campers. That gave fifty to sixty girls and the same number of boys.

Gemma checked her watch and then held up her wrist for the other two to see. 'I've been looking forward to reading hour since about half-eight this morning,' she said.

'I hated it as a camper,' Sarah replied. 'But the quiet is going to be *heaven*.'

'What do you do while everyone's reading?' I asked.

The three girls exchanged a look as if I'd just asked how many feet they each had.

'Read,' Amy said.

That idea had not occurred to me. I had never been a reader, except for when forced at school.

'I'm going to nap,' Sarah said.

'Oooh, nap sounds good,' Amy replied. 'Maybe I'll do that.'

'You can't. One of us has to keep an eye on these terrors and I've already called bunk duty.'

Amy looked sideways at her co-counsellor, gritting her teeth, though not really.

'What are you reading?' I asked.

'*Little Women* again,' Amy replied. 'What with the bunk name and all.'

I was a microsecond from asking whether it was Alcott who wrote *Little Women* – but managed to shut up for long enough to realise that was clearly what she meant. A quick glance to Gemma was enough for me to know that she'd read my mind. There was the merest upturn of her lips, as if she was ready to pounce on the stupid question that, thankfully, did not come.

'Anyway,' Amy declared, 'we can't stand around chatting to the caretaker all day. We've got some badminton to watch – and then we've some peace to enjoy.'

They were already a half-dozen steps away, heading back towards the campers, when Amy turned and smiled at me. 'See ya around, Joe,' she said.

5

BOOK

I didn't see Amy for the rest of the day as I took my lead from Luke in what there was to do. After reading hour, we packed the umbrellas back to where they'd started, then set up the mess hall together, ready for the evening meal. Meal times at camp were strictly breakfast-lunch-tea. Dinner didn't exist.

Each meal was bookended by Luke and me unfolding the tables, setting up the right amount of chairs per bunk, doing the same for the directors' table – and then, afterwards, wiping everything down and putting them away again. The exception was tea, where the tables and chairs could be left out ready for morning.

Amy's accusation of being the caretaker was becoming hard to deny.

Luke said we were allowed to eat with everyone else if we wanted – though he usually ate in the kitchen with the cooks. It was hard to blame him given that mealtimes were the loudest part of each day.

The boys and girls all ate together and it was a mass whirl-wind of high-pitched voices talking over each other, with cutlery banging into plates and cups clanking off tables and, sometimes, the floor.

On that first day, I had lunch at the top table with the directors. Then, after laying out everything for tea, I cycled home without eating. With Luke camping on site and me biking in, there was never an issue with me leaving early and him staying on.

Those rides home, both before and during camp, were always met with a growing sense of dread and the unknown. Of not knowing what would be waiting on the other side of the door. The simplicity of Michelle or me describing a day as 'good' or 'bad' for Mum was like standing directly underneath a plane as it took off and calling it loud. It would be true – but it wouldn't begin to explain the way the sound engulfed a whole body. How the boom made it feel as if every part of a person's soul was being swallowed by something indescribably explosive. 'Loud' would be a foreign word in the same way that 'good' or 'bad' was meaningless.

By the time I got home, I was feeling the burn of what was a first full day of work in my life. My shoulders ached from the lifting and carrying, and my legs were dead from the cycling and endless walking. I don't think I knew the phrase 'hard day's work' until that first evening. I wanted to settle, rest and do very little.

Before I headed inside, I could see the curtains were still drawn, which was rarely a good sign for what was to come. I wheeled my bike through the house and left it at the back door, then took a breath and opened the door into the living room. The murk cascaded out, swamping the light of the kitchen like a hand closing around a flame. Mum could go days at a time without leaving the living room, except to use the toilet. She'd keep the curtains pulled and the heat would build until it became like walking into a steam room. It would often be hotter inside than out and the air would be thick and hard to breathe.

Mum never seemed to notice any of that. She'd sit on the sofa and stare in the vague direction of the television. The blinking lights of the screen would burn through the lightless room, sending bluey-green slivers across Mum's unmoving features.

'Are you OK?' I asked.

Mum blinked as the television's light danced across her face. She mumbled something I didn't catch and that likely wasn't important. It wasn't worth asking her to repeat herself because if she wanted to be heard, she'd make sure she was.

I crossed the room, squinting against the flickering light and picked up what turned out to be a slice of bread that was at her feet. There was a litre glass bottle there, too, empty except for a sliver of clear liquid at the bottom.

It had been one of *those* days.

'Have you been shopping?'

She spoke without glancing away from the TV. There was a game show on the screen, though not one I recognised. We'd had cable installed the year before, which opened up a whole televisual world beyond the five main channels. Despite ever more options, Mum seemed stuck on UK Gold, with its revolving schedule of decades-old repeats. Michelle said there was comfort in the familiar.

'For what?' I asked.

'Food. There's nothing in the fridge. Nothing in the cupboards. Do I have to do *everything* around here?'

'I don't have any money, Mum. I've been at work all day. I only just got home.'

She continued staring towards the corner of the room, not acknowledging that I'd spoken. I examined the slice of bread I'd picked up. It was hard to tell in the dim light but there didn't appear to be any signs of mould – or an explanation for why it was on the floor. With Mum at that time, it was better not to ask.

'Where's your sister?' she asked. There was a snap to her voice. A demand.

'Probably working late.'

I waited for a moment, wondering if there was more to come. When it became clear there wasn't, I moved back into the kitchen and closed the door behind me.

It's not a nice thing to admit but it was always a relief to close that door. Her presence in the house, *her* house, was so overwhelming sometimes, so bleak, that leaving was the only option.

I checked the fridge and the cupboards and, though it wasn't quite true that there was 'nothing' within, there certainly wasn't much. The idea of tinned peas on a handful of shattered cream crackers left me wishing I'd eaten at camp.

As I was scraping away the wall of frost that was supposed to be a freezer compartment, wondering if anything interesting was hidden beyond, the front door opened. I looked down the hall as Michelle kicked it closed with her heel and wrestled half-a-dozen plastic bags full of shopping towards the kitchen.

'You're allowed to help,' she said – although, by that point, a pair of apples were already rolling back the way she'd come.

We got everything onto the counter and then started refilling the fridge and cupboards together.

I squeezed a box of Shredded Wheat into the cupboard next to the fridge. 'Did you pay for all this?' I asked.

She handed me a carton of long-life milk. 'What do you think?'

I put the milk into the cupboard, next to the cereal, then Michelle took it back out again and put it in the fridge.

'Do you want something to eat?' she asked.

'I can—'

'I'll do it. It's fine.'

We finished emptying the bags and then my sister pulled out a Lion bar and lobbed it across to me.

'Got that for you,' she said, before nodding towards the living room.

'Not a good day,' I said, though I kept my voice down.

She nodded and then made a clucking sound with her tongue, wondering how to approach the evening. This wasn't uncommon.

'Do you know who wrote *Little Women*?' I asked.

Michelle turned back to me, an eyebrow raised. 'Why?'

'All the bunks at camp are named after authors – and there's one I don't know.'

She didn't need to think. 'Louisa May Alcott. It takes a chapter or two to get used to the language but you should read it. It's good.'

I must have pulled a face because she followed it up almost immediately.

'It's not just for women, despite the title.'

'What's it about?'

She started looking for something among the newly filled cupboards. 'Growing up.'

'I always figured it was about... I dunno, women who were little.'

Michelle eyed me over her shoulder. 'C'mon, Joe. You're not with your mates now.'

She didn't say it harshly but I found myself looking at the floor, hoping she'd look away.

'What did you want to talk to me about?' I asked, wanting to change the subject.

When I risked a glance up, I realised Michelle was back to skimming through the cupboards.

She didn't reply at first, which was a reply in itself. The hairs on the back of my neck rose as I waited.

She eventually turned to face me, a box of dry spaghetti in her hand. 'Spag bol?'

'What did you want to say?'

I think a part of me knew before she said it. It was one of those things both unexpected and yet entirely predictable.

'I'm moving into my own flat,' she said.

We stared at one another for a while, locked in a distant embrace, each knowing what the other was thinking. For me, it was horror at being left with Mum. For her, it was an apology for something entirely necessary.

'It's not far away,' she said. 'I'll drop by all the time to check on Mum and make sure there's food in the cupboard. I'm at the garage every day and you can come over in the evenings or the weekends if you need a break.'

She didn't need to spell out from what I might want a break.

I tried to think of something to say but it was impossible to get past the vision of me being alone in the house with Mum.

Michelle filled the kettle and switched it on, then ran her finger along the top of the spaghetti box.

'I'm not hungry,' I said.

She put it down on the counter and sighed. 'C'mon, Joe...'

I didn't storm out but I certainly stomped my feet on the stairs as I went up to my room.

Michelle followed me up half an hour later or so. She knocked on my door and, when I said nothing, she nudged it open and then stepped inside.

'For you,' she said, passing a plate across to where I was lying on my bed.

A part of me wanted to huff and puff, to be annoyed at her, not the situation – but the bigger part of me was hungry. I pushed myself up and took the plate.

'I didn't know we had cheese,' I said.

'I hid it at the back of the fridge, underneath the bag of spinach.'

'That is a pretty good hiding place...'

Michelle smiled down at me and then sat on the bed at my side. Our combined weight made the mattress sink and she watched and waited as I bit into the cheese toastie. My favourite and always my first choice. It was molten hot, of course, but I doubt there's ever been a bad cheese toastie made across human history. Fire was invented to melt cheese and I will never believe otherwise.

'Thank you,' I said, though it was more of a mumble. I wasn't quite able to accept reality right then. I wanted to be angry.

'I'm going out in a bit,' she said. 'I'll check on Mum first but she was sleeping when I came up. It should be quiet.'

'Who are you seeing?'

'A friend.' She produced the Lion bar from somewhere and put it on the bed next to me. 'You left this.'

I picked it up and moved it to my other side as I continued to eat the toastie.

Michelle stood, saying she'd be right back, and then she disappeared across the hall into her room. There was the sound of a cupboard opening and closing and then she was back.

'You can have it,' she said, as she put a paperback of *Little Women* on my side table. I glanced across to it but didn't want to touch it with my greasy fingers. 'I'm sorry,' she said, still standing.

'What for?'

'You know. I would've gone a while back but I didn't want to go before your exams. It feels like now's the right time.'

I stared at the half-eaten sandwich and chewed what was in my mouth. Chewed and chewed because it meant I didn't have to reply. It was a hostage situation, although I wasn't sure whether me or Mum was the one who'd been kidnapped.

'It's not your fault,' I managed, which was more or less the most adult thing I'd ever managed to say at that point.

We stayed like that for a while, her standing; me sitting on the bed. I nibbled around the crusts, leaving the cheesiest parts for last.

'I have to get ready,' Michelle said, as she turned and disappeared back to her room, closing both our doors on the way.

I finished the toastie and the Lion bar as I listened to my sister getting ready through the wall. Elastica were playing, though not loud enough to attract Mum's attention from downstairs. I wondered if she'd say goodbye on the way out but, when the music went quiet, the next thing I heard were footsteps on the stairs and then the front door clicking open and closed.

I thought about going downstairs to wash up my plate but it was quiet down there and not worth the risk of antagonising Mum. Instead I washed my hands in the bathroom and then returned to examine the book Michelle had given me. The cover had a painting of a tree with four women underneath, each wearing the enormous dresses that signalled the sort of BBC period drama I went out of my way to avoid. The pages were a crispy yellowy-brown and, inside the front cover, 'Michelle Miller' had been printed in blue ballpoint.

The first few lines didn't hold the unfathomable weight of the Shakespeare I'd been forced to endure at school – but they weren't quite in English, either. Not a type of English I recognised, in any case. I put it back down, then picked it up and pushed it into the bag I took to camp.

My back and shoulders continued to ache as I lay on my bed, trying not to wriggle too much, not wanting the creaky frame to echo through the floorboards. I watched TV with the volume as low as it could go while still being able to hear it and waited, wondering what time Michelle would be home.

6

NEWSLETTER

The Camp Sycamore newsletter was put together by a different bunk each day. As journalistic endeavours went, it wasn't up there with *The Times* but it *was* the biggest staple of day-to-day life around camp. A large part of it listed the day's activities, with individual bunk schedules, so everybody knew what they had on. It also proved useful to Luke and me, because we knew which equipment had to be dragged across the field and when.

Each edition also saw a 'profile of the day' – and day two's happened to be Sarah, who was Amy's co-counsellor for Alcott on the girls' side. There was a smiling photo of her taken the day before, in her fresh white Camp Sycamore T-shirt that had the small tree logo on the front.

I skimmed the newsletter, though quickly got distracted because there were badminton nets to put up and football goals to arrange.

If it hadn't been for her profile, chances were I'd have never talked to Sarah that day. She was unspooling a ball of wool when I saw her close to the Alcott bunk. I stood over her, accidentally blocking the sun as she looked up and took me in.

'It's cold in the shade,' she said.

I moved to the side, then mumbled something about liking Blur myself. Her eyes narrowed momentarily before she realised I was talking about the favourite band she'd listed in the profile.

She shrugged. 'One of the girls from Dahl put me on the spot and I didn't know what to say. Blur was the first thing that came out.'

We remained there for a moment, an unquestionable awkwardness hovering – probably because my mates and I preferred Oasis and The Verve and I didn't know that much about Blur. Seemingly, she didn't either. I couldn't remember why I'd started talking to her in the first place.

I mumbled something about having work to do and turned to make an escape when she made me stop.

'I heard things about you,' she said.

I turned and she hadn't moved. The wool was at her feet and she was frozen with strands stretching from one hand to the other.

'Like what?' I asked.

She nodded towards the boys' side of the field. 'Some of the guys know you from school. Gemma, too.'

It wasn't an answer, although I had a reasonable idea of what they might have said about me – especially Ian. This was another of those things that was unexpected, even though every part of it could've been predicted.

'I have to get back,' she said, even though she wasn't moving.

I took the cue and headed back towards the staff lounge, looking for Luke and whatever might be up next. It was hard to forget what Sarah had said, and how much Amy might have heard as well.

The rest of the morning was spent in much the way that they all would be. There was carrying and fetching, putting up and pulling down, hunting around the supply tent and wishing someone had organised it better. Not bothering to do it myself.

Luke joined in with a game of football a little before lunch and I lay on the grass, watching as the counsellors let the younger boys run rings around them. That was allowed to continue until any of the older ones had the ball at their feet – at which time the tackles got harder. I was better off out of it and enjoyed the sun, knowing it was preferable to sitting at home.

I didn't fancy lunch among the screaming masses, so headed towards the staff lounge with Luke. He led me out to a patch of grass at the back, hidden from the main site and next to a larger tent that housed the kitchen. There was a lad a couple of years older than me wearing chef whites and a blue hairnet. He was sweating around his face and puffing away on a cigarette as he nodded towards Luke with recognition. The smell of something meaty was strong, overwhelming that of the cigarette.

'Neil, Joe; Joe, Neil,' Luke said – which was probably the best way to sum him up as a person. There were no complications around the introduction, only our names and that was that.

Neil lowered his cigarette and blew out a plume of smoke, before nodding towards me. Another person of apparently few words.

With us introduced, Luke said he'd be a minute, then he nipped back into the staff lounge before re-emerging a minute or two later with a supermarket carrier bag. He passed it across to Neil, who checked inside, nodded, and then put it down at his feet.

'Whatcha after?'

'Cheese and pickle for me and him and a couple of Calippos.'

Another nod. Neil stubbed out the cigarette on the ground and then dropped the remains into a muddy bucket before picking up the bag Luke had given him and disappearing back into the kitchen.

'What was that all about?' I asked.

'I'm trusting you now,' Luke said. 'Passing down the knowledge that was passed to me last year. Are you ready?'

He spoke earnestly, as if about to hand down a thousand-year-old prophecy.

'I guess.'

He shrugged. 'Good enough. Basically, there's the tuck shop where everyone can buy crisps and chocolate. One of our jobs is to sort the stock. There are new deliveries every Tuesday and Friday, so when you unpack everything, put a few things to the side.'

'Like what?'

'Cans of Coke. Chocolate bars. That sort of thing. Everything's logged in this big exercise book. Just write down the new stock minus whatever you've taken and that's it. Share it with our friends in the kitchen and we're all winners. They'll make you whatever you want to eat. Call it a... *bonus*.'

Almost as if to prove the point, there was a swish of tent flap and then Neil returned with a pair of paper plates, each containing cheese and pickle sandwiches. After handing those over, he reached into the pocket of his apron and pulled out a pair of ice lollies which he also passed across.

'Pleasure,' he said, without prompting, before turning and heading back into the kitchen.

Luke and I sat on the grass at the back of the tents, out of sight from anyone else. It might have been illicit food – but it was unquestionably tasty.

The lolly was already soft, so I started with that. The order for Luke was largely irrelevant given the speed at which he ate. He wolfed down everything and then stretched back onto the grass, splaying his arms wide and letting the sun drench him.

'Plenty of money to be made all summer if you're up for it,' he said.

'How?' I asked, suddenly interested in how the expenses I was being paid could be supplemented.

He propped himself up on his elbows, squinting towards me. 'The counsellors don't finish 'til eight, which is when all the campers have to be back in their bunks. Full lights out for everyone is ten – but counsellors can have two hours off between eight and ten *if* their co-counsellor will cover. By eight, all the shops are shut. Everyone gets Saturday night off but the shops are closed then too. Some have parents who live around here but most live on-site for the whole six weeks. The tuck shop is limited and there's no easy way for them to get supplies. If you're happy to take requests, it's a goldmine out there.'

'Requests for what?'

'Fags mainly – or whatever else the tuck shop doesn't sell.'

There was relish in Luke's voice as he talked about his, or possibly our, financial prospects for the coming weeks. When the talk was over, he hopped up and said he was heading into the mess hall to eat with everyone else.

'Nothing better than two lunches,' he added, though I declined the invitation and returned to the empty staff lounge with the remains of my sandwich.

I was almost done when the flap that linked the lounge to the mess hall opened momentarily. There was a flash of sound, which dwindled almost immediately as it closed once more.

Amy stood a little inside the lounge, looking from side to side before she focused in on me.

'Too good to eat with the likes of us, are you?' she asked.

'Way too good.'

That got the merest hint of a smile. 'What've you got there?'

'Roughly a quarter of a cheese and pickle sandwich.'

The smile became a curious half-frown. 'We're stuck with tomato out there.'

'What's wrong with tomato?'

She perched on the corner of the second sofa, a short

distance away from me. 'I don't trust anything that's not quite a fruit and not quite a vegetable.'

'It's definitely a fruit.'

'Is it though? I know that's what they say – but nobody's making a tomato crumble, are they? You don't go into a bakery and ask for a tomato strudel.'

Strudel was another thing I'd never heard of at the time – but I certainly wasn't going to admit it.

'The kitchen made me a sandwich,' I said.

'I didn't know they did requests.'

'Special privileges for assistant counsellors.'

'That's discrimination.'

'That's what you get for calling us caretakers.'

Amy snorted at this and then stood to return to looking around the lounge.

'What are you after?' I asked.

'Napkins.' She turned and eyed me suspiciously. 'You always seem to be where I'm heading.'

I tapped my temple. 'Psychic ability.'

Amy ignored that as she found a handful of napkins close to the bin. She held them up, as if lifting a trophy, and then turned to go. I wanted to ask if she'd heard the same things about me that Sarah apparently had, although I didn't think I wanted to know. I likely knew the answer anyway.

She was almost back at the flap when she stopped again. 'Nice top. Did you get it in New York?'

I'd put almost no thought into my clothes when I'd dressed that morning. The white and black T-shirt with New York City written on the front had been on top of the pile, which more or less summed up my attitude to clothes at the time.

'It used to be my dad's,' I said. 'Something to do with John Lennon having one like it.'

'Did your dad get it in New York?'

That was my turn to laugh. 'I doubt it. More like a market

stall somewhere. He didn't really go abroad. He thought Bristol was in the north.'

I thought it was funny but this seemed to confuse Amy more than anything else. Her eyebrows arched to almost meet in the middle.

'Why are you wearing your dad's clothes?'

It must have been something in my face because none of it felt very funny any longer. She started to add something, possibly even say sorry – but I'd already answered.

'He died two years ago.'

It was impossible not to think of my friends when I thought of what happened to Dad. That wouldn't usually be a problem but my friends and the camp were two opposites.

There was a garage at the side of my friend Dan's house. His parents never used it to park the car, so, over time, he – and therefore we – had taken it over as our own space. Dan had a PlayStation in there and he, Mark, Pete and me would spend hours playing ISS Pro football against each other. We'd slump on the sofa that had once sat in Dan's living room before his parents got a new one. Apart from the PlayStation, everything was hand-me-downs, or nicked from outside people's homes when they'd left things out for the binmen. There was a lamp and two rugs, a calendar two years out of date that we'd kept because the women within were all topless. We'd found a dart-board in a skip and liberated some actual darts from the Red Lion pub. Mark turned up one day with a toaster that he said came from a bin at the back of the school but which looked far too new for that.

Our diet was close to ninety per cent toast at one point as we'd sit in Dan's garage with a loaf of bread and tiny tubs of Flora stolen from the school canteen.

Even as fourteen- and fifteen-year-olds, we did our fair share of drinking in that garage, too. More than our fair share. Dan's parents were the sort who figured we were going to get drunk anyway, so we might as well do it in their general vicinity. As long as we paid for it, they'd buy us crates of lager, through which we'd plough across a weekend.

As we'd drink more through a Friday and Saturday night, the games of PlayStation football and darts would devolve into dead arms and dead legs.

Mark was the loudest of us. The competitive one who couldn't take losing at darts, PlayStation, or anything else. I always saw Pete as the biggest follower of our foursome, going along with whatever the rest wanted to do. The truth might have been that *I* was the biggest follower. Then there was Dan. He was the smart one who could have more or less picked whichever group of friends he wanted. He was top of our IT class and could easily have been in with the computer nerds. If not that, he was decent at cricket, football, rugby and more or less everything else. Then he got on with the girls in drama – which meant he actually talked to them, unlike the rest of us.

That was me and my friends. That was my life. Our lives.

And then one August day, as we sweltered in that garage space, there was a knock on the internal door. Dan's mum appeared and looked directly to me and I knew something was wrong without needing her to say it. She was pale, her eyes wide and unblinking, as if she'd seen something that couldn't be unseen.

'Your mum called,' she said, still focusing on me. 'She said your sister's on her way, so you should wait outside.'

She glanced towards the row of empty unbranded supermarket lager cans that we'd placed against the wall and then turned and rushed away.

The other three looked at me. Even though we didn't know what she was talking about, or why I had to leave, it was so out of the ordinary that the joy of the place had gone. The little in-jokes that ran and ran, the niggly digs at each other, and the endless threat of getting a dead leg if someone let their defences down had all passed. In more ways than one, that briefest of parental visits had been sobering.

We opened up the main garage door and I walked out into the evening sunshine. There was orange in the sky and heat on my arms. My friends waited with me, nobody speaking, nobody daring.

Michelle pulled up a few minutes later and she didn't talk either. I got into the passenger seat and she started to drive before I'd fully closed the door. When I got it shut and turned to look at her, she was fully focused on the road and unblinkingly absorbed in the same way Dan's mum had been.

'What's wrong?' I asked her.

'Not now.'

That was all she would say. The radio was off and no tapes were playing. The journey from Dan's house to ours happened in a vacuum of unspeakable horror. Of knowing something awful had happened but not knowing what.

When she pulled onto our street, there was a police car parked outside the house in the same spot as Dad always parked. Michelle pulled in behind it and then turned off the engine before resting her forehead on the steering wheel.

And thinking of Dad made me think of that evening because the two are one. As Amy had asked about my T-shirt, I thought of those repelling magnets. Of Dan, Pete and Mark on one side – and camp on the other.

I'm not sure how long I sat on that sofa in the staff lounge, staring and saying nothing – but it was Amy who followed up with a solemn: 'I'm sorry.'

Her voice had me blinking back into the tent, two years on from those thoughts. I wanted to tell her all of it right there. About Dad and everything else that had happened since. I'd never really said any of it out loud at that point. I had placated teachers and adults with smaller snippets of how I felt, but the bulk of it, the worst of it, had been only for me.

'I didn't know,' Amy added. She was frozen, those napkins in her hand with the other reaching towards the tent flap.

'No reason for you to know,' I replied.

'It's a nice T-shirt,' she said. 'It suits you.'

I looked down to the top, Dad's top, and there was nothing for me to say.

'I've got to get back,' Amy said. 'One of the girls has dropped a yoghurt and it's gone everywhere, and...' She held up the napkins, pressing the point. 'Sorry,' she said again.

And then she was gone.

LAGER

It was probably that one moment which changed the course of my week at camp. Being there suddenly felt like a mistake. There was barely any money involved and, with Ian seemingly doing all he could to turn strangers against me, it wasn't clear what I was getting from it. The biggest indicator of my changing attitude is that I have almost no idea what I did the rest of that day. Luke showed me the beginnings of his black-market enterprise, which included Mini Rolls, Jammie Dodgers and packets of Monster Munch – but that was about it.

At home, Michelle had returned with a stack of flattened boxes. She reassembled them in her bedroom and started packing ahead of the move. She said she'd told Mum – but our mother was pretending none of it was happening. When I checked in on her after camp, she blamed me for the living room being too hot, even though I'd been out all day and she'd been sitting in there with the windows closed and curtains drawn.

Because of that, I went back to basics and spent the evening in the way I had hundreds of others.

Dan's garage was so hot that we'd done what we almost never did and opened the main door a little. We had a fan set up next to it, though it didn't feel as if much cool air was making its way into what had become an accidental sauna.

The ISS Pro of two years before had become FIFA '99 – and I was as bad at that version of PlayStation football as I was the old one. There was a definite hierarchy when it came to playing games in the garage. We'd play mini tournaments that were usually won by Mark or Dan. With everything belonging to Dan, he was the only person Mark would tolerate losing to. Pete was a lot better than me, which meant his occasional victories would be met by Mark's strong cries of 'luck', or his irrational annoyance at the PlayStation controller itself. *My* even more occasional wins were far harder for Mark to take. They would be met with a bin being kicked across the garage, or accusations of cheating.

On that night, I'd managed a flukey victory and, partly because of the heat, but mainly because of his defeat, Mark declared that he'd had enough of the garage. He said we should go into town – and so we did.

The four of us hurried through the streets. It was still light and we must have been such a strange sight in those days. Because of that unending threat of a dead arm or leg, we'd never leave our sides open to one another, meaning our walks anywhere would end up as a bizarre blend of speed-walking, or sideways crab-stepping. Whoever walked closest to the kerb was at constant risk of being nudged into the road – and there was no respite for whoever was on the other side. There would have been almost no journeys that didn't involve one or more of us being shoved into a bush, or over a low wall.

The warmth of those evenings egged us on even further and, by the time we arrived at the Red Lion, the four of us were a desperate collection of sweaty, giddy teenage boys.

Our town had four or five pubs all within five minutes of each other – but it was the Red Lion where everyone underage knew they could get served. It was an open secret that nobody dared say out loud in case it might go away. Knowledge of such a thing seemed to pass via osmosis from underage teen to underage teen and there were times when the beer garden at the back was filled with more people from our year at school than actual adults.

The four of us passed the tables at the front of the pub, which were all surrounded by groups who were chatting, drinking and smoking. Every door and window was open inside in an attempt to dampen the heat. Sweat used to dribble down those walls on the hottest days, with smoke spiralling around the ceiling. The floor could be so sticky that it was like walking on a bed of gum.

We hadn't reached the age of buying rounds, so the four of us marched up to the bar and ordered our drinks individually. There was as much adventure in our picks as there was the on-tap choices – which meant we always went for either Foster's, Carling or Strongbow.

Michelle had given me £80 the previous Christmas and said to make it last. I was certainly doing that seven months on, as I dug out £1.40 for a pint of Foster's, before the four of us headed out to the beer garden.

The Red Lion was not only the cheapest pub, and the only one in which nobody bothered about ages, it was also the one with the best garden. The green banked down towards the canal, stopping only at the fence that separated it from the towpath. There were at least thirty picnic tables, plus space on the grass itself. When the World Cup had been on the previous year, they had big screens set up. It was like trying to have a beer while a riot was going on. Goals would lead to drinks being thrown and people dancing on the tables. By the end of a night, especially the one when England were knocked out by Argentina, there were fights. Men rolled around on the lawn, with pieces of their ripped shirts left on the grass behind.

Even on a regular evening, there was still an edge to the

atmosphere. A sense that a wrong word here, or an accidental shoulder-bump and spilled pint there, could lead to a mini war.

Perhaps it was that which led to us taking a picnic table at the furthest point from the pub. We sat at the fence, next to the towpath, plonked our drinks down and steadily got drunk.

Pete had taken up smoking at around that time and he sat puffing away as we all watched on and stuck to our drinks. Mark said something about finding some 'babes', which would have been ludicrously unlikely, even if we weren't sixteen.

Conversations were rarely earnest at that time, especially as the cheap lager took hold, but we weren't constantly laddish. Dan asked Pete if he'd heard back from the college he wanted to attend – and he'd had an offer dependent on him getting five Cs or above. There was an unspoken thing where we all knew Dan and Pete would go off to do their A levels, before going to university, while Mark and I would probably get jobs.

It wasn't so obvious at the time but we were separated in ways that weren't really apparent to teenagers. Dan and Pete lived in the new-build houses, near a park and primary school. Mark and I lived in the old houses, close to the factory that shut down when we were all kids.

It was Michelle who pointed out those differences to me at some point around that summer. She said that all the nicer cars she worked on came from that new-build area of town – and, when I asked why, she stared at me as if I'd asked whether water was wet. Sometimes the obvious is only obvious if somebody points it out.

On that evening, we sat and we laughed and we drank – and it was good to be out of the garage for once.

Mark was leaning back on the wooden bench, resting on the fence and almost horizontal.

'Did the cricket teams get posted?' he asked.

'We're all in the twos,' Dan replied – although 'all' wasn't quite true because I didn't play in any of the town's cricket sides. I just watched the others. Dan glanced sideways to me, as if remembering. 'You coming on Saturday?'

'I dunno.'

This lack of commitment forced Mark to sit up straighter as he reached for his pint. 'You're not working with *that lot* this weekend are you?'

'I dunno...'

Fate is a weird, unpredictable thing – and it might have been that day when I learned what an odd sense of humour it has. As Mark was talking about '*that lot*', a couple ambled along the towpath, paying no attention to the booming noise from the beer garden. I saw them before they saw us – and Ian and Gemma were happily minding their own business, taking their break between eight and ten, until Mark spotted them.

'Dicko!' he bellowed, for Ian had the unfortunate last name of 'Dickinson'.

Mark was tipsy at best, outright drunk at worse, and he jumped up, sitting on the table to get himself higher.

Ian saw him then, saw *us*. He hesitated for a moment as if to turn and head back the way he'd come. Gemma took a little longer to realise what was happening and, by the time she did, she was almost level with us and Ian had no choice but to catch her up.

'Dicko!' Mark called again. 'Look who it is. The Dick. The Big Dick. The Big Dicker. Dick King Smith. The Dickwick Papers. The Dickster. Dicky. Little Wicky Dicky. Dickhead. The Head. Sherbet Dick. The Dick Fit Fitter. Branston Dickle. Crocodile Dickdee. Dicky Dicky Bang Bang. Leonardo DiDickio. Dicky Martin. Compact Dick. Sony Dickman. Dick Cheese. The Cheese. Dicklodocus.'

He continued through the list of nicknames that had been attributed across something close to a decade – and the only impressive thing was that he'd somehow remembered them all.

Or *almost*. Pete was off his seat at this point. 'Dick And Mix!'

It wasn't the first time I was embarrassed to be around my friends – but it was unquestionably the time when I most wanted to be anywhere but with them.

The thing was, after Dad's death, I had nobody else. Or it *felt* like I had nobody else. My friends became my life. Those first weeks without Dad were spent in Dan's garage, still being bad at PlayStation and darts. There was an unspoken amnesty for a while as nobody quite knew what was safe to say to me – but as soon as Mark had left himself unguarded, I went in hard with my knee and gave him a dead leg. Then, as he spun and hopped, I'd punched him in the shoulder for a dead arm to match.

And then life was normal again... or as normal as it could be. It became open season once more for dead arms, dead legs, random headlocks and nudges off the pavement.

Getting past what happened to Dad didn't happen because of anything that came from school, or Michelle, or Mum – it came from Dan, Mark and Pete.

But there, in that beer garden, I wanted nothing to do with them.

Even though I hadn't spoken, it was me on whom Ian focused first. There was defiance and then he turned to Mark.

'The thing is, I can change my name anytime I want – but you're stuck with that face...' He smirked, which was the worst thing to do – and he knew it.

Mark was on his feet, leaning across the fence, spitting and furious. 'You what?'

I was definitely scared of Mark back then. There was a side to him that could snap without warning, especially if he'd been drinking. That makes it sound as if he terrorised us but it worked both ways. Someone in the year above had said something about my dad – and it was Mark who responded by wrestling him to the floor. It was Mark who took the school suspension. He could be the most loyal of friends and the worst of enemies, all within the space of a moment.

That's why I was careful that day on the edge of the towpath. I tugged on the back of Mark's T-shirt, pulling him back towards the table and away from Ian and Gemma. Ian had a curious, excited look on his face, daring almost, as if he wanted Mark to jump the fence. Gemma had only contempt.

'Just leave it,' I said. 'What's the point?'

Mark was on me then, spinning and poking a finger in my face. His breath was every one of the six pints we'd got through. 'What's it matter to you? You his friend now?'

I glanced across to Ian, who was still watching on with something close to amusement.

'It's not that,' I said, as I angled myself away, so Mark could see the beer garden behind us. People were watching by that point, wondering – or perhaps hoping – whether a bit of free entertainment was about to begin. Getting served underage in the Red Lion was easy enough – but probably not so for anyone who caused trouble.

For a moment, it felt as if Mark didn't care. As if he'd barge me away and then leap the fence to defend his masculinity anyway. It was dangerously unpredictable – because *he* was dangerously unpredictable – and, as usual, it was only Dan who could talk him down.

'Joe's right,' Dan said. 'No point, is there?'

Mark turned between us and then straightened his T-shirt before returning to his seat.

Ian laughed gently but provocatively before he muttered something to Gemma and then the two of them continued on their way.

They might have gone but the menace lingered. 'You're turning into one of that lot,' Mark said, point in the direction they'd gone. There was anger in his voice.

I almost asked 'what lot?' but instead replied with something about it being 'just a job'. I hadn't told any of them it was only £25 a week in expenses.

Mark wasn't placated. He went through another list of Ian's various nicknames, grumbled a series of baseless threats to nobody in particular – and then huffed his way inside to go to the toilet.

A part of me felt out of place at camp – but that was nothing compared to how wrong it felt to be sitting at the back of the Red Lion that evening. Without my friends, I'd have had no one when Dad died. With them, I had no idea who I was.

8

VIDEO

I was running an extension cord across the boys' field the next morning when Ian strode past me. I called after him and he paused for a moment before turning with a flourish and huffing loudly.

'What?' he said.

I was mumbling, not quite sure how to phrase things. 'I wanted to say that I'm sorry about last night.'

'You *want* to say, or you *are* saying?'

'I'm sorry. I don't think he meant anything by it and, um...'

I looked up from the ground and Ian was staring back, eyebrows raised. 'Is that it?'

'I don't know what to say.'

Ian folded his arms and watched me, waiting. When it became clear I really didn't know what to say, he spun and started to walk away again. He'd only taken a couple of steps when he turned back. He shook his head. 'Look, I know it wasn't you saying all that stuff. I know it isn't you at school – and, honestly, I don't care that much. Call me whatever you want. I'm going to stay with my aunt in Stratford in September. I'm going to college there and the chances of us ever seeing each other again are basically nothing. I am done with Mark, Pete and all of you. Say sorry, don't say sorry. Mean it, don't mean it. Whatever.' He paused for breath, lips clenched together momentarily. 'You can't be two people. If you stand by and watch, you might as well be the one doing the shouting.'

Ian took one more step away and then spun back again.

'I'm only telling you this because Gem reckons you used to be all right.'

When he walked away that time, he continued walking. I watched him go as he bounded across the field, speeding up as he got closer to the boys from his bunk. They welcomed him with a cheer and then he led them in a conga back to the bunks. It was impossible not to see the contrast from the way he was with those boys to the way Dan, Mark, Pete and I were together. The joy on one side and whatever it was we had on the other.

It felt as if I'd missed out on something growing up – except there was little time to dwell on anything in that first week at camp. One job bled into the next into the next until I was back carrying those large umbrellas across to the girls' field for reading hour.

I had almost finished setting up when I spotted Gemma for the first time since the previous evening. My smile was unreturned as she mumbled something I didn't catch, and probably didn't want to, as she turned and walked off towards her bunk.

Life felt like such a mess in that moment. Michelle was moving out, Dan and Pete would be off to college, and I'd be left with Mum and Mark. Even Mark had been talking about some sort of job with his uncle's tarmacking company.

I had none of that – and was lost in a spiral of self-pity as I drifted across to the furthest edge of the field and found a spot of unblemished grass to settle. Aside from mealtimes, the main respite in my day came around reading hour. The umbrellas took up quite a bit of space in each field and, until the hour was finished, they couldn't be removed. No other activities could be set up until after the hour, which meant Luke and I had that time free to do whatever we wanted.

I had my bag and a lukewarm can of Coke, so took out the book Michelle had given me, determined to do something with my time.

It was hard-going in those first few paragraphs of *Little Women* but as I neared the end of the first chapter, and the story neared Christmas, I realised I was taking it in without needing to re-read.

I also realised I was being watched.

One of the campers, a young girl, was standing a couple of metres away, watching me with a perplexed look on her face. She had ginger hair and freckles, the sort who'd burn from simply looking at the sky on a day like that.

'Have you read that before?' she asked.

It was Thursday by this point, four days in, and she was more or less the first camper to talk to me.

'No,' I said.

She replied with pride in her voice. 'I've read it three times. And watched the Winona Ryder movie. Mum videoed it off the telly but she reckons there's at least two more from ages ago. They've not been on the telly, though.' She paused for a moment and then: 'Have you seen any of them?'

It was impossible not to think of the videos we sometimes watched in Dan's garage. The *Nightmare on Elm Street* and the *Child's Play* movies were hardly a varied mix.

I told her I hadn't and then asked her name.

'Charlotte,' she said, 'although Mum calls me Lot.'

'What are you reading for reading hour?'

She beamed at this question and took a step closer. '*The Magician's Nephew*. I brought *all* the Narnia books – and I'm going to read them *all*.'

'How many are there?'

'Seven.'

'That's a lot of books for six weeks.'

Charlotte seemed confused by this. 'I read a book every week. How many do you read?'

For her, it was a natural question. There was obvious logic, in that, if someone of her age could read a book a week, then someone older could surely read more. I pictured the tatty *FHM* and *Loaded* magazines that lay around Dan's garage, none of which counted as a book.

And then, as if from nowhere, Amy was at Charlotte's side. Those clouds of how messy my life was cleared momentarily. She placed a gentle hand on the younger girl's shoulder and the pair of them looked down upon me as I continued to sit on the grass.

'How many books *do* you read a week?'

There was a playful smile behind Amy's question.

'As many as I can,' I said.

She grinned some more at that and then tapped Charlotte on the arm. 'Time to head back,' she said. 'It's time to meditate.'

Charlotte gave one last look at me and then skipped away back to the rest of the campers. Amy, meanwhile, continued to look down on me.

'Don't laugh at that,' she said, noticing some change in my face.

'I wasn't.'

'It's five minutes to calm them down before reading hour begins properly. We can hardly call it "five minutes for you all to shut up" – so meditation time it is.'

'I'm not judging. If you want to sit cross-legged and chant at the moon, you go for it.' I gave her half a smirk, letting her know I was joking.

She was about to say something back but it felt as if she changed her mind as she noticed the book in my hand. I twisted it around, allowing her to see the cover.

'It's my sister's,' I said.

'Sure it is.' She waited a beat and then: 'What did the kitchen make for you today? Caviar and champagne?'

'Sparkling wine instead of champagne – but we did have caviar.'

She pulled a face. 'Yuck. Have you ever had it?'

'Nope. You?'

'Mum and Dad hosted some sort of fundraising thing last Christmas. There were loads of people over and they served caviar then.'

'What does it taste like?'

Her nose twitched and she twisted her lips into one another. 'Kind of like... fishy salt. Or salty fish.'

'Sounds like a bad fish finger.'

That got another snort of laughter. I was collecting them, cherishing every one.

'That's what you should get the kitchen to make for you,' she said. 'Fish finger sandwiches.'

9

SUITCASE

My days were already largely based around trying to do jobs in the general vicinity of where I might bump into Amy. I was helped by the fact that Luke's black market was far more popular with the boys than the girls. Whenever jobs needed to be done simultaneously in separate fields, he would send me off to the girls' side while he worked on the boys'. The extent of his wares was never entirely clear but even I'd heard rumours that he sold a porno mag, specifically a *Razzle*, to one of the counsellors in the boys' bunk.

In the afternoons, after reading hour, each bunk spent time writing letters to their parents. It was my job to collect everything ready to be picked up the next day. It also became my job to sort each day's incoming mail, which included letters from parents replying to their children. It all feels so quaint in retrospect. The final year or two of a dying form that had been in place for a century before us.

I photocopied the newsletter each day and became something of an expert at where the toner went and how to fix the endless paper jams. George, Fiona or another of the directors would find me to say something like 'It's doing it again' – and then I'd hurry back to the main office and jab a needlessly complex series of buttons, before opening up the photocopier to yank free a half-torn sheet of paper. There were times when it felt as if the machine's default state was flashing with error messages.

Moments of free time were often spent putting out fires around the camp, though thankfully not literal ones. The days went quickly and each time Amy saw, and acknowledged me, offered another little shot to keep going.

On that particular day, I ate at camp, finding a spot in the mess hall and watching as Charlotte parked herself next to Amy and spent the entire meal firing questions at her. It was an odd feeling to be jealous of an eleven-year-old girl – though I certainly was.

Around all that, I did my best to avoid Ian. I had no idea what to say to him, or how to go about making anything better. He had a point, probably more than one, but it felt as if all I could do was say sorry. If that wasn't accepted, what else was there?

Each bike ride home continued to be accompanied by that growing dread that the curtains would be drawn and the air dusty. That Mum would have had a Bad Day and be spoiling for an argument over something as stupid as a dripping tap or a creaky stair.

When I got home that day, the signs were all there with the curtains shut. I took a breath as I let myself into the house – and the lack of TV echoing through the wall was something of a surprise. Perhaps a Bad Day hadn't been so bad.

I checked the living room with hesitancy but, even though it was gloomy and dark, there was nobody there and the television was off.

'Mum...?'

My call drifted around the house, unanswered, though there was a creak from the landing above. I followed the sound up the stairs, though paused at the top when I saw Mum sitting on the ground, her knees hugged to her chest. She was rocking back and forth gently, eyes wide, staring towards Michelle's open door.

That too-familiar sinking feeling in my stomach was back – but it only lasted until I got to the top and peered around the corner into my sister's room. Michelle was folding clothes into a suitcase, which was resting on a stack of sealed boxes. She turned, her features dark until she realised it was me.

'I didn't hear you come in,' she said.

I stepped to the side, so she could see Mum on the floor, even though she must have already known she was there.

'What's going on?' I asked.

It was Mum who answered from behind me, her voice hissed and harsh. 'Ask *her*.'

'Nothing's going on,' Michelle replied calmly. 'It's just that Mum doesn't want to believe I'm moving out tomorrow.'

There was a snarl to Mum's tone. 'You think you're better than us, don't you?'

Michelle turned back to folding and packing her clothes. 'Of course not.'

She continued putting things in her case, keeping her back to us as she moved methodically and deliberately. She was drawing out the moment, not to delay the packing, more to put off the continuing argument.

I waited in the doorway for a while, waiting to be the peace-keeper if things really blew – but then Michelle stopped and turned. She leant against the stack of boxes and took us both in.

'Mum's got a job,' she said. 'She starts on Monday.' There was a scathing moment of silence. A viciously judgemental pause and then: 'That's if she wants to turn up.'

When I turned to look at her, Mum had angled herself away and was staring off towards the bathroom door.

'Barry at the lumber yard's offered her a job,' Michelle

continued. 'I ran into him earlier and he said he's been waiting on an answer for three weeks. I told him she'll be in on Monday.'

Mum mumbled something that I didn't catch. She was no longer rocking or fidgeting. It was always hard to tell how much was an act with her. It felt as if she simultaneously wanted attention and to be left alone.

When I turned back to Michelle, she was watching me. 'I'll come back on Sunday night to sort her out an outfit, then again on Monday to take her to Barry's place.'

An image of Mum at the lumber yard, lugging long planks of wood, flitted through my mind. 'What's she going to do there?' I asked.

'He said there's work to do in the office, plus their whole stocktaking process needs working on. There'll be phones to answer, that sort of thing.'

Mum was still muttering behind us, the subject of the conversation, though not a part of it.

'This is what she really needs,' Michelle said. 'It's what we *all* need.'

She was right, of course – it's just a shame that Mum would end up in the hospital long before we figured out what she actually needed.

10

FISH

For something that had initially been so uncomfortable, that moment on the landing left me with a sense of hope the next morning. It was Friday and Michelle was going to be moving out that day – but if we could get Mum to work on the Monday, figure out some sort of routine, then perhaps everything *would* end up being all right.

At camp, there was an early delivery of drinks and snacks, which Luke left for me to sort out. I filled the vending machine with cans, crisps and chocolate, then logged everything left over in the tuck shop stock book. I knew it wasn't right but there was such ease to counting forty cans but writing thirty-six in the book. It's easy to blame Luke for introducing me to the scam but it was my choice to go along with it.

On that first Friday, I had a grand plan.

As lunchtime loomed, I retrieved a bag of pilfered snacks and headed out to the green at the back of the staff lounge. I opened the tent flap to the kitchen and asked for Neil, who emerged shortly afterwards, drying his hands on his apron. I passed him the bag and he checked inside, taking things out and putting them back again, before he looked up and took me in.

He rolled his tongue around his mouth. 'That'll do 'til next week,' he said. 'D'you want something now?'

It's hard to remember why I felt so giddy in the moment. As if I'd planned an elaborate bank job and had escaped with ten million, while the police were busy on the other side of town. I told him what I wanted, which was met with a shrug as he disappeared back into the kitchen. I waited alone on that green, unsure if I was doing something wrong. I was on the brink of leaving when the flap swished again and Neil returned with a plate containing my request.

By then, lunch was in full swing in the mess hall, with the usual clamour of voices and cutlery, of chaos and organisation. I opened the flap that linked the staff lounge and the mess hall, somehow managing to catch Amy's eye almost immediately. I nodded behind me, towards the lounge, and she responded with a somewhat perplexed frown before saying something to Charlotte at her side. She stood and rounded the tables, heading towards me as I retreated into the lounge. By the time she got there, fork in hand for some reason, I was trying to sit casually on the sofa as if I hadn't in any way summoned her.

'I'm pretty busy,' she said.

'I got you something,' I replied, nodding towards the plate that sat on the table near the door.

Her frown softened a little as she approached the table and then angled herself to look more closely at what was on the plate.

'I'll give you one thing,' she said, nodding towards the mess hall, 'a fish finger sandwich is a lot nicer than the salads we've all got in there. It's roughly eighty per cent lettuce.'

She picked up the plate – and it was only then that I realised my lack of thought process. I'd been so excited at thinking up the great Fish Finger Sandwich Escapade™, that I'd not *actually* considered it properly. Her options were either to eat quickly in front of me – or take the illicit food back to her table to have with the others. Neither was sensible.

I said something about ketchup packets, also on the table, in a weak attempt to justify my idiocy. She ignored those, though took a bite of the sandwich, which she chewed while angled away from me.

It was hard to know whether she saw my naivety as arrogance in the moment. That trying to get her attention with a sandwich was down to my own inflated ego and self-belief, as opposed to the precise opposite. I felt like such an idiot – but then she was kind enough to give me an out.

Amy picked up a handful of napkins and wrapped the sandwich. 'I'll eat it later,' she said.

Neither of us mentioned how cold it would be, how the bread would have hardened. It would end up in the bin, of course, but, such was my desperation to impress, I didn't think of that at the time.

'Thank you,' she said.

There was a second or two of awkwardness that this moment hadn't worked out the way I'd hoped, and then she moved towards the tent flap. Suddenly, I found myself speaking.

'Can I have a minute with you later?' I asked.

There was a moment in which I was sure there was horror in her eyes. That our little talks from the past few days had been a mirage and I'd read everything incorrectly. Perhaps it was there, or perhaps it wasn't – but her reply was an unsure-sounding: 'Um, yeah... um... when?'

I said something about my sister moving out in the evening, so having to be gone by five, and she blinked back, understandably taking none of it in.

'Find me at reading hour,' she said – and, before I could reply, probably before I could embarrass myself any further, she was gone.

Time slowed after that. Lunch seemed to go on for an age and, by the time everyone had left for Luke and me to start clearing, it felt as if it should be late in the afternoon. There was a big clock high on the canvas of the mess hall but those minute hands were frozen. We cleaned and we cleared, we folded away the tables and stacked the chairs, so the mess hall could be used as a craft space before tea. I had to fetch some things from the supply tent and then deliver a parcel to the directors' bunks. Job after job and still that clock hardly moved.

I couldn't stop thinking about that moment of confusion on Amy's face. Telling myself I'd misread everything and was about to make more of an idiot of myself. I considered going home and not coming back, in case I *was* wrong. Perhaps I would have done if there hadn't been that non-stop work.

That afternoon was the hottest of the first week, probably the hottest of the summer to that point, and I sweltered as I set up the umbrellas when it was time. Campers started sheltering under them immediately, wrapping themselves in drenched towels to stay cool. I kept an eye out for Amy but she was busy close to the Alcott bunk, doing some sort of activity with Sarah and a few of her campers.

As reading hour started, almost every patch of grass underneath the umbrellas was occupied for the first time. There was a tap at the side of the field and counsellors were traipsing back and forth to fill cups and bottles with water.

I went to the same spot as the day before. I'd been planning to use reading hour as precisely that, to read at least another chapter of Michelle's book, but it was so hot, I couldn't fathom doing much more than resting in the shade of a hedge. My skin was itching from the heat and sweat kept running in my eyes. Trying to scrub it away seemed to do little more than rub it in, which left me squinting as my eyes streamed.

It was at that point when Amy arrived. She stood over me for a moment but then edged around so that she was sitting in the shade, too. She was holding a can of Coke that she ran up and down her arms, trying to cool off.

'I heard they're cancelling afternoon activities,' she said. 'Too hot. Everyone's got to stay in their bunks or under shade.'

'That sounds like an easy afternoon for all of us.'

'Speak for yourself. The campers have barely stopped running since Monday. Everyone will be hyper after reading hour, heat or no heat.'

She pressed back onto the grass, propping herself up on her elbows before opening the can and gulping some of it down.

'What did you want?'

Somehow, I'd almost forgotten that it was me who'd asked for a minute with Amy. She'd told me to come and find her. When I hadn't she'd come to find me instead. She was looking at me expectedly but the rehearsed speech I'd gone over so many times in my head felt stuck.

'Luke said all the counsellors get Saturday night off,' I said.

Amy wasn't looking at me, which was perhaps for the best. She was laid on the grass, eyes closed.

'Only 'til ten,' she said. 'About half the campers are five-dayers, so they get picked up on Friday and go home for the weekend. The rest are seven-dayers and stay through. Because there aren't as many campers, the directors keep an eye on everyone from after tea Saturday, until ten.'

'He said counsellors can stay out later if their co-counsellors cover...?'

It was a question but there was another that was unasked behind it. At the time, I wondered if Amy knew what I was really asking – although she clearly did. I realised a lot later that girls are far more clued into that sort of thing than boys. Certainly more than I ever was.

Amy didn't reply at first, to either the asked question, or the implied one.

'Sarah's not bothered about staying out late,' she said. 'She reckons she went out a lot last year and that there's not much going on. I'm going to do most of the weekday evenings to give her a break – and she's going to do weekends.'

I'm not sure why, but I suppose I felt a little twinge of annoyance at the idea there wasn't much going on in town. It was *true*, of course, but the town was still mine. I grew up there and it was one thing for me to say how rubbish it was but another for someone else.

'It's not that bad,' I said, lying to myself as well as Amy.

'What is there to do?' she asked.

'There's the gorge. You can walk all the way to the top and look down over the camp and the town.'

Amy pushed herself up and opened her eyes. She rotated to take in the gorge that towered high over us and then glanced towards me with a sceptical look on her face. 'Oooh, a big rock.'

The sarcasm was impossible to miss as she laid back down and closed her eyes again.

'What time can you stay out 'til?' I asked.

'When?'

'On Saturdays. If Sarah covers, when do you have to be back?'

She didn't reply at first, probably because I still wasn't asking the question that was implied. I could feel a panic beginning to take hold that I wouldn't actually be able to get the words out.

'Theoretically,' Amy said, 'eight on Sunday morning. That's when breakfast happens, so if you were still out then, someone would notice. Some of the girls who live around here were saying they might go home for a night and sleep in a proper bed.'

'What about you...?'

There was another delay in the reply. She was toying with me, of course, though I was too immature to realise it at the time. I almost asked the question again but then:

'Nah... I'm here for the long haul. I'm a proper seven-dayer. Besides, Mum usually has some sort of dinner party, or gala, or garden party every weekend. It's much better being here.'

My mouth was dry. All the supplementary questions had been used up and I had nothing left to ask, except the only one I wanted to. I looked down upon her, figuring that I could say the words and then, if she said 'no', I didn't need to ever see her again. This was a temporary job, for little money. I could go home at the end of the day and never come back.

And so, out it came: 'Iwaswonderingifyoumightwantto-gooutwithmeonSaturdaynight?'

Amy pushed herself up again and opened her eyes. Her pupils flared from the change in light as she took me in.

'Was that Welsh?' she asked. 'I have a friend who speaks Welsh but I only ever learned "nos da", which she reckons means good night.' A pause. 'It might be a swear word. I hadn't thought of that until now. I could've been going around swearing at Mum every night...'

I stared at her, somewhat panicked. 'It's not Welsh,' I managed. There really was no alternative. 'I was, um, asking, um, if you, um, wanted to, er, go out, um, with, um, me, on, er, Saturday night... um.'

It was in the open, sort of. A genie out of the lamp, down the street with no intention of ever returning.

There was a moment of quiet, as if everything had stopped... everything except me because, for some reason, I was still talking.

'I mean, it's no worry if you don't... and I was just thinking... and it was just an idea... and it's totally up to you... and... um...' I had to shut myself up. If I kept talking, there was a good chance I'd end up asking her to elope to Gretna Green, or something even madder. If there was anything madder.

That final um hung, as if it was echoing around the field. I had never asked a girl out before that, nor had anyone asked me.

I knew the answer a moment before she gave it. Her gaze darted past me, towards the umbrellas and the rest of the girls' field.

'I can't,' she said.

'Oh, yeah, that's fine, I... er—'

'I've already got plans with Ian and Gemma. They were going to show me the sights. The Eiffel Tower, Times Square, the, I don't know... taxi rank.' A pause. 'The famous gorge...'

'Of course. That sounds great. Brilliant.' Every word was ending on an upturn as if I was Australian, or rattling out a series of new questions.

'Come with us,' she said. 'I don't know what they've got planned but it'll all be around town.'

She'd barely made the offer before I talked myself out of it.

'Oh, it's just I usually see my friends on Saturdays. At the cricket club...'

It was easy to see why this sudden shift confused her. Was I asking her to come to the cricket club, or out in general, or... what? I don't think I knew.

Amy shook her head slowly and shot another glance past me towards the field. 'That doesn't sound like my thing,' she said. 'When are you back here? Do you work weekends?'

I managed something about having Saturdays off and then alternating Sundays with Luke but, in all honesty, I could have been babbling about anything.

'Are you in on Sunday?' she asked.

'It's Luke's week,' I think I replied.

We remained there, cloaked in awkwardness until Amy pushed herself up onto her knees and then stood. I looked up to her but she was standing between me and the sun, her features shadowed in darkness. 'Enjoy your cricket,' she said. 'Hit some sixes, or whatever it is you do.'

I thought about telling her that I didn't actually play but that petulant, childish side of me had already made up my mind that I wouldn't see her again. I didn't know how to cope with rejection at that age. I didn't understand that we'd met days before, had exchanged a few brief conversations, and that I was putting her on the spot. Of course she was going to say no.

'Is it sixes?' she asked. 'Or fours?'

'Both.'

I think she nodded, although the shade made it hard to know. 'See you Monday,' she said.

'Definitely,' I replied – knowing this would certainly be my final day at camp.

11

VAN

When I got home that evening, a small mustard yellow van was parked at the front. A faint navy British Telecom logo was still visible on the side panel and the back doors were open, with a pair of rusting steps lowered to the ground.

The front door of the house was open and, as I went to walk inside, Michelle was coming out with a box in her hands. We each stepped back until I moved to the side to let her past.

'Where'd the van come from?' I asked.

'Borrowed it from work for the weekend. I can get everything done in one trip.'

I trailed her to the back, where she pushed the box inside. It was more like a car than a van, except that the whole of the back had storage space, instead of seats.

'Nice colour,' I said.

She laughed and said that the garage had bought a couple of ex-BT vehicles at auction, with the idea of fixing them up and selling. I didn't mention that they'd need to paint them first.

Inside the house and the living room door was closed. Michelle said that Mum was still pretending the move wasn't happening, which sounded about right. I helped my sister carry boxes and her suitcase out to the van and then climbed inside and pushed everything to the back. The van was unquestionably overkill given she didn't own anywhere near enough to fill it.

When that was done, I sat on the tail of the van, legs dangling out the back as Michelle stood over me and stretched high. She groaned in pleasure as I heard something click and then she put her hands on her hips and arched backwards.

'I'll be back Sunday to help Mum get ready for work,' she said.

'What if she won't go?'

'I'll make sure she goes. She needs structure. It wasn't always like this.'

She said that as if I'd somehow forgotten how things used to be, although I suppose part of me had. This had become the norm in such a short period that I couldn't see past it.

Michelle reached for her bag and removed a piece of notepaper that she passed across. 'That's my address,' she said.

I read it and then looked up. 'I don't know where this is.'

'You do. It's those new flats they built where those fields out past the garage used to be. If you start at my work, go along there, turn right at the Spar; left, right, right – and then it's number 11a.'

I knew I wasn't going to remember any of that. 'Why 11a?' I asked.

'Because it's above eleven.'

'What about twelve?'

'There's a twelve as well.'

'None of that makes sense.'

My sister smiled down on me and it felt as if there was a hint of sadness there. It was the end of something for both of us. The start, too.

She nodded towards the house and then locked the van before we headed inside together. We ignored the living room and went up the stairs. Our rooms were opposite each other and, though my door was closed, hers was open. Light cascaded out, spreading across the landing and turning the usually gloomy space into something bright and alien.

We went into her room, where the walls were bare and there was nothing left except the carpet, bed and a pillow without any case. The curtains were open and so was the window. The warmth of the day seeped through the space but there was a freshness, too.

Before I knew it, Michelle had her arms around me. I instinctively tried to pull away but she clasped me tighter. We were the same height back then and our heads slotted onto one another's shoulders. I felt her breathe in and out.

'I get four brother-sister hugs a year and this is one,' she said, her voice muffled and behind me.

I don't think I held onto her. My arms probably hung loose, like some sort of useless shop dummy, though I stopped fighting her off as she held me. I didn't really *do* hugging back then.

When she let me go, she stepped back and smiled gently with her lips tight together. Her voice cracked when she spoke.

'It'll be all right,' she said.

'You're not the one who has to live with her.'

'I know...'

Anger burned, as much as I tried to fight it. The injustice of what Mum had become. The frustration that Michelle was getting away and not me. The worry of what life would be.

I only realised I was crying when she reached and brushed something away from my cheek. The tears had come from nowhere, bubbling up from down deep. Crying had never been a thing for me until after Dad died. I'd never seen him cry and it was as if, without him around, I had permission. I tried to turn away but Michelle held me again, gripping me so hard that there was no chance to escape, even if I wanted. We stayed like that for a while, probably until I stopped.

Afterwards, it was all embarrassment and apologies, both of us, though me more than her.

'I'll be back Sunday,' she said.

I grunted something that was probably 'yes', though any words were stuck in my throat. Michelle said she had to go and pick up the keys, so I followed her out of the room and then sat on the top step as she headed downstairs. I pressed back, letting that top step dig into my back, and listened as my sister opened the living room door to tell Mum she was going. I didn't hear a reply and it didn't take long until that door closed and the front one opened. She called a cheery 'see ya' but I pretended I didn't hear.

Then the door closed.

Then the van started.

Then she was gone.

And that was it. Just me and Mum, plus that inescapable, drowning sense that something awful was going to happen.

12

CIDER

Mum slept on the sofa that Friday night. When I went downstairs the following morning, I opened the living room door a crack to allow a sliver of light to puncture the space. It was enough to see her chest rising and falling, so I crept inside, collected the dirty cups and plates and then backed as quietly as I could into the kitchen.

The mugs were stained brown with tea and one of the plates was coated with some sort of greeny-brown sludge that I figured was best not to think too much about. I washed everything in the sink, trying to do so as silently as possible, then left it all on the draining board. When that was done, I filled the kettle and went searching for teabags, before leaving a couple on the counter. It wasn't much but it would save Mum a few jobs later – plus lower the risk of returning to her raging about something I either had or had not done.

After that, I headed outside, which was like walking into a wall. It was even hotter than the Friday; the sort of day where doing much of anything is a full workout.

By the time I'd walked across town to the cricket club, my clothes were stuck to me and I was gasping for something to drink. I bought a Coke from the bar and then went back outside, where I sat in the shade of a tree at the edge of the boundary. Dan, Mark and Pete were all fielding – which meant there was going to be a lengthy period of me waiting and not doing much else.

I half watched, mainly looking up whenever there was the sound of the ball hitting a bat, or if the players got particularly excited about something. As well as that, I skimmed in and out of Michelle's book, careful not to lift it too high in case someone might catch a glimpse of the cover.

The setting was something spectacular. I didn't play, though I'd heard from enough people who did that it was one of the most scenic grounds in the area – and something of a treat for visiting teams. It was hard to argue with that as I half watched the figures in white chase around under a perfect sky dwarfed by the grandeur of the gorge beyond.

Around an hour passed until Dan was sent out to the boundary to field. I walked around to his position and rested against the fence. We spoke in fits and starts as he moved in and out, though much of the talking was done by him as he asked my opinion about the game. I rarely knew what I was talking about when it came to sport but he wasn't listening anyway. He said that his captain didn't know what he was doing, that some fielder was in the wrong place. Something about a spinner.

Discounting the barman's 'what can I get you?', I realised Dan was the first – and only – person I'd talked to that day. I wanted him to stay, for him to ask me how camp had been, but it wasn't long before he was called back towards the central part of the field, never to return.

After that, I returned to my spot in the shade, alternating between watching and reading.

The innings took around three hours to finish and then all the players disappeared into the clubhouse for something to eat and drink. I could have gone in if I wanted – but, on the times I did, it always felt like gate-crashing someone's wedding. The players ate together and I simply hung around.

I bought myself another drink and then sat on the chairs outside the pavilion, waiting and pretending this was a fun way to spend a Saturday. Going to the cricket club over the weekend had been my routine for a few summers as my friends moved into the adult teams. I found myself wondering whether I'd been pretending about enjoying it for all that time. I was living through other people; listening to their victories, successes and failures while creating none of my own. I really was a follower.

I don't know why it suddenly occurred to me that particular afternoon, other than that, during the week at camp, things had been happening *because* of me, not despite. Simple things like the umbrellas being set up, so the kids could have shade, or the benches set up so they could have somewhere to sit.

A while passed and then Mark emerged from the changing rooms. His kit was stained green from the grass, with smudges of dark red from the ball. He was wearing white pads, gloves, and swinging his bat from side to side. He did a jog on the spot and then a couple of squats before starting a slow walk out towards the middle at the side of another batsman.

Pete and Dan came to sit next to me, both also wearing pads and holding their bats. They stretched their legs out, the metal spikes of their shoes click-clacking on the concrete. We watched as the opposing team returned to the field, followed closely by the two umpires. Mark was already in the middle, pacing and waiting.

'How's camp?' Dan asked.

'All right,' I said, glad he'd asked but not wanting to commit to saying it was good or bad. I'm not sure we ever described anything as 'good' to one another. 'It's money, innit?'

That was my justification for spending the summer away from my friends. None of them were working – and they'd have been bemused if they knew how little I was making.

'I heard your sister was moving out?' Dan added.

'How'd you know that?'

'Everything gets around, doesn't it?'

That much was true. Our town was small enough that very little happened without someone's cousin's aunt's best friend's cat seeing it and reporting back. I let that sit for a moment, not wanting to talk about it.

'She went yesterday,' I said, hoping it ended this strand of conversation.

'How's your mum with it?'

I felt Dan looking sideways towards me, sensing his genuine interest. I couldn't face him, couldn't give a proper answer. I should have said that she'd taken it appallingly and that I was here so I didn't have to be there. That I dreaded what lay ahead.

Some things simply could not be shared, though. It was how we'd always been as friends. We never talked about Dad's death, we simply fell back into the routine of low-level violence and teasing. Of PlayStation, darts and Dan's garage. At the time, I thought that normality was what I needed.

'She's fine,' I said.

Out in the middle, Mark was hunched, tapping his bat into the ground and sending a series of earthy thumps reverberating around the green. He looked up, waiting for the bowler to run in for the first ball. A few seconds later and it was all over. He lunged forward, swishing the bat in an arc. There was a woody-sounding *thwick* and then, as the ball carried through to one of the fielders behind the stumps, all the opposition players leapt in the air.

I felt both Dan and Pete tense as we all knew what was going to happen. The replacement batsman pushed up from his seat and started walking to the middle, swinging his bat and doing little jumps on the way. He and Mark didn't exchange a word – and the rest of the home team were silent as Mark strode past into the changing room.

Moments later, there was a thunderous bang of Mark's bat being flung against something and then a second *thump*, which sounded like a door being kicked.

The players on the sideline acted as if nothing had happened, though the ones in the middle were exchanging amused glances.

As the game continued, there was minimal conversation off the field until Mark emerged from the dressing room a few minutes later. He was out of his whites, in shorts and a black vest with flip-flops. Without a word to his teammates, he stormed around the boundary until he slumped in roughly the spot where I'd been sitting during the first innings.

The day didn't get a lot better from there.

The team were thrashed and neither Pete nor Dan scored many more runs than Mark.

As was the custom, win or lose, we regrouped in the bar after everyone had showered and changed. The clubhouse always smelled of shower gel on those evenings. The older players' wives and girlfriends often showed up for a couple of drinks, although that didn't mean a gentler edge.

Lager might have been our drink at the Red Lion – but it was strictly cider at the cricket club, and not the standard Strongbow. I never saw it on sale anywhere other than the club, but Death Rat was seven point one per cent and pumped into glasses with small chunks of apple. Nobody ever bothered about ID at the cricket club, either.

I'd been sticking to soft drinks during the day but, after his early end to the afternoon, Mark had already raced through at least three pints of Rat. I had a sense of what might be to come and perhaps should have left after the game. There was an inevitability to everything and, I suppose, a part of me relished it all.

As the evening drew in, Mark continued drinking – but the four of us were keeping up, even though he'd had that head start. We were sitting around a circular table, a little away from the bar, when Mark returned from the bar with another pint. He plonked it on the table hard enough to make some of it slosh over the top and then dropped onto the stool with enough force to make the legs squeak across the floor. He almost fell but righted himself and acted as if it hadn't happened.

'What's going on with you and Dicklodocus?' he demanded.

I picked up my pint, taking a sip and using up the few seconds to ignore the question. Pete and Dan were both silent but Mark's stare didn't drop as I put down the drink.

'Nothing,' I replied. 'We work at the same place.'

'You're not bumming him, are you?'

I didn't answer that, knowing there'd be no correct answer, regardless of what I said.

Dan shuffled in his seat and glanced between us. 'C'mon, mate,' he said to Mark, 'let it go.'

Mark was cradling his drink by then but he whacked it back onto the table, making it spill a second time.

'God's sake, I'm just having a laugh. What's wrong with that? We used to have a laugh, didn't we?'

Nobody replied and the four of us sat, drinking, not daring to say anything that might make it worse.

The evening continued around us as the opposition players left as one big group. Numbers temporarily dwindled but then the first team arrived back from wherever they'd been playing and the place swelled once more. Players swapped stories of how their various days had gone – which only made it worse when a series of first-teamers came across to commiserate with Mark over his first-baller. He seethed silently, but Mark knew better than to show the older members of the team that he was still bothered by it. They'd never stop ribbing him otherwise.

We continued drinking.

One more pint.

Two.

Three.

I didn't even like the stuff.

Words became more slurred. The exaggerations over the day's success and failure were more pronounced. I kept thinking of Amy, wondering what she was up to a mile or so away with Ian and Gemma, wishing she hadn't said no. Or wishing I hadn't said no when she said I should go out with them.

I was scared of Ian, not in any physical way but because he was the bigger person. He'd told people I was a bully and he was right. I'd never stood up to Mark, always relying on Dan to talk him down when things were heated. Even worse, I sometimes allowed myself to be egged into things. I'd be the one calling other people names. Making their lives miserable. I couldn't hide behind the façade of being present but not involved.

One more cider.

Another.

We were all underage but nobody cared.

Another drink.

It was seven point one per cent but we were throwing it back like it was Coke.

We didn't only pick on others. Of our four, Pete got it as bad as anyone. There was once a crease in his trousers during a biology lesson. It was three years ago but he was called 'Boner' every day after. And, because he was Boner, there was also Bones, Little Bones, Boneyard, Boney M, The Creamer, Creamery, Cream Dream, Fresh Cream, Whipped Cream, Double Cream – and so on. He laughed along but there couldn't have been any way he enjoyed that.

My name was too short, so I was Joey – or, because we found out a baby kangaroo was a Joey, I was sometimes called Roo. Years before, Dad was caught doing thirty-nine in a thirty, so Mark called him, and therefore me, Speedy Gonzalez. That became Gonzo – but then, after Dad died, it went away.

Dan was Dan The Man, or Dan With The Plan – but his name is too short as well.

Mark had it easy, too. He was Marco, Marky or Marky Boy. Sometimes Markster. It was mainly just Mark, though.

Except, in the way people who say the meanest things to each other are often those who are closest, there was one other nickname.

Mark's dad was sent to prison for a few weeks when we were ten or eleven. It was something to do with nicked shopping from an Iceland, and not his first offence. Pete called Mark 'Jail-bait', which was the one and only time anybody ever said it. Nobody risked it a second time.

But our roundabout, slurring conversation was only going one way that night and, after another drink, Mark had circled back to where we were.

'Are you bumming him, then?'

Dan started to say something but Mark talked over him, poking a finger towards me.

'He can talk for himself.'

I finished the cider, wincing and hating every last drop. The bitterness dried out my mouth and I don't think there was ever a time when I actually wanted one.

'What do you want me to say?' I replied.

'It's a simple question. Are you bumming him, or not?'

I pushed back the stool and stood but Mark wasn't letting it go.

'C'mon, Gonzo. Are you bumming him?'

And in the moment, with my sister leaving, with Amy saying no, with *me* saying no to her, with my pitiful idea that a girl might go out with me because I gave her a sandwich I'd exchanged for stolen goods – and, maybe worst of all, with Ian showing me a mirror of who I was, I felt as if I had nothing.

It was the cider but it wasn't. The alcohol had only enhanced what I already felt.

The town was *pathetic*.

My life was *pathetic*.

I was *pathetic*.

'Piss off, Jailbait.'

The next bit was slow motion. One of those scenes in a Western where somebody walks into a bar and the music stops. Where everybody looks and they all know what's about to happen a moment before it does.

Dan lunged forward to stop it but I was already ahead of him as I threw the first punch. I was never a fighter, nor a lover, I suppose – but there was something burning in me that night.

The punch barely landed. At best it glanced Mark's cheek but, more realistically, it missed. He spun slightly from his seat, standing at the same time – and then it was on. We were on the floor, nose to nose, chest to chest, trying to fling punches at one another's head and body. A glass went spinning and smashed somewhere nearby. We could have rolled into the broken glass but neither of us was thinking. Mark's forehead pressed hard into mine. I could smell the booze on his breath, perhaps even taste it as we were so close. I was trying to fire punches at the side of his head but my arm was clamped tight to my body by his as he tried to do the same.

A table went spinning, then a stool. Another glass shattered and then a table was on top of us. Cricketers stood around us, trying to get us apart, and there were flashes of their going-out shoes as our elbows flew and knees collided.

My chest was hammering so hard that I could feel the blood rushing around my body. We rolled in the crisp shards and sandwich crumbs, back and across the cider-stained sticky patch of floor. There were no real blows but our sweat rained on each other. There was spit and froth and wide eyes and growling threats about who was going to kill whom.

And then, finally, there were other people's hands on us, yanking us up and apart. Someone had a grip under my right armpit, while someone else had me under the other. I flailed my legs and fought, trying to kick Mark; trying to kick anyone in the general vicinity. People were shouting, someone was crying, another glass was dropped – and then I was being hauled towards the door.

It was cold by then.

Dark.

Street lights glowed in the distance but the only light in the car park streamed from the windows of the clubhouse.

Someone pushed me hard in the chest, shoving me away from the building, telling me to go home. I was panting and there was snot on my top lip, while sweat continued to pour from my face.

I must have lunged towards the door, wanting to get back inside, because I was pushed away again, harder this time. I ended up on my arse, the cold, gravelly tarmac of the car park shaking me free of the frenzy as it suddenly dawned on me where I was and what had happened.

Someone asked whether I was done and I nodded, then lay back on the cool, hard ground, trying to catch my breath.

The stars twinkled high above and the moon flared white. A large part of me wanted Mark to storm out and start kicking me in the side, the legs, the head. Make it all go away.

It took a minute, maybe two, but then someone did end up standing over me, offering a hand to pull me up. Dan gripped my wrist with his hand and pulled until I was sitting. It was only then that I realised my palm was grazed, with flecks of dust and grit stuck to the raw flesh.

'Do you need help getting home?' he asked.

'No.'

He handed me my rucksack and then crouched to offer me his shoulder as I managed to stand. My knees ached and something was stinging over the top of my eye. From inside the club-house, someone was still shouting; maybe Mark, maybe not.

'We can call a taxi if you want...?'

'Don't bother.'

I started walking away from him, heading towards the lights of the road. My whole body was throbbing by then; knees and elbows especially. I stomped and sulked my way across town, sticking to the shadows and not wanting to be seen.

The town was noticeably busier, swelled by tourists and probably counsellors on their evening off. Faint songs from the pubs competed with each other for prominence and the night smelled of cigarettes. People were laughing, someone was singing. With the heat of the day gone, they were ready to enjoy themselves.

And then I saw them on the other side of the street. Ian, Gemma and Amy were walking in a line, laughing about something, and almost skipping with delight. They crossed the road a little along from me, taking the turn that led to the hill back up to camp.

I held my breath, frozen in the darkened gap between street lights, wanting to be anywhere that wasn't there.

13

GORGE

I didn't get hangovers back then, not real ones anyway. There was none of that day-long paralysis that followed a heavy night. Instead, I'd find myself avoiding light as if some sort of vampire. At worse, I'd have a throbbing ache somewhere around my temples that was easily cured with a couple of paracetamol.

By the time I woke up in the early afternoon of Sunday, the worst thing I had going on was a dry mouth. I popped a couple of painkillers from the bathroom cabinet and drank down a couple of glasses of water, then sat on the toilet, examining my injuries from the night before.

There were grazes on both knees and a scratch around my right elbow. My left palm was scuffed, although a lot of the skin had seemingly healed overnight. There was a scratch across the top of my eye that had wept blood overnight and crusted into my eyebrow. Much of it was superficial. I'd had worse when I used to join in with the playground football games at school. Those were all a big free-for-all of flailing legs and deliberate trips.

I did my best to clean the blood from my brow and then headed downstairs. Mum was in the living room and, for once, the curtains were open. The lack of circulation still made it musty and dank but it was an improvement from any other day that week. I almost asked if she'd heard me get in the night before but she was focused on the television and there was little point in potentially setting her off.

Instead, I sat in the armchair and watched with her. It was another game show, the colours washed out of the old recording, the men's suits too big, their heads balding, the music cheap, the prizes worthless. Everyone looked so old in those days.

Mum spoke without turning to look at me. 'You off every weekend?'

'Only Saturdays,' I replied. 'I alternate Sundays – so I'll be in next week.'

She waited a moment, perhaps absorbing the information, perhaps waiting for the guy with the massive glasses to get the answer wrong.

'You should be out there doing something,' she said. 'Can't sit around here if you're going to drop out of school.'

'I haven't dropped out, Mum. I'm waiting to see what grades I get.'

It was a lie couched in truth. I *hadn't* dropped out and I *was* waiting to see what grades I got. I also had little to no intention of going back to do A levels, regardless of what happened.

'Your dad wouldn't let you sit around.' It felt like an accusation – and Mum would never have brought him up unless she was trying to get at me.

'I'm *not* sitting around, I've been working all week.' I pressed back into the chair, not in the mood. 'Besides, Dad's not here.'

There was a third point I wanted to make – that *she* was the one sitting around all day – but I'd already destroyed at least one relationship that weekend.

It hadn't always been the way it was at home. Mum had been made redundant at the start of the year. She used to work for the council in the planning department. Her bosses had let everyone get through Christmas and New Year, then decided to make about ten per cent of the workforce redundant. She got a few cards when she left, a bit of a collection... and that was it. Michelle and I assumed she'd look for a different job but things gradually slipped.

When Dad died, the house had been paid off, so there was no enormous financial need for her to work. Michelle had been covering the day-to-day stuff.

In those first couple of weeks, Mum went out to meet work friends here and there. She met Michelle at the garage and they would go to a café during lunch. She picked me up from school if it was raining. The decline was somehow both steady and rapid because those first couple of weeks quickly gave way to none of those things happening. She stopped changing her clothes and opted to sleep on the sofa with the TV on. She drank tea all day and harder stuff all night. The television was a constant companion, with me at school and Michelle at work.

A part of her seemed to have died with Dad, another when she lost the job she'd had for ten years or more. The first few weeks after Dad died were awful, but it was only after Mum lost her job that things got really bad. Like she might have been able to cope with one terrible thing – but not two.

Michelle and I tried to help, tried to take her places, and keep the house stocked with food – but there was only so much we could do. She was the parent, after all.

I began to spend more time at Dan's garage. Michelle had things she had to do after work. Anything that meant we didn't need to be at home.

Meanwhile, Mum's days were the same... except those Bad Days became so bad that she was unbearable to be around. Our desire to help her slowly ebbed away with the vicious mood swings, the hurled mugs, the tantrums and, eventually, those long silent spells in the stinking living room.

And, on that Sunday, as she talked of Dad not letting me sit around, another Bad Day felt close.

I left the living room, then the house entirely as I grabbed my bike from the back of the house and part-cycled, part-wheeled my way down to town. The pubs were beginning to fill again, noise levels rising to a clamour as residents and tourists ambled in, ready to finish off the weekend.

I didn't want to risk running into anyone I knew, especially not anyone involved with the cricket club, so I cycled up the winding road towards the gorge. The houses thinned as I moved further out of town, replaced by cars parked on the verge. I continued up and up, legs searing from the effort, until I reached the stile next to the large green and white National Trust board.

My bike disappeared over the top of the stile and then I followed, backpack over my aching shoulders as I set off along the rocky path towards the top. The trail was lined with trees and generous shade. It was warm but I wasn't going to stop for anything. I passed a few people on the way up and there were sideways glances because of the bike I was dragging – but nobody spoke to me. In that moment, it was exactly how I wanted things to be.

I let the sense of anger rumble and churn. By that point, it was probably more anger at myself than anything or anyone else.

The trail eventually opened out onto a large craggy rock-face. There was a series of signs about staying away from the edge, being careful on wet rocks and not feeding the wildlife.

Given the number of cars around the bottom, the top of the gorge was surprisingly empty. There were a couple of picnickers and some guy hovering close to the edge – but there was enough space that I was largely alone. I dropped my bike and crept towards the lookout, crouching and enjoying the rush as the ground hurtled up to me and away again.

Nobody cared about the warning signs. The whole point was to get as close as possible to the lip.

I waited for my head to clear and then looked down on the speckled white tents that decorated the green of the campsite below. Dots moved from place to place and, beyond, the town sat still and pristine. The big houses were in the distance and I took a moment wondering if I could figure out which was George's. They all looked the same.

The cricket club was there, too. More green among the buildings. Beyond that was fields and forest, untouched and unoccupied all the way out to the shimmering horizon.

My legs dangled over the side as I sat on the very tip of the gorge, leaning back, and then lying, on the rock as the sun beat down.

A few people came and went, standing close to the edge and taking their photos. A woman said something to me about being too close but I didn't recognise her and certainly didn't listen.

There was a part of me that wouldn't have minded if the rocks had crumbled away, me on top. I wondered what people might say afterwards. Whether Dan would call me a good friend, whether Michelle would talk about how much I'd be missed. I thought about what Ian would say, or think. If it would be some sort of comeuppance.

The craggy, awkward surface dug into my back and I thought about Mum. How she'd been through so much. I pictured that police car outside the house when Dad had died and wondered what she'd do if another turned up.

It was after that I shifted away from the edge. I sat further back on the rock in the shade, reading Michelle's book, and actually taking it in that time. I was a few chapters in when I realised I was actually enjoying it. I had always thought books and reading were for weirdos or snobs. That they were something I'd never understand.

Except, on those rocks, I figured out that it wasn't about the book itself, it was about the story within.

Reading was… fun – and it actually passed the time.

The sun was still high, the sky still blue – but I'd left my watch somewhere, probably at home, and when I realised I was completely alone at the top, I figured it was time to head home.

It was easier getting down and there were a few spots where I was able to freewheel on my bike along the trail.

By the time I got home, Michelle's car was parked outside. I let myself into the house and carried my bike through to the back, before dropping it and heading into the living room.

Michelle was there by herself. The TV was muted and she looked up to take me in, before standing and crossing the room to get a better look.

'What happened to you?' she asked.

'What?'

'You're burned red, for one. Plus there's a cut over your eye.'

'Fell off my bike,' I said

She frowned a little and I wondered if news had gone around the town about my fight with Mark. She would hear sooner or later, if she hadn't already.

Luckily, she changed the subject before I had to.

'Mum's making sure her work outfit still fits,' Michelle said. 'She'll be down in a minute.'

After the mini argument that morning, I'd forgotten that Mum was starting work at the lumber yard the following day.

'She had a shower,' Michelle added. 'I helped her dry her hair, and cooked her beans on toast…'

'Is it a Good Day?'

Michelle didn't reply – but we both knew why. It was too big a question. As if any positive answer would jinx it.

'What's the flat like?' I asked instead.

'Great. It feels bigger than it is because there are cupboards built in, plus a big wardrobe. So much space.'

'Have you unpacked?'

'More or less. You should come over next week. One night after we're both done at work. Bring your friends if you want.'

If she had heard about the fight then she was acting as if she hadn't. I wondered if there was an edge to the offer, a challenge for me to tell her what really happened with the cut above my eye.

As if on cue to avoid me having to explain any of that, there was the sound of footsteps on stairs and then Mum appeared in the living room. There was that moment again, time stopping, because it was like going back to the past when Dad was around and she'd be at work every day.

She wasn't wearing anything special. A dark skirt and white top, the sort of thing she always wore to the council offices, but there was something reassuring about seeing her as she used to be.

Mum looked to me and then to Michelle. 'This OK?'

'You look great, Mum,' she replied.

Despite everything, despite the hope which flared that things would work out, I still couldn't quite bring myself to say it. She was still Mum, after all.

I garbled something about it being fine, which made Michelle laugh. 'Don't go too overboard,' she said.

Mum didn't smile or laugh but there was a twitch to her eyes. Understanding, perhaps.

Michelle said she'd be back in the morning to take Mum to work – then she turned to me and asked what time I had to be at camp. I wanted to say that I was done and wouldn't be going back. That things hadn't worked out and it wasn't for me.

Except, with Mum going back to work, I couldn't quite do it. I couldn't let her down if she was going to try to get her life, *our* lives, back to some sort of normality.

'Eight,' I said. 'I start at eight.'

14

FIVER

Mum was sitting in the kitchen when I got downstairs the next morning. I was still half expecting to find her asleep on the sofa. It was Monday, the start of a new week: a clean sheet, a new leaf and all that. There was a plate in front of her with two slices of toast. She'd nibbled at one but the second was untouched. She was wearing the same outfit she'd tried on the day before, with her hair tied back neatly.

When she smiled at me and asked how I slept, there was weariness in her eyes. A night of fractured sleep, or, perhaps, months. Finally, she'd made an effort.

I said I'd slept fine and she pointed out I was going to be late for camp if I didn't get going. It was quarter-to-eight – and she was right – except there was no way I was going to leave without waiting to see Mum get into Michelle's car.

We sat together in the kitchen, not saying much – which was better than sitting in the living room and arguing. She asked if I was hungry and I said I'd eat at camp. All the while, she picked at her toast, not eating it.

It was ten-past-eight when Michelle arrived and beeped her horn. Mum picked up her bag from the kitchen counter and gave me a blank look before I ushered her to the front door. Michelle waved, full of eagerness, and I found myself waving back.

I waited and watched, half expecting Mum to kick off her work shoes and bolt along the road. She'd dive into one of the side alleys and disappear into the web of the estate as Michelle and I tried to track her down.

She didn't, of course. She got into Michelle's car, closed the door behind her and reached for the seat belt.

It was all so normal – and yet that was the thing which had been lacking in our lives for what felt like such a long time. It barely seemed real. An imposter or an invader, who looked and talked like Mum but certainly didn't act like her. Not the her she'd become.

Michelle waved again and then shunted the car into gear before driving off. I watched them go around the corner, still partly wondering if Mum would open the door while the car was moving and bail out.

Barry's lumber yard was on the other side of town, a few minutes away in the car, and I thought of all the junctions and lights where Michelle might have to stop on the way. All those little opportunities for Mum to make a break for it.

Before he died, Dad had run a landscaping and gardening company. After his death, one of his friends, Barry Dennis, bought out the remaining assets of the business and folded them into his own. There were no Miller's Landscaping vans on the roads – but there were ones belonging to Dennis Landscaping. Barry had repainted Dad's vans and had his own logo stencilled over the top. He'd even used the same shade of brown.

That buyout was the main reason Mum no longer needed to work to pay the bills – and there was some degree of irony that he was trying to encourage her to go back.

I waited on the street for a minute or two, that image of Mum escaping not quite leaving me, until I figured I should get to camp. I grabbed my bike and pedalled hard across town, arriving a little after half-past and dumping my bike on the grass between the staff lounge and the kitchen.

It was a rush and I already had a lengthy explanation planned for Luke regarding my lateness. There was an alarm that didn't go off and a shower that only had cold water. My bike had a puncture...

...And I didn't use any of it, because the first person I saw when I walked into the staff lounge was Amy. She was reading through the day's newsletter, the pandemonium of breakfast raging in the mess hall behind, when she looked up and took me in.

'What happened to you?' she asked.

'What?'

'You're all red and there's a scratch above your eye.'

It was almost exactly what my sister had said to me the day before.

'Trying a new look,' I said, hoping for a laugh that didn't arrive.

'How did you really get that scratch?'

'Fell off my bike.'

She huffed with something approaching annoyance and I wondered what the problem was, until I realised it was nothing to do with my grazes.

'You've cost me a fiver,' she said.

'Why?'

'And Ian. You've cost him a fiver, too. He's gonna be annoyed.'

'What happened?'

'*You* happened. I didn't think you'd show up this week – and Ian was convinced you were done. It was only Gem who thought you'd be here. She was like, "You'll see. He'll be there." We both owe her a fiver now.'

I thought Amy might be joking, although there was little

humour about her scowl. I wondered why Gemma had such faith in me, given our limited conversations in the past decade.

'Why did you think I'd not be here?'

She pouted her lips slightly and raised an eyebrow. For a moment, it felt as if she knew everything I'd been thinking when I asked her out. That I didn't know what to do with rejection, even though it wasn't her fault.

'Just a feeling,' she replied, somewhat cryptically.

I don't think I wanted to push for any further explanation, so I changed the subject.

'Did you have a good night?' I asked.

She blinked back into the lounge. 'On Saturday? As good a night as you're going to get around here. It's not like we took in an opera and then went to the Ritz for cocktails.'

It was a foreign language. Ideas of which I couldn't conceive. 'Is opera your thing?' I asked.

A snort: 'Opera is *nobody's* thing. People just pretend to like it.' A pause: 'Have you ever been?'

'No.'

'You're not missing much. It goes on for ages.'

'What time did you get in?' I regretted asking as soon as I'd said it. It's not like I wanted to check up on her, more I was interested in what kind of night she'd had.

Amy threw up her hands. 'You're worse than Mum!'

'I didn't mean it like that. It was because of the ten o'clock curfew and…'

Amy waved it away with a swish of her hand. I'd not seen her in two days and she'd caught the sun in that time, her skin turning a soft golden brown. 'Two or three,' she said airily. 'That eight a.m. breakfast bell comes *way* too early when you're hungover. Then it's only a few hours until the five-day campers are back – and there are parents to entertain and…' she tailed off. 'Anyway, in summary: good night, back by four.'

'I thought you said two or three?'

That got a grin. She took a small half-step towards the flap that led back to the mess hall and it felt as if she was about to leave. I tried to think of something to say that might keep the conversation going but I was blank until she stretched a newsletter across in my direction.

'Did you know it's Craft Week?' she asked, as I took it. 'There's a big gallery show on Friday and prizes for the top-three. The counsellors are already losing their minds over which bunk is going to win. We were barely out of bed this morning when we heard the Potter girls doing some sort of chant they'd made up. They rhymed "Beatrix" with "fearless" – and said everyone else was going down.'

'That is a terrible bit of rhyming.'

'At least it's close. You try coming up with something to rhyme with Alcott.'

I stopped to think. 'Small... dot...?'

'Yeah, that's how we're going to gee ourselves up to beat the other bunks. Rhyming Alcott with small dot...'

Amy was pretending to be annoyed, everything coming through a smile.

'I didn't realise you were so competitive,' I said.

'Neither did I. Is it too much to ask that every other bunk bows down and admits Sarah and I run the best bunk on site?'

'I heard Gemma's bunk is a very tight ship. Lot of good campers in there.'

Her eyes narrowed. 'We are going to crush them. Don't you worry about that.'

We grinned at one another. After the weekend, with Mark and Mum, the world was suddenly lighter again. It was inconceivable I'd thought about not returning.

'Anyway...'

She was conspiratorial by then – and I suddenly realised she'd been in the lounge because she was waiting to see if I actually would show up. Everything we'd spoken about was a prelude to what she really wanted.

'You can help,' she added.

'How?'

'When the gallery goes live on Friday, everybody gets a vote for their favourite. That's every counsellor, director, support staff, camper... caretaker...' There was a twinkle in her eye. 'It's a *private* vote. You write the number of the thing you like on some paper, put it in the box – and that's it. Nothing's got a name on it – just numbers.'

'But people in each bunk will know who did the work.'

'Exactly. Sarah and me figured all the campers' and counsellors' votes will cancel each other out. They'll just vote for their own stuff. So the people who'll decide will be, well... you lot.'

It might have been insulting and exclusive but it wasn't. It felt as if I was being drawn into Amy's world, which was more than fine by me.

'You want me to vote for something done by someone in your bunk.'

A nod. 'I could give you a little nudge. Something like "vote for the painting of the lion" or whatever. Then you get your little mate, Luke, to vote the right way. Have a word with your friends in the kitchen and get them to do the same...'

She bobbed a little on the spot, having said everything she wanted and waiting for the reply. I made her wait a few seconds, drawing it out.

'Are you trying to get me to rig an election?'

Amy stretched and gently slapped my arm. I realised later it was the first time we actually touched. 'Joe Miller! That's such a dirty word. Are you accusing me of corruption?'

'I mean... it *is* corruption.'

She grimaced but it wasn't enough to hide the upturn in her

lips. 'I suppose I prefer to think of it as vote *persuasion*, rather than vote *rigging*.'

'Even though there's rigging involved?'

A snort. 'Look! I'm *one person* asking *another person* for a favour. If you want to put a label on that, it says a lot more about you than me.'

It was my turn to laugh.

'Will you do it?' she asked.

'I'll see what I can do.'

Amy smirked again and thanked me, then moved towards the mess hall. She hovered for a moment more. 'See you at reading hour,' she said – and it wasn't a question.

'See you then.'

It was only after she left that I realised I'd never told her my last name.

15

CIGARETTE

It was a conversation that lasted a few minutes – but it was as if nothing from the weekend had gone wrong. Those dark thoughts from the top of the gorge belonged to someone who wasn't me. The cricket club wasn't something I needed to think about. Everything was good again.

I found Luke not long after speaking to Amy and he laughed before we'd exchanged a word.

'What happened to you?' he asked.

'Fell off my bike and—'

'Not that, you look like you've just won the lottery. What are you so happy about?'

I made up something about a joke I'd heard from one of the kitchen staff – but Luke wanted to talk about other things anyway. His dad had gone on a 'booze cruise' to Calais on Saturday. From what I could tell, it had been with the sole intention of buying enough cigarettes for Luke to flog to various counsellors. He showed me the inside of his duffel bag, which was crammed with cartons of cigarettes.

He offered to sell me some at cost but I said I didn't smoke and that I'd leave the selling to him. I was beginning to think the biggest reason Luke had for returning to camp for that second year was that he was going to make enough money over six weeks to carry him through to the following summer.

By then, the two of us had a routine and we set about our usual jobs while the rest of camp went about its daily business. As I was working in the girls' field, Sarah made a point of catching my eye and nodding – which I presumed was an acknowledgement that she was also in on the vote rigging.

When I was emptying the bin from behind the Dahl bunk, I asked Gemma how she was going to spend her ten pounds, won from her betting on me. She gave a blink of astonishment, surprised that I knew, but then shrugged and said it would likely end up being spent in the tuck shop. 'Or on Saturday night,' she concluded.

Lunch came and went and then it was time for the umbrellas to be set out for reading hour. There were more clouds in the sky that Monday and the edge of the heat had dampened since the blazing weekend.

By the time Amy found me, I was in the spot close to the fence with *Little Women* in my hand. It wasn't only me looking out for her any longer.

She peered over me and then sat cross-legged a short distance away.

'You're just opening it at random pages to pretend you're reading, aren't you?'

'I'm up to the bit where Beth has a fever.'

Amy made an O with her lips and sucked in a breath.

'That's not a good sign,' I added.

'I don't want to spoil anything...'

'You sort of already have...'

She winced slightly. 'Sorry about that. It's not what you think... but it sort of is.'

Amy looked across to the campers underneath the umbrel-las. Some were sitting and reading, others were laid on their sides. From what I could tell, some were sleeping. Sarah was sitting next to one of the counsellors I didn't know and they were talking quietly to one another.

Luke had been right on that first day when he said this was the best hour of the day.

'Read to me...'

I turned to look back at Amy, who was lying down herself. Her eyes were closed, her body rising and falling gently.

'Read what?'

'Your book, obviously.'

'From the beginning?'

'Wherever you're up to.'

'Out loud...?'

Amy's eyes opened and she shielded her face with a hand. 'I'm not telepathic, so I don't mean read it in your head to me.'

She was amused and friendly – and there was something so wonderfully peaceful about the moment.

Amy pressed back onto the grass and closed her eyes again. Her bottom half was in the shade and she kicked off her shoes, then wriggled her toes before settling.

I stared for those few seconds. Her black hair was splayed away from the rest of her and I couldn't stop thinking about how strange it all felt. I wondered later, much later, if it was the first time I'd ever felt completely trusted by someone to whom I wasn't related. It was an alien idea for Dan, Mark, Pete or myself to let down our guards in such a way around each other. Yet here she was, within touching distance, her eyes closed, *trusting* me.

I skipped back a page and started reading chapter eighteen. It was impossible not to be self-conscious, to curse myself for every mispronounced word or stumble – and there were plenty.

The last time I'd read to anyone out loud was at primary school, when everyone had to take their turn to read to the teacher.

That afternoon felt like something that should be embar-rassing, and it was a thing that would have been, in another time or place. But Amy was putting her faith in me, so I put mine in her. It was only her who could hear, after all.

I read as best I could. Sometimes I had to stop and reread an entire line but Amy never laughed or made me feel stupid for not getting something first time. There was a moment where her breathing became shallower and I thought she might have fallen asleep. When I stopped reading, she whispered a soft 'keep going' – and so I did. I read the whole of the chapter, up until the doctor arrived and said that Beth would probably pull through.

When I was done and folded the cover closed, Amy propped herself onto her elbows and opened her eyes. The shade had shifted in the time I'd been reading and was now engulfing everything from her neck down. She blinked with sleepiness and hid a yawn in her elbow before sitting up properly.

'That was nice,' she said.

'Yeah...'

'Same time tomorrow?'

It was only three words, an invitation to do something that didn't seem like the sort of thing someone like me would do.

Except I was that person – and I would do it again.

'Same time tomorrow,' I replied.

16

DIRECTORY

It was quarter-past-seven when I arrived home – and the upstairs and downstairs curtains were open. Seeing that felt like more of the weight had been lifted. Mum had spent the day at work, come home, and not retreated to the grimness of the darkened living room. There might even be a chance she'd be persuaded to open a window. It was as Michelle had said: she needed a routine.

I let myself in and wheeled my bike through to the back, then went looking for Mum. I assumed she'd be in the living room, feet up and resting after the day – but there was nobody there. The TV was off and the remote still marooned on the windowsill where it had been left that morning.

Something started to itch at the back of my neck as I called for her. I hoped for a voice from up the stairs, something cheery and welcoming, but nothing came. I checked for myself, heading upstairs and looking into each room. I even went into the back yard, even though none of us ever did anything out there other than empty bins.

She was nowhere.

That feeling of being in Dan's garage when his mum came

in to say Michelle was picking me up was one that never left me. Not entirely. Every time it felt as if even the smallest amount of bad news was about to emerge, I'd feel a tingling around the back of my neck. It would spread quickly until it took over my entire body and I'd be left with all-over pins and needles. Later, much later, someone I know described it as mild PTSD – and maybe it was.

I felt it that evening, when the house was empty and Mum was nowhere to be found. Everything I did afterwards happened through a haze. Like looking through rippled glass, when the shape or shadow of a person might be recognisable, even though the picture isn't completely clear.

The phone was screwed to the wall next to the kitchen, with the directories in a drawer underneath. I searched through the Yellow Pages, eventually finding Barry's lumber yard under 'Building Services'. There was a phone and fax number – but the phone rang and rang to the point that I was about to give up when a man's voice finally gave a gruff 'hello?'

'Is that Barry?' I asked.

'No – and I'm just closing up, so it you want something, it'll have to be in the morning.'

'It's Joe Miller,' I said quickly, hoping he wouldn't hang up. 'I was wondering if my mum's there?'

There was a pause of a second or two and it was only the heavy breathing that let me know somebody was still at the other end. 'Who?'

'My mum was supposed to start there today. Jacqui Miller, or Jack.'

Even I could hear the panic in my voice by this point.

'Oh,' the man said, before pausing again. 'Yeah, I think...'

There was the sound of something shuffling, perhaps something being picked up and put down again.

'She left,' he said. 'Walked out this morning. Slammed a few doors, shouted a bit. I don't think anyone's seen her since.'

I wanted to reply but the words were stuck and I ended up coughing or gasping.

'She... what?' I managed eventually.

'I told you. She walked out.'

'Why?'

'I have no idea, kid.'

'D'you know where she went?'

The man sighed and the air must have gone directly into the receiver because the hiss at my end made me wince.

'I still have no idea,' he replied. 'And I've got to go.'

I started to say something else but was barely halfway through a sentence when I realised he'd gone. I stared at the phone itself for a few seconds, then the Yellow Pages, as if there might be answers there.

I thought about asking the neighbour whether she'd seen Mum at some point during the day – but we'd not been on great terms since she'd threatened to call the police on me for kicking a ball against a 'No Ball Games' sign. When I told Dad, he'd set his stereo speakers up against her wall and blasted AC/DC until Mum came home and told him to stop.

Odd how things like that stick in the mind. At the time, I thought he was sticking up for me – but, in truth, we were both wrong.

Unsure of what else to do, I grabbed my bike from the back and cycled into town.

It was close to eight and I hadn't expected much different – but Michelle's garage was locked up for the night. All I had was the address she'd written for me, though I didn't know where her flat was. She'd said it was past the garage and then right at the Spar – but the directions after that was a series of lefts and/or rights, which didn't mean an awful lot.

There weren't many options, so I cycled along to the Spar anyway and took the right. I tried various combinations of lefts and rights, looking for anything numbered 11a.

Twenty valuable minutes passed until I saw a new red-brick building across the street from a petrol station. I slowed and took in the numbers, until I saw an 11 downstairs, with an 11a directly above.

Getting up to the flat was harder than it looked. There was no sign of steps facing the street – and I had to hide my bike behind a bin and then leap the wall at the back to find an accessible set of stairs. I later found out that the only unnumbered door at the front would have opened onto a set of stairs had I tried.

I thought I had the wrong flat at first – because the person who answered 11a was a man somewhere in his early twenties. He was wearing shorts that were too short and a top with rolled-up sleeves. There were no shoes on his feet and, as he opened the door, he was mid-laugh before turning to me.

'Sorry,' I said, 'I think I've got the wrong place, I'm—'

I didn't get any further, because Michelle's voice echoed from the inside and then she was at the door, standing next to the mystery man.

'Joe...?'

She said my name like it was a question. She was bare-footed, too, wearing a floaty skirt I'd never seen before.

'I didn't expect you round today,' she added.

I must have been staring at the man.

'This is Connor,' she said. 'Con, this is my brother, Joe.'

Connor stretched out a hand but all I could do was stare at it, as if I'd forgotten what hands were. It took me a couple of seconds to remember why I was there.

'Have you seen Mum?' I asked.

'Not since this morning. I was going to go to the phone box and call the house in a bit. Ask how the day went. I thought she could call the phone box back and—'

'She's not home. I called the yard and some guy said she

walked out this morning and never went back. He said she slammed some doors.'

Michelle's face fell, slowly at first. She'd been smiling when she first got to the door, still enjoying whatever it was she and Connor had been laughing about.

Whoever *he* was.

Her face grey now, she reached for a pair of shoes on the ground next to the door. 'Can you get my keys?' she asked. I thought she was talking to me at first – but it was Connor who moved. 'I need to go out.'

17

GULL

The sky was starting to turn purple as I threw my bike into the back of Michelle's car. Hints of orange bled around the sides of the buildings but the street lights were already beginning to switch on.

Neither of us said much as Michelle drove around town. She kept it slow along the high street, ignoring the idiot behind who was beeping his horn and then angrily overtook with a flourish of Vs. We drove past pubs and chip shops, their internal lights seeping onto shadowed pavements.

Mum was nowhere.

We were almost out the other end when Michelle swerved to the side of the street and jumped out of the car, leaving her door open and the engine idling. There was a woman walking – and Michelle called to her, then they talked under a street light until Michelle did some sort of fake, not-very-reassuring laugh that was riddled with nerves.

She wasn't laughing when she got in. 'She's not seen her,' Michelle said.

There was no point in saying that I had no idea who the woman was.

We did another lap of the main shopping area and then Michelle pulled in next to a phone box and stretched across to claw a fifty-pence piece from the glovebox.

'Call home,' she said.

I did as I was told, feeding the money into the payphone and carefully tapping in the numbers that I knew was ours.

It rang and rang – and I could picture the sound echoing through the empty house. In days gone by, Dad would have been hurtling down the stairs, saying he'd get it. Not that day, though. Not ever again.

Back in the car, I offered Michelle her fifty pence back but she waved it away.

'We're going to have to call the police,' she said. It was perhaps more of a sigh than a sentence. A resignation that neither of us wanted to feel. 'If she walked out this morning, she could be anywhere,' Michelle added. 'Got on a bus, got in a taxi. Gone to the train station. Literally anywhere. She—'

'What if she did get on a bus?'

Michelle turned and looked at me. She muttered a slightly confused 'Huh?' – but then she got it.

She drove quickly out of town, following the unlit country lanes towards the seaside. The hedges were high, the verges narrow. Every time full beams seared across the carriageway, Michelle dipped her own and then cursed at the wasted time as she had to slow.

Aside for weekends, our town was dead after six or so. Everywhere except the various Spar and Londis shops, plus the pubs and chippies, were closed.

It was a different story at the seaside, though. It took us almost forty-five minutes to get there and, as we reached the front, there were people still packing the pavements on both sides. Men in three-quarter shorts and football tops marched along, beers raised aloft as they sang about something I couldn't make out. Behind them another group of men, this time all dressed as nuns, were doing the conga.

Michelle drove slowly, partly because so many people were walking in the road – but also because it meant we could actually look at those we were passing.

By the time we reached the pier, cars were parked nose to tail. The jingling sounds of the arcade games seeped onto the streets, competing with the screeches and screams of those playing. Music boomed from the pub across the road and there were people outside, arms raised, singing along.

Michelle came a stop, double parked and blocking the street, ignoring the beeps from the cars behind. 'Go find her,' she said.

'What about you?'

'I'll find you.'

It sounded ridiculous but there wasn't much chance to argue. The driver behind had leant on his horn and people were starting to look. I quickly got out, shut the door and made a point of walking in front of the car behind, showing him the Vs and letting him know what I thought of him. The glorified egg of a man shouted something back but I had already disappeared into the crowd by then.

The air was thick with chips and vinegar as I continued onto the pier. There were kids everywhere, ice creams and candy floss in hands. Blinking orange lights burned through the dark and the steady *ding-ding-ding* from the arcade was louder there than anywhere. Tourists were feeding coins into the penny machines, with others angrily thumping hands on the glass with frustration at the crane games.

I weaved in and out of the horde, ducking under arms and sliding sideways through gaps between people. By the time anyone could chirp an 'oi', I was already past.

At the back of the arcade, there was the long wooden deck of the pier. Gloomy lamps stretched the length as it ate into the ocean below. The tide was in and the water a mirrored, murky black under the night sky.

Mum and Dad used to bring Michelle and me to this resort every year. I'd be the one playing on the penny machines and getting annoyed because the cranes were incapable of actually picking anything up.

'*They're all a con,*' Dad would say – and then I'd be back the next day, not learning my lesson.

The four of us would be in a caravan together, where each movement in the night would cause the whole place to rock. It would be half-three in the morning and Dad would shout at me to stop fidgeting. Anyone going to the toilet after ten or before seven was effectively starting a war.

I loved it.

We went there because it was cheap and close – but also because Mum and Dad met there in the seventies. They had been at the same school but somehow never ran into one another. He'd been there with his friends, she'd been with hers. He'd been trying to win something by throwing darts at cards. He'd been awful, 'a complete joke', in Mum's words, but they'd seen one another and that was it. They were married a year later. Different times and all that.

As I weaved around the dwindling number of families on the pier that night, I tried to remember the last time I'd been. It had to have been four or five years. Even thinking of the resort, of that pier, had felt too much after Dad died. That place was him. It was Mum.

And there she was, sitting on the bench at the furthest end of the pier. It had felt still and warm on the pavement but the wind was thrashing knives of ice out there. Mum was still in the clothes she'd had on that morning. She was shivering as I sat next to her and gulls chirped around us, roaming on the pier hunting for soggy, dropped chips.

'What happened, Mum?' I asked.

There was no reply and I reached to take her hand. She let me hold it and her skin was glacial.

'Shell's in the car, Mum,' I said. 'We should go.'

I squeezed her fingers but that made me shiver. The water raged below us, the birds continued to fight, their claws skittering across the wooden decking at our sides.

When I stood, she allowed me to pull her up. I looped an arm through hers and we turned and started back towards the arcade, one step at a time, right foot, left foot, surrounded by other people's joy, sinking in our own melancholy.

18

RAIN

It rained the next day. Not the sort of misty drizzle that would last all day, more a wall of water. An assault on anything that wasn't a fish.

It woke me at around half-five and I pulled myself out of bed and headed to the window wearing only a pair of boxers to look out at the gloomy skies. For some reason, it hadn't occurred to me that it might rain while I was at camp. It felt like the sort of place that would exist in nothing other than sunshine.

I watched the rain fall and listened for any sound that might come from Mum's room on the other side of the wall. After we got back the night before, Mum and Michelle had sat in the car for a few minutes as I was sent inside.

When they came in, Michelle had helped Mum up to bed and they stayed in the room for a while before coming out. I was waiting on the top step, presuming an explanation would come, but Michelle had told me to go easy on her.

There was something about the way she spoke that made it sound as if she knew what had happened to make Mum run off. I asked why Mum had walked out on the job but all Michelle would say was that it was complicated. That I wouldn't understand. Like I was some child.

I said I'd ask her myself – but Michelle had stuck out an arm to block my way and used the voice she almost never used with me. The one that was closer to a growl than anything else. Something not to be messed with, or questioned.

'Leave it,' she'd said – and so I did.

She'd left and said she would check back before work the next day, which left me alone in the house that might as well have been empty.

That morning of the rain, I waited in my room and listened for movement. When nothing came before half-seven, I opened Mum's door a crack to make sure the duvet that covered her was rhythmically rising and falling. I considered waking her, asking if she wanted something to eat, but Michelle would be on the way and I wasn't sure I wanted to run into her that day.

I found my winter coat on the floor at the back of the cupboard in the hall. It was thick, with white foam spilling from a hole in the side, and far too warm for the day – but it was the only thing I owned that was remotely waterproof.

As I quickly found out while cycling to camp, whatever waterproofing it might have once had was long gone. The water went through the coat *and* my T-shirt. My jeans clung to my legs like leggings and there was water pouring into my socks and shoes with every pedal stroke.

When I got to camp, I dumped my bike at the back and squelched my way into the staff lounge. There was a towel draped across the table – but it offered little against the waterfall coming off me. When I took off my shoes, I had to empty the liquid as if tipping a cup upside down.

Camp was quiet that Tuesday, with most campers confined to bunks in the bad weather, except for mealtimes. Luke and I had so little to do that we ended up playing cards with some of the kitchen lads. I was as bad at that as I was at PlayStation and darts.

It was wet the next day, too – although the rain was less of an onslaught. Luke and I cleared the mess hall after lunch and a local artist came in to talk about different types of creativity. Every camper was there but she misjudged the audience and ended up droning on about the history of art as the children shuffled, yawned and exploded with laughter when someone near the front farted.

I learned many things across those weeks of camp – but the biggest was that, to children, if not adults, there was nothing funnier than a fart.

Across those two days, I barely saw Amy. Reading hour was abandoned because everyone was in their bunks anyway. The most I saw of her was when I delivered mail. I cowered under the lip of the bunk in an attempt to avoid the worst of the rain – and it was Sarah who answered. She took the mail and, as I was about to go, she turned and called for Amy.

Our conversation lasted a minute at most. It was a gloomy grey inside the bunk, with only a couple of dim lightbulbs, and I could see the shapes of the children over her shoulder, watching and listening.

Under those observant eyes and pricked ears, we made nothing but small talk about the rain and how damp the field was. Whether it would drain quickly and what the forecast looked like for the rest of the week. She asked what I was up to and I told her I was mainly playing cards. She puffed out a breath and said that was more or less what they'd been doing.

There wasn't much to say after that, not with such scrutiny. We said goodbye and I delivered the rest of the mail before heading back to the staff lounge to play cards.

At home, Mum had slipped back into her routine of television and the sofa. That image of her dressed for work with clean hair had been a cruel mirage.

The rain had fed into all our moods over those two days, as if life was on hold until the sun decided to return.

On the Wednesday, I'd not long returned from camp when there was the sound of the front door opening. Only three of us had a key – and Mum and me were at home – but it still felt surprising to see Michelle waiting in the doorway as I washed up Mum's mugs in the kitchen sink.

'Are you ready?' she called along the hall.

'Ready for what?'

'Didn't Mum tell you?'

'Tell me what?'

Michelle closed the front door and walked into the kitchen.

'I came over at lunch,' she said. 'I was going to pick you both up to come over to the new flat. Mum said she'd tell you.'

We both turned to look at the closed door that led into the living room.

'She didn't say anything,' I replied.

Michelle groaned and then picked up a tea towel to dry the mugs as I washed. We did Mum's dishes together and put everything away – then, as I put on my shoes, Michelle went to retrieve Mum from the sofa.

Mum was certainly talking by that point. She said she didn't want to see Michelle's flat, it was too far, too late, too much hassle.

Michelle was a lot calmer than I could ever be. She patiently and calmly dealt with all those complaints – 'You might like it if you see it', 'It's only across town', 'We don't have to stay long', 'It's no hassle for you, you just have to come' – while I was sitting on the stairs, fighting to stop myself telling Michelle to just go.

It was a silent drive across town, with me in the back of Michelle's car and Mum in the front, staring aimlessly out the window. Michelle parked and took us up those stairs at the front and then opened the door to 11a. There was no guy in too-short shorts this time. No sign of anyone living there, except Michelle.

The living room and kitchen shared the same space, with the carpet giving way to lino in the corner. There was one small bedroom, with a double bed, a TV, tape deck with CD player in the corner, and two speakers.

'It's not much,' Michelle said but, for the first time, I started to think about how much I'd like a similar space as my own. Somewhere I wouldn't have to worry about making too much noise, or leaving open a door. A place where I could sleep and not have to be concerned about what might be going on downstairs or in the next room. A kitchen in which I didn't have to do someone else's dishes day after day.

I was drifting and dreaming, though it didn't take long for Mum to caustically sear away at those thoughts.

'Who chose those curtains?' she asked. They were green and I hadn't noticed them, though Mum started tugging at them until Michelle ushered her away.

'They came with the flat,' my sister replied.

'Why is the ceiling so low?'

I looked up at the dimpled white above and couldn't see anything odd.

Mum had already moved on, though. She was by the second window, pointing at a dark smudge on the white sill. 'Why hasn't that been cleaned? And what about your bed? It's as if I never taught you how to tuck in the corners. Don't think I missed those shoes on the floor, either. And what about that tap?'

She crossed to the kitchen, where the tap dripped a long, steady droplet into the sink before forming another.

'This place is a death trap,' Mum said. 'Full of mould as well. Horrible.'

Mum continued listing her complaints and observations and, as she did, I watched Michelle wince and shrink. Her arms got closer to her body, her knees sank, and then she was sitting on the arm of the sofa.

Outside, the rain continued to batter the windows, hammering onto the glass, but it felt darker and harsher inside.

Mum was pointing at the front door by then but I was no longer listening to what she was saying. And then I was speaking. Then I was shouting.

'Why can't you just be happy for her?'

Mum stopped mid-word and turned slowly to look towards me, mouth still open. Michelle was staring, too – though I think I might have been the most surprised of us all. I could feel the momentum slipping as I spoke but I was in too deep.

'You're always criticising, always moaning. Who cares if her bed isn't tucked in, or the curtains are green? You can't be bothered to get off the sofa most days. Who cares if—'

'Joe...'

It was Michelle who spoke. There was a deftness about her tone. A kindness I couldn't stand. She should be angrier than me.

'It's all right,' she added.

'It's *not* all right.' I turned to Mum, unable to keep it in any longer. Those months of frustration when I was supposed to focusing on exams and school – but, instead, I was dreading the walk home. Fearing what might be waiting. 'Why are you *like* this?'

I was shouting and the question hovered between the three of us. The elephant wasn't in the room, it *was* the room.

Nobody spoke and I realised I was crying again. Michelle took a step towards me but I couldn't face either her or Mum. Then I was out the front door and down the steps. I was running and my clothes were sticking to me. I hurtled through puddles and across roads. Headlights flared and there was a stream running along the high street. Still I ran and I felt invincible, as is if I could keep going forever, as if I'd use fury as fuel and I would never have to stop.

But I did stop.

I was at the cricket club, with no particular memory of the route I'd taken to get there. Hair plastered my cheeks, my forehead, and water was pouring down my back.

I was cold and wet and... angry. Angry at Dad for dying, at Mum for not dealing with it... at everything. And as ever – *more* than ever – I was angry at myself.

19

HAND

I didn't go home that night. I realised the next morning that Michelle and perhaps even Mum might have been concerned about where I'd gone. There had been times before when I'd slept at Dan's and I figured they'd have guessed I was there and didn't want to be bothered. They didn't know I'd managed to not only fall out with them but my friends, too.

I slept under the covers that were in the middle of the cricket pitch. They were a domed metal with space underneath to let the grass breathe, while protecting it from rain. There's no way I should have been able to sleep in my wet clothes as the rain thundered on top of the metal – and yet it was the best night's sleep I'd had in months.

When I woke, it was light and the sun was up. There were clouds in the sky but much more blue. I crawled out from under the covers and groaned with pleasure, perhaps relief, as I stretched and the warmth swam across me.

My clothes were damp but not as drenched as the night before, so I walked across town, sticking to the sunny side of the various streets, until I got home. I was more or less dry by the time I got there and, after letting myself in, I headed upstairs. In usual circumstances I'd have moved around as quietly possible – but I made little attempt that morning. When I showered, I stood under the head and let warm water run across me until I felt more like a person who hadn't slept on the ground the night before.

It still feels like one of those things that didn't happen, even though it did.

I found clean clothes and then headed back downstairs to get my bike from the back. I had already wheeled it through the house and was about to cycle off when I stopped myself.

Mum was asleep on the sofa, underneath a blanket, with the muted TV strobing across the darkened room. I watched her for a minute or so, making sure she was breathing, wondering if it was Michelle who'd tucked her in down there.

When I left, I closed the doors quietly second time around. I took a slight detour on the way to camp, stopping at the garage and leaving a message with Michelle's boss to tell her I was fine. He huffed and shrugged as if it was a massive task – but he said he'd pass it on – and then I was off to camp as if it had been a perfectly normal morning.

I was late, but not by much, and times were already becoming fluid in that second week. As long as jobs were done, nobody seemed to mind when we arrived. Luke never made a fuss of my timekeeping because I told him I'd empty the bins each day, which was the job he *really* didn't want to do.

The staff lounge was empty when I arrived, though the din of breakfast was raging on the other side of the tent flap. I picked up the newsletter to find out what was going on for the rest of the day, though was instantly drawn to the photo of Amy in the top corner. Her head was tilted slightly and she was giving a half-smile as if to say she was tolerating her picture being taken, though she didn't entirely approve.

I knew that look well, having given it in more or less every photo that had ever been taken of me. There were even some from when I was still in nappies in which I was giving the photographer a bit of side-eye.

Amy was that day's profile and I read through her answers, before returning the newsletter to the pile. I changed my mind half a second later and picked it up again, then folded it into my pocket.

I was about to go searching for Luke when George strode in from the mess hall. I hadn't seen him in anything other than passing since the previous week and the rain hadn't seemed to have dampened his spirits. He clapped his hands together in enthusiasm as he said my name and asked how the past few days had been going. I said it was fine, which was only true if we were strictly talking about camp goings-on.

'I was looking for you, actually,' he said. 'Can you pick me up something from the house? The courier dropped off two boxes of marker pens but they were sent there instead of here for some reason.'

I checked my pockets and pulled out the key he'd given me the week before.

'The parcel should be around the side, behind the gate,' he added. 'But there's one other thing.'

'What?'

'Fee was there last night and she thinks she might have left the kitchen light on. Can you check? While you're there, you might as well check the others too.'

I told him it was fine and had taken a step towards the back and my bike when I stopped.

'Do you sleep here?' I asked.

George seemed a little surprised at the question, or perhaps the directness. He blinked his eyes open wider. 'Fee and I rarely get home while camp's running. We're here five or six nights a week – and always at weekends when counsellors have more freedom to go off site.'

He yawned, which seemed so out of character for a person I

pictured as having endless energy. He was one of those adults who actually felt like an adult. A person aware, and in control, of everything around him. A yawn was almost a sign of weakness. I think he sensed it too because, when he finished, he chuckled kindly.

'We plan all year for this and, when it comes around, we never stop.'

I asked if he needed anything else but he said the light check and pens was all.

It felt exhilarating to ride that morning. Water was running along the edges of the kerb but the road was otherwise dry and my own night of sleep had done me good.

At George's, the parcel was around the side, as he'd said. I put it in my backpack and then left my bike on the driveway as I let myself into his house.

There was never a time when I entered in which I wasn't blown away by the scale of the place. I was used to the semi-detacheds of me and my friends – or Michelle's two-room flat. The idea of living somewhere so large felt inconceivable. I wondered what he did with all the space if it was only him and Fiona. Aside from the kitchen, living room and bedroom, what more could anyone need?

My footsteps echoed on the hard floor as I headed through to the kitchen and turned off the lights. Even without the lights, it was so white, like some from an advert. I also couldn't get over how clean everything was. There were no greeny-brown foam marks around the taps, or dust in the sink. No mug rings on the counters, or crumbs around the toaster. As for the toaster itself, it was chrome and shiny; not faded grey plastic like we had at home.

George had asked me to check the other lights, so I told myself I was doing just that as I spied inside every room of the house. There were two living rooms: one filled with packed bookshelves, a desk and computer; then a second one with a television and two big sofas. Upstairs, there were four bedrooms, all of which were larger than anything at my house. Even the small one had enough space for a double bed. There were also three bathrooms – one connected to the biggest bedroom, and then one more on the upstairs landing and a final one downstairs.

At the time, I couldn't think of a house I'd visited that had more than one.

The main bedroom also had a wardrobe large enough for someone to walk into. It was as disorientating as it was impressive. It was my first proper glimpse of another life, another world. Of seeing that not everybody lived like I did.

I was standing in the downstairs hallway when the wave of self-consciousness grasped me. I felt so small among the surroundings. So unworthy. I don't think I ever quite got past that when it came to houses like that. It was as if the level I'd been born into was where I deserved to be. There was me – and then there were people like George.

I fought away that disorientation and, after double-checking I'd turned off the kitchen light, I hurried out of the house and locked it.

Back at camp, I found George and gave him his parcel. He asked about the lights and I lied, saying they hadn't been on. I was many things back then – but never really a liar – and I don't think I ever figured out why I said it.

I was about to head out and look for Luke for the second time that day when George stopped me. He had the sort of voice that halted people and there was never a time when he said something that didn't leave me compelled to reply.

'What are your plans for after summer?' he asked.

I think I stared at him gormlessly, because he followed it up quickly.

'Are you doing your A levels?'

'I'm not sure,' I said. 'I'm waiting on my grades. They're due in a few weeks.'

'I'm certain a smart lad like you will get what you want.'

His direct stare was so penetrating that I wilted under it. 'I was thinking about maybe getting a job...'

George nodded along, not judging, and I had a curious desire to ask what he thought. I almost did – but then Fiona came into his office, holding a printer cartridge in her hand. We hadn't spoken that much since the start of camp but she seemed delighted to see me.

'Just the man I was looking for,' she said. 'I'm told you know how to fix the printer.'

'More the photocopier...'

'Must be more or less the same thing...?'

I didn't bother attempting to point out the differences, instead taking the cartridge and heading off to fix the latest electrical problem. It was years later that I thought I should have probably gone into photocopier maintenance as a career. I certainly had the intensive on-the-job training for it.

The rest of the morning passed as usual after that. There was more to do without the rain but I preferred it that way. There were only so many hands of cards that could be played as the elements thrashed away on canvas.

By the time lunch came and went, the fields had dried out under the baking sun. It was business as usual, so Luke and I set up the umbrellas in the respective fields ahead of reading hour. After the weekend and the rain and the arguments, there was an excitement building within me as I took my spot on the edge of the field and waited.

In retrospect, it was presumptive and probably arrogant – but, as soon as the campers had settled, Amy came and sat across from me. It's difficult to describe the relief of seeing her. Partly, or perhaps largely, through my own attitude, I'd managed to antagonise more or less everyone else I actually knew.

'Thank God the rain stopped,' she said. 'One more day and it would have been a mutiny. Everyone was driving everyone else crazy being stuck in the bunk all day.'

'I spent two days playing cards.'

'Pfft. All right for some. I sent Sarah out to take a walk this morning because she was losing her mind.'

'What about *your* mind?'

She started to answer and then stopped. 'I think I'm OK, actually.' A pause. 'Thank you for asking.'

We sat for a little while, not speaking – which was something that would usually have been awkward. With my friends, we would barely last a few seconds until someone felt the need to break the silence with a joke or a minor act of violence. It was as if remaining quiet too long might expose the cracks in our friendship.

'I saw your profile in the newsletter,' I said.

'I couldn't get out of it. Everyone has to have their day.'

'Do you really like Skunk Anansie?'

'Love them, don't you?'

I stumbled over an answer – 'I mean, sort of, um—' but she cut me off with a laugh.

'It's more to annoy Mum,' she said. 'She sees a woman with a bald head and gets worried I'll shave off my hair.'

She tugged at a few strands, as if to illustrate the point.

'It might suit you,' I said.

Amy laughed away the suggestion.

'What music do you like?' I asked.

A shrug. 'Everything. Nothing.' She stopped for a moment and then added: 'Do you think that's weird? Everyone has a favourite band but I'll listen to whatever's on.'

I told her I agreed, though it didn't seem as if she quite believed me. After that, I took out the folded newsletter and read her profile back to her. She laughed much of it off, though held up her hands to show off her chipped fingernails when I said her favourite colour was black.

'I don't think I know anyone whose favourite colour is black,' I said.

'It's more to annoy Mum again.'

'Are all your likes based on things your mum doesn't approve of?'

She pouted her bottom lip and hmmed. 'That's very perceptive... but it's a weird question, isn't it? Who cares about a favourite colour, number, letter, or anything like that? It's not like we go around asking people about their favourite toe. Why are we always ranking things?'

'Aren't you trying to get me to rig an election?'

She snorted at this, which made my day's goal complete. Every time she did it, the sound was followed by a beaming smile and, when it was for me, it felt as if we were the only people who mattered.

'Well, there is that,' she said, 'but that's more about *subverting* the system. Fighting injustice and all that.'

Amy checked over her shoulder and then turned back and lowered her voice.

'Speaking of that, Charlotte's entry is the best from our bunk. All the girls are going to vote for her and so's Sarah and me. That's eleven votes – and Charlotte reckons she knows a couple of girls in Lewis that might defect as well.'

'You make it sound like a spy film.'

She stared at me, deadpan and unsmiling. 'It's much more serious than that. Dahl have a chant going now. Something about Roald and bold and gold... total nonsense...' She tailed off and then picked up again. 'Anyway, Charlotte's done this black and white pencil drawing of an elephant. There was no frame of reference, so I have no idea how she managed it with us all sitting in the bunk. It's perfect, though. Seriously, really good.'

'You want me to vote for the elephant?'

'Exactly. Nobody will know the numbers of each piece until the gallery opens tomorrow – but vote for the pencil elephant and get everyone you know to do it.'

'I'll see what I can do... but you know this is all sounding a bit banana republicky.'

'Oooh, get you with the fancy terms.'

'It means—'

She cut me off, wearing that serious face again, and I wasn't sure if it was joking this time. 'I know what it means.'

A couple of seconds passed and then her features broke.

'I'm not just saying this – but Charlotte is really good. She was telling me how her dad's working in America and that she hasn't seen him since the start of June. He's some sort of diplomat.'

She put the emphasis on the 'P' – *dip* – sounding disgusted. I figured it was more the fact he was away as opposed to his job.

'Her friends are on holiday with their parents in various places and she's been sent here to be out of the way. I mean, *she* didn't say it like that but...'

Amy didn't finish the sentence and I wasn't sure what to say to her. She must have recognised this because she pressed back onto her elbows.

'Have you got your book?'

I dug into my bag and held up Michelle's copy of *Little Women*.

'Have you been reading it without me?'

I almost laughed at that. I'd spent two days playing cards – and my evenings either searching for Mum or arguing with her. The idea of reading away from here hadn't crossed my mind.

As Amy lay back and closed her eyes, I started to read to her once more. The language was coming easier by that point. I allowed myself a few gentler, longer pauses in between para-graphs, mainly to watch how the sun was making Amy's skin glow. Or how her eyelashes twitched slightly as she relaxed. There were little things about her that I'd never noticed in another person before. How the area at the bottom of her neck was slightly concave, how she had lighter freckles around her hairline compared to the ones near the front of her face.

I read... and she listened... and it was... lovely.

There were a few minutes where everything else melted away and it was just two people and someone else's words.

Only a few minutes, though.

I wanted to tell her about Mum and Dad, and Michelle. About that guy who opened the door at Michelle's flat. About Dan and Pete and Mark and why Ian hated me. Of how it led to me rolling around on the dirty floor with what used to be one of my friends. That Dan, Pete and Mark had been a big part of my life and then, in that moment, they weren't – though I didn't know if that was good or bad.

I didn't say any of that to Amy. I read the whole chapter and then, when I was done, she pushed herself onto her elbows and sat up properly. There was a moment, just a moment, when she reached and touched my hand.

'I enjoyed that,' she said.

And in that moment, just that moment, I knew I was feeling something I never had.

20

BALLOT

That hour with Amy was the spark that carried me through the rest of that day and into the next. I hadn't seen Michelle since running out of her flat on Wednesday and, by Friday morning, Mum was still in the living room. She'd barely moved since Michelle and I brought her home from the pier on Monday.

She was at least awake on the Friday morning, which was an improvement on the previous day. I asked if she wanted a cup of tea and she said she'd make one for herself. I waited in the kitchen, sitting on the stool and watching her make herself breakfast. I think a part of me was afraid she'd burn herself on the kettle, or drop something on her foot. Things had changed since the pier, or perhaps since I shouted at her when we were at Michelle's.

Mum buttered some toast and made the tea, then leant against the counter as she bit into her breakfast.

It wasn't much in any wider way but, in context, this felt like a lot for her. A step forward, perhaps.

'How's camp?' she asked, which took me by surprise to such a degree that I replied with a quick 'What?'

She repeated herself and I said something about it being 'all right.'

I figured that would be the end of the conversation but she was actually listening. 'Is that "all right" as in "really good", or "really bad"?'

I wasn't used to having back-and-forth conversations with her, certainly not at a regular volume, but she bit her toast and looked at me with something that felt like genuine interest.

'Good,' I said. 'It's been good.'

She nodded and then put down her plate, before looping her fingers through her mug and holding it close to her chest.

'I feel so tired all the time.'

There was a lump in my throat. It had arrived out of nowhere, as if I'd swallowed a stone. I suppose it was something like the admission I'd wanted for months. Not the main thing, of course. What I really wanted was my mum back – but, in that moment, the acknowledgement that things weren't normal would do.

I didn't think I'd be able to reply but I croaked out: 'Why did you leave the job? I thought it'd be a new start...?'

Mum sipped her tea and turned to look out the window that faced the barren back yard. 'You wouldn't understand,' she said.

'That's what Michelle said.'

She didn't reply to that and neither of us spoke for a while. I wondered if I should apologise for shouting at the flat – except, deep down, I wasn't sorry.

I wanted the moment to continue because it felt like our first proper connection in a while. Unfortunately, the clock on the wall had other ideas.

'I have to go,' I said.

'Have a good day.'

I went out to the back and wheeled my bike across the kitchen before I stopped. 'Will you open the curtains today?' I asked.

A pause and then: 'Yes.'

'And a window?'

There was a longer pause that time. 'We'll see.'

Mum and I had only swapped a few words – but I was feeling so much better as I cycled to camp that day. It dawned on me later that my moods were swinging as wildly as anyone's at the time. I'd feel full of darkness and gloom, then one small interaction would change everything.

At camp, I was barely off my bike when Gemma accosted me on the grass at the back of the staff lounge. I'd not spoken to her since finding out she'd made ten pounds from me turning up on Monday.

'I was wondering when you'd get here,' she said.

'I'm not late!'

She wasn't listening. 'It's the gallery show later and I need you to vote for one of my girls.'

I laughed at that. 'Considering it's supposed to be a blind vote, there's a lot of counsellors trying to get me on board.'

Her eyes narrowed. 'Amy, obviously. Who else?'

I wondered if it was obvious to everyone that Amy and I had been spending time together but didn't get much opportunity to think on that because Gemma was firing names at me, almost entirely of counsellors I didn't know.

'Has Gavin asked you?' she said. 'What about Hannah? Or Anna? I wouldn't trust any of that Blyton lot. Have they offered you something?'

'None of them,' I replied.

'Ian?'

'I don't think he's talking to me.'

Gemma nodded at that. 'Hardly surprising, is it?'

'I've said sorry but he won't accept it.'

Gemma had a hand on her hip and a raised eyebrow. 'Do you blame him? You can't just bully someone for years, say sorry once, and think that makes everything all right.'

'It wasn't really—'

Gemma rolled her eyes, which was enough to cut me off. 'Pretending it wasn't you isn't going to help. For all we know, for all *he* knows, you're with your friends every night, laughing at us.'

'I'm not laughing at you. At *any* of you. I've not seen them all week.'

Gemma examined me for a moment and it felt as if she was trying to figure out if I was telling the truth.

'I don't know what to do,' I added, quieter now.

There was a clang from the kitchen and we both turned in its direction, waiting to see if something more would come from it. When nothing did, and I looked back, I realised Gemma was focusing on me again.

'I remember when we were both little,' she said. '*Really* little. We used to sit in the library at school together and talk about the books we'd read. We must have been about six and we were these pretentious little kids who'd always be banging on about reading. We had all the Famous Five books between us and swapped them back and forth.'

It was like she had opened a curtain to reveal something once lost. I'd somehow forgotten that I *had* been a reader once. It felt like another person.

'I hardly remember that,' I said.

'There were times when I'd think of you when you were that little boy. When you were off with your friends and acting like dicks. When you'd make people cry and I'd think of that boy and those books and I'd wonder what happened.'

That mirror was being held up to me again – and it was one at which I couldn't bear to look. That meant I couldn't bear to look at her.

'It's a stupid cliché,' she continued, 'but actions speak louder than words. If you want him to think you're OK – or anyone really – you have to stop being a twat around them.'

'I know...'

The air was heavy between us. Too many truths in too short a time. I felt stuck on the spot, embarrassed at everything I was – until Gemma gave me the out.

'That absolutely does *not* mean that you vote for anyone from his bunk later. If he tries to bribe you, tell him to get lost and call him whatever you want.'

It made me smile, although it didn't feel deserved.

'Who am I supposed to vote for?' I asked.

Gemma grimaced slightly. 'There is a bit of a problem there. None of my girls are that artistic.'

'That does sound like a problem for a craft competition.'

'Tell me about it! Anyway, the best we've got is a knitted Eiffel Tower.'

I tried to picture it. 'That sounds quite good.'

Gemma caught my eye. 'It might *sound* good but you haven't seen it. It sort of... leans. We were thinking about pretending it's the Leaning Tower of Pisa – but it looks nothing like it.'

'Does it look like the Eiffel Tower?'

Gemma hmmed. 'Maybe if you squint and don't get too close.' She considered that for a moment and then added: 'Anyway, none of that matters. Vote for the Eiffel Tower of Pisa – and get all your kitchen mates to do the same. And that Luke guy. And anyone else you know. Potter think they've got this tied up and I can't wait to see their faces...'

I told her I'd see what I could do, which was far short of the promise she wanted. There wasn't a lot of time for me to get rigging – because, as soon as breakfast was done, Luke and I started converting the mess hall into a gallery. The chairs were cleared, the tables wiped down and we set up a dozen easels around the space.

We were almost done when there was the beep of the van from the lane at the back of the camp. That was the signal that the tuck shop delivery was there – and Luke had no problem with me sorting it out that day.

I did as I had the first week, putting some items into a bag at the side, restocking the vending machine, and logging everything else into the stocktaking book.

After that, I returned to the mess hall, where George and Fiona were laying out the various pieces of art around the space. I'd expected mainly drawings and paintings – but that was far from the case. Someone had sculpted a rhino out of clay, there was a couple of cross-stitches, a knitted George and Fiona, a hand that was drawn in charcoal – and those were only a selection.

There was also the pencil elephant, of course. And the Eiffel Tower of Pisa.

The more that was laid out, the more I realised that I was ludicrously bad at art. I'd known that from school, of course, but the campers were years younger than me and infinitely better. It probably said a lot about me, none of it good, that I was surprised at the quality.

George, Fiona and one of the other directors laid everything out and then stood in the corner to make sure they were happy it all had equal prominence.

'We've got some great campers this year,' George said, though it took me a moment to realise he was talking to Luke and myself. We'd been standing off to the side, waiting to hear if we needed to do anything else.

Luke and I both agreed – and then George went around the room placing a numbered sticker next to each entry. At the front, there was a large box with a slot on the top. Slips of paper and the pens I'd picked up were on the side.

George did a second lap, this time simply looking, until he was back at the front. He picked up a piece of paper and wrote a number I couldn't see, before folding the scrap and putting it in the box. Fiona and the other director had apparently already decided, because neither bothered with a lap before adding their votes to the box.

Fiona said she had things to do and then she disappeared with the other director, leaving Luke, myself and George in the vast mess hall.

'You two can get your votes in before we open for business,' George said. 'There's a crowd outside already and I'm going to go out and talk them through the procedures.'

'What are they?' Luke asked.

'Eight people maximum in the gallery at any time,' George replied. 'Hopefully that will give everyone space and time to make their choices. I think we all want to appreciate each other's work. We're all winners here.'

He clapped his hands and then strolled out of the tent and onto the field.

I exchanged a shrug with Luke and then we walked around the perimeter of the mess hall. The Eiffel Tower of Pisa was indeed leaning – though it also looked a bit like a melting pyramid. I couldn't imagine it would be getting many votes away from Gemma's immediate campers. Not without a little assistance, in any case.

Charlotte's monochrome elephant was number thirty-three. It was perhaps a little more simplistic than I'd expected given Amy's praise – but still a lot better than I could do. Not to mention the fact that Charlotte was eleven. Also, it was definitely in the top three pieces I might have picked in any case.

'Has someone got to you?'

I turned to look at Luke, who was standing by the ballot box.

'Huh?'

'Someone's got to you, haven't they? It was the same last year. None of the counsellors want to lose to any of the others. They're all out there trading votes as we speak. There was some sort of voting bloc last year where the boys and girls from Potter joined together to vote for this sunflower thing one of them had made.' He chuckled at the memory. 'This is the most corrupt election you'll ever be a part of.'

'Someone's got to me,' I said.

'Go on then, give me a number.'

The elephant was thirty-three and the Eiffel Tower of Pisa was nine. I looked at both and then made up my mind.

'You sure?' Luke said.

'No,' I replied. 'But now I've got to go and convince the kitchen lot to vote the same way.'

'Should be easy after this morning's delivery...'

Luke might have winked but it could have been the light. Either way, the rig was on.

21

TROPHY

Everyone ate lunch on the field that day, with the mess hall left clear for campers, counsellors and directors to view the gallery. It was Friday and the five-dayers would be getting picked up by the parents in the late afternoon and early evening. There was a party-type atmosphere, with so much laughing and excitement around the fields. Nobody was in their bunks and there were impromptu mixed games of football and tag going on in different areas.

It was warm that day but comfortable. A little after three the bell went for everyone to assemble at the front of the mess hall. Campers sat on the grass, along with some of the counsellors, while others stood at the sides. The directors were there, too, standing at George's side as he balanced on a low table that was unnecessary given his height.

I was at the back with Luke, who was finding the entire thing hilarious. 'I've never rigged an election before,' he said, a little too loudly.

'It's not rigged,' I whispered back.

He laughed but didn't reply.

George had no need for any sort of loudhailer, he simply

spoke a little louder than usual, which was plenty enough for everyone to hear. Third place was a girl from Potter, who'd sculpted the rhino. Luke had to turn around to stop himself from laughing as she stomped to the front, furious at not winning. Fiona offered a small trophy and a bronze rosette, both of which were snatched away. The girl was halfway back to her spot on the floor when she had to be called back for photographs.

Second went to a boy from the Alcott bunk. He'd painted the moon, which would have been another piece that went into my possible top three. The crafted craters and crescented dark side had been created with genuine precision – and he got a large round of applause as he picked up his cup and silver rosette, before holding it up for his counsellor, Ian, to see.

I couldn't look as George said it was time to announce the winner. He asked for a drumroll and the campers clapped their hands and stomped their feet until...

'The winner of Camp Sycamore's craft week 1999 is...'

The pause lingered long until the eventual:

'Charlotte from Alcott girls.'

There were cheers from Charlotte's side of the crowd and not quite boos from some of the others, though there was unquestionable grumbling.

Charlotte dragged Amy up to the front and accepted her trophy and rosette with the beaming grin never leaving her face.

Luke nudged me below the ribs but I ignored him as I turned and set off to take down the badminton nets that had been left up.

Cars started arriving after that as the five-dayers headed home for the weekend. It was always busy in those hours, the comings and goings, the hellos and goodbyes.

Amy found me a little before tea as I was connecting a hose to the tap at the back of the girls' field.

'Glamorous work,' she said from behind me.

'Someone's got to do it,' I replied.

She walked forward until we were standing a pace or so apart. 'Thank you,' she said.

I couldn't quite look at her. 'I don't feel too good about it. I thought the moon was better.'

Amy considered that for a few seconds. 'I thought so, too.'

'Bit late now.'

'If it's any consolation, Charlotte's delighted. She'll still be thinking of it for years. That moon kid's dad is on the board at the National Gallery in London. He'll be fine. He'll have had his name down for some fine arts college since the day he was born.'

I thought on that for a little while, wondering if it made me feel better. I couldn't tell. Talk of things like fine arts colleges was one more thing that was a different world to me.

'Are you going to ask me out again?'

I couldn't escape Amy's stare in that moment.

The words wouldn't come: 'I mean, um, I didn't really, um... It's just...'

There was sympathy in the gentleness of her smile. 'Come out with us tomorrow night.'

'Who?'

'Ian, Gem and me.'

I almost winced at Ian's name and there was no way Amy could have missed it.

'Where are you going?' I asked.

'Does it matter? Meet us at the gates. Technically, we get off at eight but it was a bit after seven last week. Come out. It'll be fun.'

'Is this because Charlotte won?'

That got a little snort. Half a one. 'No. You should have come out last week. The offer was there. It's still there now.'

It should have been an easy answer but I couldn't quite say it.

'I asked him,' Amy said. 'I talked to Ian.'

'What did he say?'

'I wouldn't be inviting you out if he'd said no...'

She turned and followed my stare back towards the boys' field. I thought about Gemma and actions speaking louder than words.

'OK,' I said, quietly. 'I'll meet you here.'

From beyond the hedge, somewhere in the girls' field there was a loud cheer.

We stood for a moment, each wondering what came next.

'I've got to get back,' Amy said. 'Sounds like we're celebrating tonight.'

'Champagne all round?'

'Sherbet dips all round. They're gonna be so high.'

She stepped away and then turned back.

'See you tomorrow,' she said. 'And don't be late.'

22

BLUE

Although I didn't play, it was strange to have a Saturday without cricket. As with so many other things, the routine of watching Dan, Mark and Pete had somehow become a repeating part of my life. The week since the cricket club fight was the longest I'd ever gone without talking to one of Dan, Mark or Pete since we were around eight years old. During term time, we'd see each other in and out of school – and we had been inseparable during school holidays. Even when Dan went on ski holidays in December, Mark would still be the ever-present around town.

We'd had fall-outs in the past – but nothing serious and nothing that lasted more than a weekend. Nobody would ever apologise but we'd make it up by pretending none of it had happened, then carry on in the precise way we had before.

But then, that second week of camp, I'd gone seven days without really thinking of any of them. None of the three had gone out of their way to contact me – and I hadn't them.

Without cricket, I spent Saturday willing the clock to go faster. I spent time in my room and cycled around town. I went past the garage, though Michelle didn't seem to be working; and

I cycled around her flat, wondering if I'd spot the mysterious Connor again.

I didn't.

The anticipation and nervous energy I had around finally seeing Amy away from camp was dampened by the fact Ian would be there. They were two ends of the seesaw and I was somehow supposed to balance it all.

I tried to waste as much time as I could until it was time to head up to the campsite. I cycled there and left my bike behind the staff lounge, then walked across what felt like a half-deserted site. It was so quiet compared to the usual bedlam of games and activities.

Campers were leaving the mess hall in ones and twos, heading across towards their bunks. Far from the party atmosphere of the previous afternoon, it was like the hangover that followed.

Ian, Gemma and Amy were leaning on the gate at the front of the site when I arrived. They had been looking in the opposite direction, expecting me to come from the road that led directly to town, and it was Ian who spotted me first. He blinked, surprised I was there.

'Looks like it's time,' he said.

Amy and Gemma both turned and took me in. Gemma's smile was slight but Amy's much bigger. 'We were wondering if you'd show,' she said.

Every time Amy and I had talked before, words had come naturally and easily but, with others there, I couldn't think of anything to say.

Ian instantly became the leader, walking a pace ahead of Gemma and Amy, with me another step back. He led us down the slope towards town as the three of them spoke freely about their week and the campers in their bunks. Someone in Ian's tent got up at three in the morning, every morning, for a wee. Ian and his co-counsellor took it in turns to lead him across to the toilet block and then try to get back to sleep afterwards. A girl in Gemma's bunk had brought a crocheted blanket from home that she'd been sleeping with since she was a baby. It was riddled with holes and fraying at the edges – but she couldn't fall asleep without it. Amy talked about how Charlotte had gone three days without getting a letter from home, even though she'd been writing every day.

I listened and realised how entwined they all were with the lives of the children who were only a few years younger than we were. Being a counsellor wasn't simply watching campers play games, or organising workshop sessions, it involved a full range of everything a parent was supposed to do. It suddenly felt as if this whole thing was crazy, that these responsibilities went so far beyond what should be expected. It's not as if any of us had any training – and yet here we were, essentially running a mix between a school and a games club.

If any of the others felt that, then they didn't say it. They happily discussed their bunks as we continued to walk. I resisted the urge to ask where we were going and, when we reached town, we slotted into a tighter group. Ian led us past the Red Lion, where boisterous shouts drifted from the beer garden at the back. We went past the towpath and over the canal, past the ice-cream shops and the cheesemakers.

It was busy that evening, with locals and holidaymakers from the scattered caravan parks mixing with those who were visiting for the day. The pavements were packed and people were walking along the edges of the road, as cars crept around them.

Ian led us away from all that until we were on the far side of the town, within a few minutes' walk of where I lived. All the while, I was an interloper in their conversations about camp life. I had nothing to add and everything about the journey would have happened the same regardless of whether I was there.

Without warning, Ian suddenly veered off the pavement

into a place I'd cycled and walked past thousands of times, without ever going in. The Night And Day Café was the sort of place that my friends and I, though mainly Mark, would make fun of. We'd sometimes hear dreadful jazz seeping out from the inside, where all the instruments seemed to be playing over each other. Or there'd be a guy with long hair and a matted beard down to his stomach who'd be hanging around the tables at the front. Or a woman with a necklace made of daisies would be writing something on the board. We'd snigger and sneer, then forget all about it as we headed to Dan's garage and locked ourselves away.

I was curious as I paid attention to the blackboard on the wall outside as we headed through the front door. Colourful chalk flowers decorated the edges and, in swirly calligraphic letters, 'Poetry Night Tonight' was written in the centre.

I trailed after the other three, ducking under the low beam a little past the door that had 'WATCH YOUR HEAD!' written on a ripped sheet of paper that was taped to the wood. We emerged into a gloomy room with a low ceiling. Huge fans whirred in the corners and the air was thick and clammy.

Ian headed directly towards a couple of lads and a woman who were lounging on a big sofa underneath a chandelier that was only a fraction above head height. They were a little older than us and Ian threw himself onto the sofa as they separated to let him in. One of the boys instantly put an arm around his shoulder and said something into Ian's ear that made him roar with laughter.

When I turned from him, Amy was in the distance, edging her way through the crowd. I took a step after her but Gemma took my hand and pulled me back.

'She's going to the toilet.'

Her grip was warm and sweaty, though I suspected mine was too. I'd been in busier places but there was something about the low ceiling that made everything feel more compact.

Gemma kept hold of me and pulled me around a small group of people towards the bar. As I looked around, I noticed how varied everything was. There were teenagers and pensioners – plus everything in between. There was a woman with purple hair, another with green. A couple of men were in smart suits, others in shorts and vests. I was so used to the male-dominated spaces of the cricket club and the Red Lion – plus Dan's garage – that it was like stumbling into a new world.

As I was marvelling at something utterly normal, Gemma had found us stools at the bar. The woman serving couldn't have been that much older than us but knew Gemma by name. She asked 'how many?' without specifying what and Gemma replied with 'four'.

The server crouched and plucked four bottles that contained luminous blue liquid from the fridge at her feet. She popped the lids and put them in front of us. Gemma passed a handful of change before picking up one of the bottles. She nudged across another towards me.

'What is it?' I asked.

'Hard to know. There's definitely vodka but, after that, it's a mystery.' I must have pulled a face because she laughed. 'Try it.'

It was syrupy and sweet at first, then bitter and throat-burning at the end. Somehow as good as the best drink I'd ever had while also, without question, being the worst. As if someone had crossed a blueberry with a chemical weapon.

'Good, isn't it?' Gemma said.

'Sort of...'

It was also moreish. The moment that first swallow had gone down, I was craving more. We'd both had half a bottle each before we spoke again.

'What do you usually drink?' she asked.

'Lager... cider...'

'Course you do.'

I don't think she meant it harshly but I still found myself

twisting on the stool, embarrassed. I watched for a while as Ian and his friends joked around. They were more unruly than I could have guessed – though in a completely different way to me and my friends. We were all about nicknames, dead arms, headlocks and competitiveness. They were telling jokes or stories I couldn't hear and then laughing long and loud.

After a few minutes, Amy edged her way back through the crowd and spotted us at the bar. I thought she was going to grab a stool but, instead, she stretched between Gemma and me and plucked the two full bottles. With those in hand, she headed across to Ian and his friends, where they shuffled around to find a space for her. I started to stand but Gemma tugged on my shirt.

'Not yet,' she said.

There was no particular reason to listen to her – but I was questioning a lot about myself over that summer, with my judgement the biggest thing of all.

I twisted back on the stool until we were facing each other. 'Sorry about the Eiffel Tower thing,' I said.

Gemma waved it away. 'We were never going to win. It looked like someone had dropped it. I don't think Craft Week was our thing.'

She paused and drank from her bottle.

'Why are you here?' she asked.

'The café?'

A shrug. 'And camp. Are you going back to your friends and making fun of us every night?'

'Is that what you think?'

She held the bottle between her thumb and forefinger and let it swing like a pendulum. 'I don't know.'

'I'm not laughing at anyone – and I've not seen Dan and that lot all week.'

Gemma clasped the bottle tighter, stopping it moving, and

took me in before having another gulp. 'Everyone at camp loves Amy,' she said.

I felt the hairs rise on my arm and snatched for my bottle, then held it to my lips, not drinking but using it as a shield. I kept the bottle where it was and angled myself so I could see Amy on the sofas with Ian and his friends. She was sitting on the lap of one of them, carefully tracing his hairline with her finger in some sort of game the rest of them found hilarious. When he winced and scratched his own eyebrow, she slipped off his lap as everyone burst into applause and laughter.

'Is it that obvious?' I asked.

Gemma nudged me with her elbow. 'She comes and sits with you every reading hour. How much more obvious do you want it?'

Over on the sofas, one of the boys was on Ian's lap, tracing his hairline with the very tip of his finger. He'd been doing it for less than five seconds when Ian shuddered and couldn't resist scratching his own head.

'What are you saying?' I asked.

Gemma didn't reply at first. We continued to watch the game as Ian ran his finger around Amy's face. She seemed resistant to him, not flinching or scratching as the people around them started to gently drum their fingers on the chairs and table. I'd never seen this sort of thing before. The way they were all so comfortable with one another was alien, yet comforting.

'Don't be a dick,' Gemma said. 'That's all I'm saying.'

It could have sounded harsh but it didn't. It was more like she was telling me to look both ways before crossing the street. An obvious bit of advice.

The rules were still unclear but, by not reacting, Amy had seemingly won on the sofas. She reached onto the table and picked up a handful of pound coins that went into her bag.

'What do you think of poetry night?'

I must have squirmed when I turned to Gemma because she laughed.

'Wait until you actually see it. A lot is rubbish but sometimes it's amazing.' A pause. 'Anyway, it's not about the poetry.'

It only took me a moment to know what she meant. There was so much laughter around us, so much joy. Despite the noise, there was also a tranquillity about it all. The Red Lion always had that edge, as if a war could break out at any moment. The cricket club was better but I'd seen plenty of arguments in there – plus rolled around on the floor with one of my best mates.

There was none of that in the café, despite the claustrophobia of the low ceilings and the shoulder-to-shoulder nature of the crowd.

'C'mon…'

Gemma took my hand again and led me across to the sofas. There were no formal introductions, they simply parted and allowed us space to sit. Everyone was drinking the same blue stuff that Gemma had bought for me. The only label on the bottle simply read 'Blue', which wasn't that reassuring about what was inside.

Amy was at the furthest end of the sofa, squished next to Ian. As soon as I sat, she stood and headed to the bar. Minutes later and she was back, plonking another bottle in front of Gemma and myself – and then handing another to Ian.

I didn't exactly join in with the games and the fun but I did laugh along, even though much of their conversation was about people and things I didn't know.

Ian bought a round next and he put a bottle in front of me without looking in my direction. Each bottle slipped down quickly and there was certainly something addictive about it. As I finished the third, it was my turn, so I went to the bar with the £25 George had given me in cash the day before. Four bottles of Blue cost £4 and I returned to the sofa and handed everyone in our group a drink. Amy and Ian were in a conversation and each acknowledged me with a nod as I returned to my spot at the other end.

There was a time when I would have minded this sort of exclusion – but it wasn't then. Gemma was telling one of Ian's friends about a drama club she was in and he said he'd been in the same one when he was younger. He was kind enough to try to involve me in the conversation, asking if I did drama. I had to lean in and shout into his ear that I didn't. Somehow, none of that mattered.

It was nine o'clock when everyone went quiet. Stools and chairs screeched across the floor and I craned my neck around a man in a leather waistcoat to see that someone was standing on a stage at the very back of the room. The speakers whined and everyone winced until a woman with massive glasses apologised.

'It's that time of the week,' she said – and people cheered and banged the table. Around me, Ian, his friends, Amy and Gemma were all bashing something as the noise bounced around the walls and ceiling until we were living through an earthquake. The woman at the front shouted someone's name and then a woman wearing what looked like a knitted tea cosy headed up to the front as the sound somehow got louder.

And that was how the next hour or so passed. Someone would go to the microphone with a thunderous welcome, they'd read their poem, and then retake their seat to an even louder reception. It felt as if every person in the room knew each other, as if this was some sort of secret club that existed in plain sight.

I had no idea whether the poems were something they'd written, or something more famous. I didn't know if any of it was any good – not that it mattered. Whoever spoke, or for how long, their performance was bookended with a tsunami of support.

I'd barely finished my next drink when one of Ian's friends

pushed a fresh bottle of Blue into my hand. I started to thank him but he shrugged it away, as if I was one of them.

As if I belonged.

At ten, without any sort of prompt, everyone got up and acted as one. Chairs were dragged towards the edges of the room and stacked; then, from nowhere, a band appeared on stage. They played songs I largely didn't know and probably didn't like, but it still didn't matter. The sound of the guitar boomed around the walls and the lyrics were far too muffled to make out. Then they played the Savage Garden song from a couple of years before that had been everywhere. Mark, me and the others would sneer and laugh at it and anyone who liked it. But, as the band strummed 'Truly, Madly, Deeply', people sang and bobbed along.

I sat on the side, still drinking as people were dancing and laughing. Ian was dancing with the tallest of his friends – and Gemma with his mate. Then they swapped and Ian was with the other lad.

I watched and I drank… and then Amy was sitting on the arm of the sofa. Her hair was damp with sweat, sticking to the sides of her face as she looked down upon me.

She leaned in, close to my ear and yelled: 'Are you dancing?'

I held up my hands and leaned in to her ear. Her hair brushed across my nose and her neck was sticky. 'I don't dance.'

It was true. I didn't dance, because of course I didn't. Mark, Dan, Pete and me laughed at the sort of people who did. It's not like there was any dancing, ever, in the Red Lion or at the cricket club.

Except Amy wasn't accepting that as an answer. She grabbed my hand and pulled me up and towards the dance floor. I was suddenly in the middle of the crowd as people bounced and flailed around me. I had no idea what I was doing but I tried to copy Amy. When she put her arms up, I did the same. If she jumped, I jumped half a second later. It was like a poorly choreographed 'Heads, Shoulders, Knees and Toes' – although none of that was her fault.

In retrospect, it was one of the most embarrassing moments of my life to that point – although I didn't feel it in that room. There were no video cameras, nobody filming. There were limbs everywhere and nobody cared what anyone else was doing.

I'd been dancing, if it could be called that, with Amy – but then she was with one of Ian's friends. From nowhere, Ian was in front of me and we were sort of dancing together. He was unquestionably dancing and I was bobbing side to side like some sort of seal poking its head above water.

It was another thing that should have been uncomfortable, for so many reasons, but Ian's laughter only made me bob harder and higher until we moved again. I danced with Gemma and then one of Ian's friends before Amy was finally in front of me once more. A strap of her vest top had slipped down her arm, exposing a bare, browned shoulder. She put her hands around my neck and leaned in, whispering – or probably shouting – 'you look hot' into my ear.

It was only as she said this that I realised I'd sweated through my T-shirt. It was sticking to my chest and back and I could feel liquid dripping into my underwear.

It should have been grim but everyone was in the same position. A triangle of sweat had formed at the front of Amy's top and, when I looked across to Ian and his friends, two of them were no longer wearing tops.

Amy unwrapped her hands from my neck and stepped across to the sofas, where she grabbed two fullish bottles of Blue from the table. She handed me one and took my hand. We snaked through and around the swaying crowd as the room shook. We were in a gloomy corridor, where we passed a line of people queueing for the toilets, and then we were out the fire door and on a patch of grass. The clammy cloying heat of the café was gone in an instant. The bank overlooked a different stretch of the canal compared to the one at the back of the Red Lion. It was quieter there, gentler.

Amy lay and I rested at her side as we peered down towards the black, unmoving water. The cloudless sky was a dark purple and the moon shone bright.

We lay like that for a while, holding hands and listening to the muffled music behind. When Amy rolled onto her side, I copied and we lay there staring into each other's eyes for a while. Hers were green in the day but black under the night, twinkling under the moon. I wasn't often lost for words around her – but I was then. Actually, it wasn't words. I knew what I wanted to do, what I wanted to happen.

And then it *did* happen, in slow motion. She leaned forward, the mildest incline of her neck, and she pressed her lips to mine. It was soft and sudden. Almost like she was asking a question, perhaps of herself more than me.

She shifted away but not far. I watched her eyes and then I risked it and leaned in myself. I could taste the Blue on her this time and we pressed into each other with much more force second time around. I had my hand on her hip and she had one on my cheek when she finally pulled away.

'Poetry night is fun, isn't it?' she said.

'The best.'

23

GRASS

Luke was having breakfast when I arrived at camp the next morning. He didn't live locally, so slept on site – but it was still his day off. He said his dad was driving in to pick him up and take him somewhere, then he left me with a list of tasks that turned out to be a blank piece of paper. 'Enjoy yourself,' he said, as he set off towards the front gate.

It was after breakfast and I was in the staff lounge by myself when the connecting flap to the mess hall swished and Amy appeared. She was in her camp T-shirt and shorts – but it was the playful smile I noticed first. She crossed the hall and took my hand, then led me out the back, past the place I left my bike each day, and into the adjacent field. We followed the hedgerow back along the line of the camp field until we were sitting underneath a tree. The boys' bunks were a few metres away, on the other side of the hedge, though we were completely shielded from view.

We'd not even spoken but we were suddenly grabbing for each other, faces pressed together. It wasn't so short or gentle that time. We were entwined in the long grass, our hands on each other's hips, arms, cheeks. In one another's hair. We giggled to each other and only pulled apart when our lips needed a rest.

There was nothing particularly funny but we laughed anyway as we lay in the grass and felt the sun upon us.

'How were you this morning?' she asked. They were the first words we'd said to each other since last night.

'Bit of a headache but that was about it.'

'Same – but Sarah handled breakfast and let me sleep in.'

'Have you got to get back soon?'

She shook her head and then reached to pluck a strand of grass from my hair, which she tossed to the side. 'Sarah's going to cover the morning and I'll do the afternoon. There's not many campers around this weekend.'

I must have smiled because she reflected it.

'Why?' she added. 'Do you have an idea about what to do?'

We kissed more but it was gentler this time and intermingled with stops to rest on the grass and listen to camp continuing on the other side of the hedge.

We were on our backs, holding hands, eyes closed because of the sun and bright sky when I managed to fumble out the words that had been in my head all morning.

'I won't mind if you want to keep this secret,' I said.

Amy propped herself on an elbow and blocked the sun with her body. 'Do *you* want to keep it a secret?'

I opened my eyes and looked into hers. 'Why would I want it to be a secret?'

'Why would *I*?'

She leaned in and kissed me again and I thought back to my first kiss a little over a year before. Mark, Dan, Pete and I had gone to a birthday party for a girl in our year. It had been on a Saturday afternoon at her house, though dragged through to the evening. I was drunk on lager, my stomach gurgling, bladder bursting when Yasmine from my maths class had waved me across to the alley at the side of the house. She didn't say a word but pinned me to the wall and shoved her mouth over the top of mine. I was so surprised that I started to pull away before I went with it. I had no idea what I was doing – and the only open-mouthed kissing I'd seen was on TV.

It lasted a few seconds until our teeth collided and then Yasmine pulled away. She swayed from side to side and I reached to catch her. She didn't need me, instead using a wheelie bin to hold herself up.

'I always wondered what that would be like,' she'd said.

I was too shocked by the whole thing to reply and, before I could, she added: 'Don't tell anyone.'

'About this?'

She shook her head. 'I'll deny it if you say anything. Tell them you made it up.'

I'd stared at her for a few seconds and then walked away. In the time after, it felt like more of a dream than anything else. At school, Yasmine pretended I didn't exist.

Back in the field, Amy kissed me again and it was nothing like it had been with Yasmine. I had no idea what I was doing but Amy seemed to. She also had the patience to guide me.

'Have you got your book?' she asked.

It took me a moment to realise she meant *Little Women*. 'It's in my bag,' I said. 'In the lounge.'

'Go get it.'

I did as I was told and then re-joined her at the tree. I read her another chapter as she lay in the grass, her arms and legs splayed, chest rising and falling slowly, eyes closed as the sun washed across her.

When I got to the end, she rolled slowly onto her side, opened her eyes and then kissed me. 'I have to get back,' she said.

'I probably have work to do, too.'

We stood and walked back to the campsite hand in hand and I was filled with a sense of everything and nothing all at the same time. Contentment is probably the best way to put it. There was no sense of wishing I'd said or done something differently. Of regret. If everything ended there, it would be OK because I had already experienced something perfect.

A couple of the kitchen staff were milling in the grassy area at the back of the lounge, so Amy and I said goodbye inside before getting on with the rest of the day.

I didn't see a lot more of her that Sunday. Because of the deal she'd done with Sarah and some of the other counsellors, she was in charge of around twenty girls for a few hours as the counsellors spent a bit of time doing other things. For the most part, it sounded as if a great number of them were sleeping off varying degrees of hangover across those Sundays.

On days things hadn't gone my way, I would remember the bike rides home in forensic detail. I'd know the times I'd had to slow and the cars that got too close when they overtook. On the good days, it was as if I'd jumped from one place to another. Like everything was light and free. The ride home that Sunday was a blink – though I do remember Michelle's car being parked outside the house. She was on her way out the front door as I was heading in.

'You look like you've had a good day,' she said.

I didn't want to get caught up in talk about Amy with my sister, so I pretended I hadn't heard. 'How's Mum?' I asked.

I looked for darkness in Michelle's face but she seemed as though she was thinking about something else. 'Not great but could be worse.' She pulled the front door into the frame, though didn't fully close it. 'I hoped you'd come round,' she said.

'When?'

'Any time after you run off the other night. I hoped you'd come by the garage or the flat. I wanted to make sure you were OK.'

'I left a message at the garage – and you could've come over...'

She nodded to acknowledge the point. 'Did you talk to Mum about why she left Barry's?'

'I didn't have a go, I just asked why...?'

Michelle took a deep breath and glanced towards her car before turning back to me. 'Didn't I tell you to leave it?'

'Yes but she's not doing anything. She just sits there and gets angry at nothing.'

'I know – but let this one thing go.'

After the weekend I'd had, the best hours of my life, I could feel those dark clouds returning. It was that house and my family.

'That's easy for you to say,' I replied. 'You moved out, you're off with some boyfriend, or whatever. It was you she was having a go at. You should've been angry, not me.'

Michelle waited, probably wondering if I had more to say. When it was her turn, she was infuriatingly calm. 'Just because I don't say everything out loud, it doesn't mean I'm not angry. Sometimes, you have to learn to keep it in.'

'What if you don't want to?'

She took another breath, held it, let it out. 'I can't answer that,' she said. 'Sometimes you have to learn these lessons yourself.'

24

TREE

The next week was exciting for more than the obvious reason. I paid no interest to newspapers or TV news – but it was impossible to miss the back-to-back coverage of the eclipse that was due to happen on Wednesday. From the campsite, we wouldn't quite be able to see the moon blocking a hundred per cent of the sun – but it was supposed to be close. I took two trips to George's house on the Monday to pick up boxes of special glasses that would allow everyone to look safely at the sun.

As well as excitement around the eclipse, after crafts, the third week was for sports. There were various badminton, volleyball, dodgeball and rounders tournaments due to run across the days. Friday was set aside for a mass sports day, with each bunk competing against the others for supremacy.

None of that led to much more of a workload for Luke and me – although that week was the one he'd been waiting for. He entered himself into a staff-only badminton tournament and, as the campers watched on and supported their counsellors, Luke thrashed all of them.

As for Amy and I, reading hour was no longer spent on site. After I set up the umbrellas, I would meet her under the tree, in the long grass, on the other side of the hedge. By the time we met there on the Tuesday, the third day in a row, there was a flattened mound of grass that had become our spot. We were doing more talking than kissing at that stage. That frantic need of the weekend had given way to something calmer. We held and we talked and we listened… and it was more than enough.

She told me that her dad worked a lot and often didn't come home during the week. Her mum had never had any sort of career – but she spent a lot of time cleaning the house, refusing to hire a cleaner.

'And she lunches a lot,' Amy added. 'It's all "let's do lunch" when she's with her friends. They go to Dad's golf club, or these little tea shops they know. Five or six of them all together, drinking champagne and avoiding bread.'

She squeezed my hand and I listened, wondering if she'd spoken about her parents to anyone else, whether it was something that had been building. I let her finish, not pushing for anything she didn't want to give up. We rested there quietly for a short while and then she changed the subject.

'What are you expecting with your exams?' she asked.

I felt nervous about the reply, knowing her predicted grades would be so much better than mine. 'Hopefully five passes. That's what everyone wants, isn't it? That's what colleges want.'

'Will you get them?'

'I don't know. I'm not good with exams.'

I thought back to the morning of my history exam, when Mum had thrown a fit because I'd made too much noise going down the stairs in the morning. She'd thrown the TV remote at me, then got angrier when it hit the ground and the batteries popped out.

'What about you?' I asked.

She squirmed slightly and I couldn't tell if it was false modesty, or actual. 'Predicted all As,' she said. 'Maybe an A-star here or there. French went really well.'

'What about after?'

I'd asked the question before I'd thought about the complications of the answer. They were such early days and the idea of what might come after camp was a distant concern. Those two and a bit weeks – and the previous three days in particular – had all been about living in the moment. Six weeks was an eternity.

'I've got a place at art college,' Amy said.

'I didn't know you drew?'

'I don't... well, not very well. It's performing arts.'

She twirled a strand of her hair and angled away, staring into the distance as if embarrassed.

'Is that acting?' I asked.

'Plus singing and dancing. A bit of everything.'

'I didn't know that was your thing.'

It dawned on me as I spoke that I didn't know that much about her at all. Not *real* things.

She smiled. 'Weren't you impressed with my dance moves on Saturday?'

'We were all a bit close. I could only really see your face.'

'True.' She chewed her lip for a moment and then added: 'Yours need a bit of work. Get those hips swaying – and you should probably try to move your feet. For a minute, I thought someone had nailed your shoes to the ground.'

She cracked into a wide grin. She was teasing but it was true.

'Do you reckon you can get all day Saturday off?' I asked.

The hope lasted less than a second as she shook her head. 'No chance. It's visitors' day on Saturday. All the parents of the seven-dayers are supposed to be coming. It's the only time the girls who sleep over will see their family across the whole six weeks. It's going to be a crazy day.' She stopped for a moment, thinking. 'Why? Do you have something planned? Were you going to show me the sights?'

'Something like that.'

Amy reached and gripped my hand, interlocking her fingers into mine. 'I'll talk to Sarah,' she said. 'I might be able to get the Saturday off after this one. She likes having a break in the evenings, so if I cover all those, I think it'll be all right.' There was another pause and then: 'I think she's got a thing for one of the lads working in Lewis. I caught them having a snog by the bins last night.'

I thought of my own first kiss, also near a bin. 'Sounds romantic,' I replied.

Amy laughed and then released my hand. She rolled onto her side and sat cross-legged, waiting for me to copy her.

'What about you?' she asked.

'I'm always up for a snog by the bins.'

That got a snort. 'I meant we only ever talk about me. I've told you about Mum and Dad but all I know is that your dad died. Do you live with your mum? A rich aunt? Ten brothers?'

'A rich uncle, actually,' I replied. 'He's loaded. Owns half of Microsoft.'

She didn't smile, she looked at me, waiting for the truth. I'd never particularly talked about this sort of thing with anyone before.

'I live with my mum,' I said. 'I've got an older sister who has her own flat. She's a mechanic and—'

'What, like cars? She fixes cars?'

In the same way that things like strudel and Louisa May Alcott had passed me by, Amy seemed stunned that my sister could be a mechanic.

'She works at the garage in town,' I said.

Amy stared off into the distance for a moment. 'I'd love to do that.'

'Would you?'

Amy thought for a second and then laughed to herself. 'No – but it would drive Mum mad, so it would be worth it.'

We sat looking at each other for a moment. It feels strange now, not the sort of thing I did before or since. I can still picture those light freckles around her hairline and darker ones towards her cheeks.

'What are you going to do if you get your five passes?' she asked.

'I'm not sure.'

'My friend, Rachel, reckons none of it matters anyway. She says you can put whatever you want on a CV and nobody ever checks. She said her brother got mainly Ds and Es – but put down As and Bs. He got a job doing something with the government in London.'

I thought on that for a moment – plus the way Michelle had said that camp would be good for my CV. Everyone had spent the last few years telling me that my entire life would rest on the outcome of those hours we spent sat in halls trying to regurgitate knowledge onto an exam paper.

'Who are your other friends?' I asked.

'Rachel's in the south of France at the moment. She goes every year because her dad's got a farm out there.'

'A farm?'

'They make wine on it. I'm not really sure – but I wouldn't say no to a holiday if it was going. Then there's Carol and Caroline. We've all been in the same classes since primary school. Carol's doing work experience at her dad's legal firm because she wants to be a lawyer when she grows up.'

'How old is she?'

'Same as us – but she said she wants it all on her CV. Caroline's doing some sort of volunteer thing at a dog rescue near her aunt's in Wales. That's for her CV too.'

I thought of my own friends and how our plans had been to spend the summer drinking in Dan's garage. If it hadn't been for Michelle fixing George's car, that's where I'd likely be. Not exactly something to brag about.

'What do you all do when you're not coming up with things for your CV?' I asked.

'I dunno... watch movies. We saw *Titanic* fourteen times at the cinema – and Caroline saw it four times on her own. Then there's drama club and dance club. Lots of things.' She paused and I knew what was coming. 'What about you?'

She must have heard something about my friends and me via Ian and I couldn't look at her as I replied. 'Pete and Dan are probably going to college but Mark's getting a job tarmacking with his uncle.'

When I looked back to her, she was staring at me.

'We have very different friends.'

'Sounds like it.'

Amy leant forward and kissed me gently, then scooched around, so that her back was resting on my chest.

'What's it like having a birthday on Christmas Day?' I asked.

She squeezed my leg and turned around as far as she could. 'Are you spying on me?'

'It was in your profile from the newsletter.'

'Oh yeah. Anyway, I get scammed with the whole "one big present" nonsense. We went skiing last year as a combined present for my birthday and Christmas, even though I don't like snow – and Mum and Dad did most of the skiing. They basically bought themselves a holiday and said it counted as my birthday and Christmas present.'

'You *definitely* got scammed.'

'I know!'

There was part of a laugh to Amy's reply but something harder bubbling under the surface, too.

'What did you do while they were skiing?' I asked.

'Sat in the hot tub a lot.' She let her head flop to the side, so it was resting on my shoulder. 'You did it again,' she said.

'Did what?'

'We were talking about you – but somehow ended up talking about me.'

I thought of the things I wanted to tell her. About Dad and how Mum had fallen apart. About the arguments and the fear I felt every time I had to go home. How Michelle had left home and how I wanted to as well, even though I knew I couldn't because it would leave Mum with no one. About how everything had gone wrong with my friends – and that I wasn't sure whether they were right for me anyway.

We sat like that, Amy's head on my shoulder, my arms around her. She didn't speak, as if inviting me to fill the space with the truth. I couldn't though – and we sat until Amy lifted her arm and looked at her watch.

'I have to head back,' she said. 'But I'll ask Sarah about a week Saturday. I hope you have something good planned.'

25

CATERPILLAR

I was cycling home that night when a largely familiar face waved at me. He had just finished reversing onto his drive and was pulling a pair of Sainsbury's bags out from the passenger seat of his car. I freewheeled across to him and stood astride my bike.

'She's a beauty, isn't she?' Barry said when he noticed me beside him – and it took me a second to realise he meant the car.

Even among the vehicles owned by those who lived in the big houses up near George, Barry's maroon Bentley stood out as something out of the ordinary. It was almost a joke around town that, wherever Barry was, his car was never far away. Or vice versa. He wasn't married – except to that vehicle. Michelle was far more into cars than I ever was and she'd been enamoured with it for years. When we were younger, both at school, she'd ask Dad if he was ever going to buy a Bentley. Dad always laughed it off. 'When we win the pools,' he'd say.

Barry had been one of Dad's friends, even though their businesses had a degree of overlap. Barry was a big guy, all belly and arms. The sort who'd go to the Red Lion to do the Biggest Breakfast challenge on a Sunday and have a chance of completing the monstrous meal. We'd never had any sort of conversation that hadn't involved one of my parents being there. The closest we'd come was at Dad's funeral, when Barry had given a speech that mentioned Michelle and me by name. I should probably remember more about it but that whole day had disappeared into a fog.

Outside his house, Barry turned between the car and me. 'Been a while since I saw you racing around on that bike,' he said. 'What have you been up to?'

It felt odd that he'd ask – but I told him I was working at the camp and he nodded along, even though I wasn't sure he knew where I was talking about.

'What do you do up there?' he asked.

'A lot of lifting and carrying. I have to set up the badminton nets and things like that...'

Something changed in Barry as I said that. It hadn't felt as if he was paying a lot of attention before but he suddenly fixed me in a curious stare, that involved his overgrown eyebrows merging to create one giant caterpillar.

'I need someone like that around the yard,' he said. 'I've got lots of little jobs that always end up being put off. I need someone with a bit of common sense. Someone who doesn't need their hand held all the time.' He looked me up and down and then added: 'Does that sound like you?'

I was put on the spot, unsure what to say. Bragging had never been a part of my family's make-up. 'I think so,' I said.

Barry roared at this, making me jump. 'Have some faith in yourself,' he said. 'You shouldn't do yourself down. You can say "yes".'

He looked at me expectantly until I mumbled a somewhat reluctant 'yes'.

'That's more like it,' he replied loudly. 'Tell you what, when you're done at that camp, you come find me.' He nodded towards the house across the pavement. 'You know where I live, or I'm at the yard most of the day. You've gotta get good grades, mind. Five or six passes, something like that.'

I thought back to Amy talking under the tree. How she said her friend's brother had invented his grades.

'I'll let you know,' I said.

'Excellent. Carrying on your dad's legacy and all that. He'd be proud. I'm thinking about opening a second yard one of these days and I need a trustworthy person to get it up and running.' A pause. 'What do you think about that?'

I didn't know what to say and it was hard to know whether it was a serious offer. It felt like one of those things adults say to kids sometimes, those vague promises of help that are only ever meant as words, not actions.

'That sounds good.'

He clapped his hands again. 'That's that then. You make sure to come see me when you're ready.'

Barry had already taken a few steps along his drive when I called after him. 'Mr Dennis?'

He turned and looked back towards where I was standing at the front of his car.

'I'm sorry about Mum,' I said. 'I know you gave her a job and she walked off but she's been having a hard time since Dad died...'

Barry eyed me for a few seconds and then put down his shopping bags on the ground. He walked back along the drive and placed a hand on my shoulder. He gripped a little too hard, making me wince, before releasing me.

'You don't need to apologise, son,' he said. 'It's not your fault. Not hers, either.' He waited a beat and then added: 'You make sure you come by after camp. I think it could turn into a great partnership.'

26

GLASSES

The curtains were open when I got home – but the living room was still dusty and grim. There were three or four mugs around Mum's feet and she was watching TV from the sofa. The programme that had been on merged into the news, with the first few minutes given over to the eclipse.

'I got something for you,' I said.

Mum didn't turn from the screen. 'Huh?'

I dug into my bag and took out one of the leftover pairs of glasses I'd taken from camp. I put them on the arm of the sofa and she pulled her gaze away from the TV long enough to look at them.

'Why would I need glasses?' she asked.

'They're special ones that let you look at the eclipse tomorrow,' I replied. 'You can't look directly at it otherwise.'

'Why are you telling me?'

'There's a viewing party on the green across from the Red Lion. You could go into town and watch it with other people. It'll be good. They say there won't be another total eclipse until 2090.'

Mum picked up the glasses and twisted them in her hand.

She put them on and took them off, then returned them to the sofa arm. Whatever she mumbled was lost underneath the sound of the TV.

I was about to say something more when someone knocked on the front door. Mum made no attempt to move, so I headed out of the living room, closing the door behind me, and went into the hall.

Nobody ever came to the house for Mum – and it wasn't going to be for me – so I'd expected Jehovah's Witnesses, or someone trying to sell something. A guy around the corner worked as a haulier and his wife sometimes went knocking on doors to see if anyone wanted to buy the various things he'd smuggled back from the continent.

It wasn't her, or anyone with a Bible. This time, it was for me.

Dan was standing on the path wearing his red England football top. He'd been staring across to the other side of the road but turned as I opened the door. We were strangers in that moment, as if we'd never met.

'Hi,' he said, quiet and reserved, as if talking to a teacher.

'Hi.'

We looked to each other for a moment and it was the same but different. We'd known each other for so long but it felt like we didn't.

'You weren't at cricket,' Dan said.

It was such an odd thing to say and yet typical of us. The weekend before, I'd been fighting on the floor of the clubhouse – but he was still surprised I hadn't been there seven days later. If not for camp, I probably would have been. Mark would have been quiet at first but, if he'd had a good game, all would have been well by the evening and we'd have been back in the routine of cider and in-jokes.

'I went out with a few people from camp,' I said.

He blinked at me, took a second too long to reply. 'Oh... was it good?'

'Yeah...'

Of our group, Dan was probably always my best friend. He could be the quietest of us – but the loudest when needed. He got the best grades by far, yet never made me or the others feel stupid for not reaching his standards.

'All that stuff with Mark,' he said, with something of a sigh. 'Look... he's sorry and everything got a bit out of hand. He was out first ball and you know what he's like. He said things, you said things. It was just the cider, wasn't it? That stuff's a killer.'

For a moment, I was back on the sticky floor of the club-house, ferreting weak punches in Mark's side as stools fell around us. We'd been so close and I'd seen the fury in his eyes, as if I was staring into his soul. He'd likely seen something similar in me, too.

'If he's sorry, then why are you saying it and not him?'

Dan rested back onto his heels and turned back towards the street. We both knew that Mark wasn't the sort to apologise for anything. In terms of forgive and forget, we all went straight to forget. We never dealt with our squabbles and problems, we pretended they weren't there.

When he looked back, Dan was trying to force a smile in which even he didn't believe. 'The lads are coming over to the garage in about half an hour,' he said. 'You should come. It'll be fun. Like the old days with just the four of us.'

I felt the pull to those weeks after Dad died when I almost lived in that garage. I certainly slept there a few times. I wondered much later if it was those weeks that shaped who I was for the year or so afterwards. I allowed myself to overlook the bad things we did because my life had that enormous Dad-shaped crater in it. I filled that adult-sized hole with three people my own age.

'Were the old days really that fun?'

Those words had been building when I said them and Dan stared at me as if I'd spoken another language.

'What do you mean?'

'I dunno… I just wonder if it was actually that good. I've never really been into cricket, or FIFA, or darts. I'm no good at any of that.'

There was a tinge of hurt in Dan's voice as he replied: 'We could have done other things.'

'I know. I'm not saying it's anyone's fault.'

We stood on the doorstep for a few seconds more but it didn't feel right to either of us. Those eight or nine days apart might as well have been a year. *Years.*

'I've got to go,' Dan said. 'Everyone will be there soon.' A pause. 'You should come.'

'Maybe another time.'

Dan wasn't going to ask for a third occasion and he took a couple of steps backwards before turning and walking away. 'See ya,' he called – and then he was gone, not bothering to look back another time.

27

MOON

Before I left for camp the next morning, I told Mum that the main part of the eclipse would be a little after eleven but that it would start at around half-nine. I reminded her about the viewing party in town but she was absorbed in the TV and it was hard to tell whether she'd been listening.

I cycled through town on the way up to camp and the high street was already busy. Bunting zigzagged across the road and a crooked 'Eclipse 99' banner had appeared outside the community hall. All the pubs were advertising 'viewing parties' and were seemingly open for breakfast. A second banner that read 'Party Like It's 1999' was above the Red Lion. I was fairly sure it had been recycled from the New Year celebrations.

The town felt as busy as I'd known it considering how early it was. Cars were parked nose to tail along both sides of the high street and camper vans were filling up the car park at the back of the Spar.

There were so many cars flooding down the hill into town that I had to get off my bike and walk the final half-mile up to the campsite.

When I got there, Luke was carrying blankets from the staff

lounge out to the main fields. Campers and counsellors were already massing on the grass, taking up spots close to their bunks and trying out their viewing glasses.

The biggest problem nobody seemed to have thought of was the greying-white clouds that were washed high across the sky. It was bright but there were no breaks – and nowhere the sun was actually visible.

I was still carrying blankets to the girls' side of the field when the first tingling wisp of cold hit. I hadn't been looking up but it was like someone had used a dimmer switch to turn down everything by the most delicate of fractions. An 'ooh' swept around the field and it felt as if everyone stopped what they were doing, put on their glasses, and looked up.

There were still clouds – lots of them – but that sense of eeriness remained. Children were talking in whispers and clustering close to one another.

After dropping off the final few blankets, I did a lap of the camp, making sure everybody had what they needed. Amy and Sarah were sitting with the girls from their bunk. Some of the campers had dragged out their sleeping bags, others looked bulky in multiple tops and jumpers. Amy had one of the blankets around her as she sipped tea from a metal mug. She saw me and nodded with acknowledgement as I continued the rounds.

Over an hour passed since the first sliver of darkness and the clouds hadn't cleared. There wasn't a lot to see but each minute felt like another minuscule turn not only of the dimmer switch but the thermostat.

I picked up one of the spare blankets and pulled it around my shoulders as I crossed to the boys' field, where there was significantly more restlessness compared to the girls. Campers were getting bored of staring at a sky that started grey and was only a bit darker. A few of the boys were kicking a ball around, though they were shadows in the murk.

It happened when I was midway across the boys' field. I'd

been walking but stopped involuntarily. I shivered and it started somewhere within the deepest reaches of my body.

Day had turned to night.

Everything felt wrong. Up was down and it felt as if I needed to hold on to something, else I would float away and into the abyss. I think I stumbled, as if I'd tripped, even though I was standing still. I wasn't sure how any of it happened but I was suddenly on the ground, dirt on my palms as I crawled on my hands and knees trying to get my bearings.

It had happened in a blink – and then there was hand on my arm, another under my shoulder, lifting me up.

'You all right?'

I couldn't see properly through the gloom – and the faintest glimmers of light seeping from the inside of bunks and tents blurred into a neon swoosh that surrounded me.

The hands stayed on my arm, keeping me upright.

'Lean on me. It's OK. It'll pass.'

It was a man's voice and I didn't have the ability to resist. The two of us stood there clasping one another under the eye of the eclipse until, eventually, the heavens wobbled and a slit of light burst from above.

I steadied myself and the hands released me.

'Can you hear the birds?' the voice asked.

I listened, straining... except: 'No...'

'I read somewhere that animals think eclipses are night. It throws off their body clocks.'

He held up his arm and, even in the gentlest light, I could see the pimple prick goosebumps speckled across his skin. I held up mine and we matched.

'I'll be a hundred and seven by the time of the next full eclipse,' Ian said.

I looked to him properly and he was staring upwards, his face half hidden by the glasses. When he turned back down to me, he took them off.

'Not that I have any intention of living that long. Who wants to be a hundred? I'll go out in a blaze of glory long before then. Comedy death, I think. Falling off a stage, something like that.'

Everything remained fuzzy and I didn't reply. Ian touched my arm, squeezing gently to make sure I was OK, and then stepped back.

'I've chosen to forgive,' he said.

I didn't need to ask who or for what – but I still couldn't think of anything better to say than 'Oh.'

It wasn't as if I thought we'd become friends but I'd assumed we'd end up broadly ignoring one another. Actually being forgiven out loud was strange. My friends and I had never forgiven anyone for anything by using the actual words.

'I'm not sure you deserve it,' Ian added. 'It's early days yet.'

I was still unsteady, or that's what I told myself. I had no idea how to respond.

'I've said a few things in the past to other people that I regret,' he added. 'Things I can't take back.' A pause. 'That's not meant as an excuse for either of us – but you said sorry. It was a bit half-arsed but I'll take it at face value.'

'Cheers.'

We stood together for a few seconds as the dimmer switch started to go back the other way.

'Your friends seemed fun,' I said.

'Ha! They are in small doses. You coming out again on Saturday?'

'Am I invited?'

'You're one of the gang now. Owen spent half the night talking about how you'd sweated through your shirt.'

'Sorry about that.'

'Oh, don't be sorry. He loved it. Not my thing but it takes all sorts.'

The world was different in the nineties but I think I knew

what he was talking about, even at our age. It was one more thing that would have been extra-terrestrial barely two weeks before.

Another notch on the dimmer switch loosened, though I held the blanket tight around my shoulders.

'I think she really likes you...'

Ian spoke softly... kindly. He wasn't looking at me, which was a good thing because I wouldn't have been able to handle it if he was. I wasn't used to anyone talking to me in such a way.

'Do you ever wonder if there's a real you...?' I asked.

It was a question that had been tickling the edges of my thoughts and, until that moment, I hadn't known who to ask. Definitely not Mark, Dan or Pete.

'How do you mean?' Ian asked.

'I suppose... at the café, when you walked in, it was like you were someone else. You went straight to your friends and you were so comfortable with them. As if, in that moment, that's where you were supposed to be. I guess I never saw you like that at school.'

Ian didn't reply at first, although I could almost feel him thinking about it.

'I've never thought of you as such a deep person,' he said.

I laughed at that. 'Me either.'

'I don't think it matters what I think – but, if you want to know, I think the real you is the you of the moment. It's why you can come to a place like this and be a different person.' He stopped and then added: 'I suppose the question is, once you leave, who are you then?'

He wouldn't have known it – but those words wormed their way deeper into my mind over the coming weeks.

I wanted to talk longer but it was getting ever lighter and campers were beginning to get up and walk about. I said I'd see him around and he gave an enthusiastic 'sure!' before he bounded off towards his bunk.

With the eclipse coming towards its conclusion, I set off back towards the main tents to find out what needed to be done in the afternoon. I was on my way into the staff lounge from one side as George entered from the other. It was an accident of timing and we both stopped, looking across to one another. He'd always been so calm and assuring – and yet I could see in his face that something was wrong.

He looked from side to side, making sure the lounge was empty – and then he came across and put a strong hand on my shoulder.

That feeling was back and I was in Dan's garage again when his mum said Michelle was coming to pick me up.

'What's happened?' I asked.

'Your sister just called the office,' he said. 'It's your mum...'

28

CLIPBOARD

George pulled up at the front of the hospital. I already had my seat belt off and was reaching for the car door handle when he said he'd find somewhere to park and join me inside.

There were two women smoking next to the no smoking sign and a man in a wheelchair who was heading out as I was going in. I was paying so little attention that I almost barrelled over the top of him before catching myself and skidding around. I think I called a 'sorry' but I was seeing everything through a swirling prism of confusion and panic.

There was a queue at the counter and I slotted in at the back. I bounced on my heels and peeped both ways around the line, trying to see what the delay was. A woman in front of me had her arm in a sling and, in front of her, a little boy was next to his mum, with scuffed dried blood running down both his legs.

My stomach was gurgling with such force that I found myself eyeing the bin next to the counter, wondering if I'd get there in time to throw up.

And then Michelle was there, off to the side, scanning the

room, looking for me. I called her name and she waved me across to her.

'What happened?' I asked.

'Come on.'

Michelle led me through a set of double doors and down a long white corridor. She was moving so quickly that I had to jog to keep up.

'What happened?' I tried again.

We rounded a corner and passed through another set of doors. The corridor was darker there and my sister slowed her pace, allowing me to slot in at her side.

'She's all right for now,' Michelle said. 'Mum had a break-down somewhere in the town, near the green. I think the eclipse might have thrown her off. Someone said she was crying and threw a few things. The police came – but they brought her here.'

I only realised I'd stopped when Michelle halted a few paces ahead and turned to look back at me. I thought of the moment I'd had on the boys' field when Ian had helped me up.

'It was me,' I said.

'What was you?'

'I told her about the viewing party in town. I said she should go. She wouldn't have been there if not for me.'

Michelle moved back towards me and gripped my hand. 'It's not your fault,' she said. 'This was long overdue. It could have happened anywhere.'

'But if I hadn't—'

'Stop that.' Michelle pressed herself up onto the tips of her toes, so we were at the same eye level. 'You're the last person to blame for any of this. You're the only one who's there every day.'

'It's just—'

'Stop.'

She lowered herself back down – and then looked past me

to where there was the sound of approaching footsteps. At the time, it felt normal for George to have appeared there but I'm still not sure how he knew where we were, or how he was simply allowed to stride along those hospital corridors unchallenged. I suppose that was him all over. Everything he did happened with purpose.

'How is she?' George asked.

'Physically OK,' Michelle replied. 'She didn't hurt herself or anyone else – but they're sending her for a psychiatric assessment.'

That moment of reassurance I had felt from George's arrival disappeared like a deflating balloon.

'What does that mean?' I asked, although I feared I knew.

'It sounds worse than it is,' Michelle said. 'Someone will ask her questions and—'

'Are they going to lock her away?'

'No...' Michelle's eyes flickered up to George and away again. 'I mean... well, no. Not like that.'

'Can we take her home?'

My sister's eyes betrayed her again as they shot momentarily to George and away a second time. She shook her head slowly. 'Not tonight.'

It felt as if the eclipse was happening again. The corridor was getting darker and colder. I could feel it sweeping across me. Squeezing.

Michelle was talking, thanking George for bringing me to the hospital. He said something about not rushing back to camp, that he would be around if I needed someone to talk to. That's how I remember it. Truth is, he might not have said anything at all.

Everything had sped up and yet it was barely moving. Suddenly it was only Michelle and me again, sitting on chairs outside a door in what felt like the furthest part of the hospital. Every now and then, a nurse would pass, or stop and ask if we were OK. I thought we were waiting to see Mum – and maybe we were – but an age had passed when someone came out of that door and asked if we were Mrs Miller's children. I tried to listen, to take make sense of the senseless, but then Michelle had a clipboard in her hand and was signing something. I wanted to ask what it was but we were on our feet again and Michelle was trying to lead me back along the way we'd come.

'Why can't we see her?' I asked.

Michelle looked to me and then back to the man who'd been speaking to us. 'Mum's not in a good way,' she said. 'We'll try again tomorrow.'

29

PILL

Michelle tidied the living room around me as the TV blinked in the background. There were crisp and chocolate wrappers down the back of the sofa, plus so many crumbs at the side that it was like someone had dumped out a smashed packet of Digestives.

Michelle vacuumed back and forth, creating neat lines in the carpet like a gardener with a mower. She swept cobwebs from the corners and crouched to wipe the skirting boards.

I should have helped, wanted to, but her way of coping was to work and mine was to stare into the void.

There was no triumph when she finished. We sat with the windows open, feeling the chill, with neither of us inclined to do anything about it.

I wanted to talk to Amy, even just to have her listen – but she was at camp and it wasn't her burden.

It was a little after one in the morning when Michelle delved into her bag and emerged with a pair of pills. She gave one to me and said I should go to bed and take it when I was under the covers. Her old room was bare, except for the bed itself and she said she'd grab some spare covers and see me in the morning.

I didn't think I'd sleep but Michelle's tablet left my eyelids heavy and thoughts drifting.

It was light when I awoke and I padded downstairs barefooted, into the kitchen and then through the open door into the living room. The back window was still open and everything was swamped by the smell of fresh grass.

Every morning, I would come down the stairs hoping Mum hadn't fallen asleep in front of the television – but then, in that moment, I'd have given anything for her to be sleeping on the sofa.

Michelle followed me down not long after and started to hunt through the kitchen cupboards. She asked if I wanted anything for breakfast but the very idea of food left my stomach lurching.

She fried herself a pair of eggs and then we sat together in the kitchen as she picked at them with a fork. The yolks spilled across her plate as she mashed everything into a gloopy puddle.

'Are you going to camp?' she asked.

'No.'

'You can if you want. I'll call if anything happens.'

I shook my head and was about to ask about her work when there was a knock on the door. Michelle had scooped a forkful of her breakfast, so I said I'd get it.

There was a sense of déjà vu as I pulled it open to reveal Dan. He was wearing a jacket with the hood up, which was the only reason I realised it was drizzling with rain.

'I heard about your mum,' Dan said. 'I wanted check if things are... um...?'

I started to speak but whatever I was saying got stuck and, before I knew it, my chest was heavy and I was gasping for breath. I only realised I was crying when Dan stepped into the house and closed the door behind us. He walked along the hall and looked into the kitchen, said something like 'hi' to Michelle and then closed that door before returning to me. He unzipped his coat and laid it on the doormat and then we sat on the floor, across from each other.

'I think it's my fault,' I said through my tears. 'I told her to go to the viewing party and she had some sort of breakdown.'

I was finding it hard to breathe and gasping for huge, rasping gulps of air. Dan waited for me to settle. I was staring at my feet and could sense him, rather than see him.

'I'm pretty sure it's not your fault,' he said.

We sat and neither of us spoke – but, in that moment, I think that's what I needed. I couldn't say how much time passed. It could have been a couple of minutes but it might have been thirty. The very concept of minutes and hours felt fluid that day.

'How is everyone?' I asked.

'Mark's Mark. He scored seventy-odd at the weekend so he's been happy all week. Pete's doing what he does. Me too, I guess. We all are.'

We continued sitting for another minute or so and then: 'Are you still coming with us to get results?' Dan asked. 'It's two weeks. We were all gonna go down together, the four of us. Remember...?'

It was something we'd talked about on the final day of term. How we'd spend the summer together and then go to the school as one to discover our fates. It had been a few weeks before but felt so quaint. A promise from another time. Another person.

'I don't think—'

Dan cut me off. 'It's just... all these years and who knows where we're going after this. It's probably our last day.'

The tears had gone but my cheeks felt tacky. I hadn't looked up the entire time we'd been sitting in the hall.

'OK,' I said. 'I'll be there.'

'We're meeting at the garage at nine. Results go up at ten – and we might go out after. The Red Lion, or—'

'I'll probably have to work at camp after.'

'Fair enough.'

We sat for a while longer but then, when Dan shuffled himself up and stood, I followed.

'I just wanted to make sure you were OK,' he said.

'Cheers.'

I looked up then and there was something in Dan's face that I hadn't seen before. He seemed older and I wondered if it was because none of this felt like a joke any longer. Even when Dad had died, we'd quickly slipped back into our old ways.

He held out his hand and I instinctively shook it. We'd never done anything so formal before. It felt strange and grown up, yet precisely the thing the moment required.

'See you soon,' he said.

He zipped up his coat as I opened the door but he hovered in the frame as if there was something else he had to say. He opened his mouth but then closed it and turned.

'See you soon,' I replied.

30

TOAST

Mum came home that night. Michelle picked her up and we had the briefest of hellos before she went up to bed. I only saw her for a minute or so but, in the day and a half she'd been away, her skin had turned grey and her cheeks had hollowed. She looked so frail as Michelle helped her upstairs and into bed.

After that, Michelle and I sat in the kitchen with Mum's collection of pills on the counter in front of us. Michelle was sorting them into a plastic daily organiser that was like a scaled-down briefcase.

'You should go to camp tomorrow,' she said.

'I don't want to leave her.'

Michelle picked up a small pink tablet and dropped it into the Monday slot. She emptied more onto the counter and began separating them.

'We can't live our lives for someone else, even if it's Mum. I'm going to work tomorrow.'

I thought of Amy and how much I wanted to tell her everything, even though I didn't think I could. We had our perfect bubble and this was a giant needle hovering, ready to pop it.

'I'm going to stay here,' I said.

Michelle finished putting the pink pills into their slots and set about dividing some white ones.

'If it's only tomorrow, then OK – but it can't be like this every day. It's not fair to you.'

She dropped a tablet onto the counter where it span and skipped towards the edge before I caught it and dropped it into the Sunday slot.

'It's not fair on Mum, either,' she added. 'She shouldn't have someone looking after her every day. She's the parent and she's not *that* old.'

There was a steady *click-click-click* as Michelle dropped more tablets into slots. Mum had to take six different tablets over the course of a day.

'What if they change her?' I asked, whispering without meaning to.

Michelle finished what she was doing and clicked each of the daily lids into place. She angled herself towards me and, for a moment, I thought she might hug me.

'They will change her,' she said. 'That's the point.'

'But—'

'She's already changed. Think of how she's been with everything that's happened. The pills are supposed to try to take her back to a point before that.'

A lump was forming in my throat again. 'They can't bring Dad back.'

She rested her head on my shoulder and it happened so suddenly that I almost shrugged her off instinctively.

'Of course not,' she said.

Michelle took a deep breath and then lifted her head.

'The nurse told me that we should think of everything as a rock. Dad died and that's one big rock. Then Mum lost her job and it's another one. Then you did your exams and it's one step away from you leaving home. One more rock. I left and it's another one. And there are lots of little ones, too. The fact she doesn't see her friends from work. Even though it's her choice, there are more little rocks. And she's wearing a backpack and all those rocks go into the bag and pin her down. Even if she wants to get up, she's struggling because they're so heavy. What the pills do is make those rocks lighter. They don't bring back Dad or get her job back – but she'll be able to stand and, perhaps, take more of those rocks out herself. Perhaps she'll get in touch with her friends again? Or she'll start looking for a new job?'

I wasn't convinced but I did understand after that. When it came to medication, I was a hypocrite anyway, because I asked Michelle for another of whatever she'd given me the night before.

I slept well again that night and was the last person up on the Friday morning. Mum and Michelle were already in the kitchen when I got down. Both were eating toast and the Friday A.M. slot in Mum's pill organiser was empty. I didn't hide the fact I was checking.

Mum's skin was still grey, cheeks still hollowed, but there was more awareness around her. Michelle went off to work and the morning was... fine. A new normal, I suppose. Mum seemed a little spaced out but we went for a walk around the nearby streets, which was something I couldn't remember doing before. We were only out for fifteen minutes or so but it was enough. She even stopped to say hello to a bouncy Labrador puppy who was all bandy legs and too-big paws. She offered him the back of her hand and he jumped up to lick her face. The owner apologised but Mum laughed for what felt like the first time in a long while. I doubted the pills had worked that quickly – though I couldn't imagine her doing that even days before.

When we got home, we watched TV together and she was actually engaged with the quiz show, rather than a passive viewer. She called answers at the presenter and cursed herself for the ones she got wrong.

'I *knew* that,' she insisted, despite evidence to the contrary.

She wanted more toast for lunch and, even though she'd already had some for breakfast, I put four slices in the toaster. We ate together from our laps in the living room and then she asked if I'd go to the shop and buy her a paper. There must have been hesitancy in me because she added quickly: 'I'll be fine. Honestly.'

I did as she asked and, when I returned, she was sitting on the sofa where I left her. The curtains and windows were open and the house felt different, as if the cloud that had hung over it had finally cleared.

I was with her for the rest of that afternoon. She read her paper and watched the TV news as I continued reading *Little Women*. I was into part two by that point and time had skipped ahead to Meg's marriage, with Jo in New York and Laurie in Europe.

Mum wanted beans on toast for tea – more toast! – but what's better than toast? I made it and we ate together again. Neither of us had much to say but, as with Dan the previous day, it didn't matter.

Michelle came round after tea and she laughed at our rounded diet of triple toast. Mum laughed too and so did I. It was the first time we'd done that as a family in a very long time. The storm felt as if it might have gone and what was left was a steadying, reassuring calm – even if it might be temporary.

It was almost dark when someone knocked on the door. Mum was alert enough to turn to me with a look a bewilderment. After his two previous visits, a part of me was expecting Dan to be there again – but it wasn't him – and it wasn't only one person.

Ian was leaning on the door frame, with Gemma and Amy standing a little behind. They were haloed by the despondent orange of the street light outside the house and each broke into a smile as I opened the door.

'Told you it was the right house,' Gemma said.

I only realised Ian was holding my bike when he wheeled it in front of him. 'Thought you might want this,' he said.

'Oh... um... thank you.'

I'd somehow forgotten about the bike but wheeled it into the hall. I left it leaning against the radiator, before returning to the front.

'We were wondering if you can come out to play,' Ian said. He spoke with a hint of a laugh.

I felt the pull stronger than ever before. Dan had asked me something similar but it had been so easy to say no then. This was different.

'I shouldn't,' I said. 'Mum only got home last night and, um...'

'It's fine if you can't,' Ian replied, 'but we've got to get back in just over an hour and it took me fifteen minutes to drag your bike over the gate.'

'*Less* than a minute,' Gemma said.

'OK but it *felt* like fifteen minutes.'

'The gate was open,' Gemma said.

Ian scowled at her with fake mischief. 'I didn't *know* the gate was open. I thought it was *locked*, which is why I spent fifteen minutes lifting it over the top.'

'Less than a minute.'

They grinned at each other and then Ian turned to me. 'Anyway, I'm just saying that, if you *can't* come out, that's fine. But if you *can* come out then we haven't got time for the whole *can-you, can't-you* thing.'

The sound of the television seeped through the wall from the living room. Mum had swallowed her pills for the day and had eaten three proper meals, even if they were toast-based.

I told them to give me a minute and then pulled the door closed before hurrying into the living room. I told Mum I was going to nip out for a bit but that I wouldn't be long. She looked away from the screen and told me to be as long as I needed. The very fact she'd turned was enough.

And then I was outside, shivering because I'd forgotten to put on a coat. The day had been cloudy and no real heat had arrived. For the first time it felt as if summer might be slipping away.

I led everyone down to the end of the road, where there was a low wall that ringed an old hardware store which had closed a couple of years before. Shutters were clamped to the floor and someone had spray-painted a garish tag across the front.

'Is this the ghetto?' Ian asked, talking partly to himself, though mainly to us.

'You're such a snob,' Gemma replied.

'How'd you know where I lived?' I asked.

It was Gemma who answered. 'Because I came to a birthday party at yours when we were about six. You invited the whole class. We did pass the parcel in your back yard and you cried because you didn't win.'

Amy snorted and Ian didn't bother to hold back as he laughed.

'You did ask,' Gemma added, and she sounded as amused as everyone else.

I laughed too and it felt as if those rocks Michelle had talked about were being lifted from my own bag.

'I can't believe you remember that,' I said.

'If only I could throw out stuff like that and remember the things I was supposed to revise.'

We laughed at Gemma this time. Four of us united as one and another rock lifted.

I told them about Mum, that she was ill and had something of a breakdown during the eclipse. She'd been kept in hospital overnight and then given piles of pills to try to make things better.

I didn't think I'd say any of it out loud but I did. It all came out as one and then... things felt a bit better. Another rock gone. A big one.

Amy had barely spoken but her voice was a soft murmur when she did. 'My mum takes pills, too,' she said. 'She tries to hide them in her bedroom drawers but there are too many. I think she gets some off her friends.'

The four of us absorbed that. She had said a lot more than the actual words.

Then Ian set us off again.

'This is why I don't have a mum,' he said.

It shouldn't have been funny – except it was. In some ways, it was the funniest thing I'd ever heard. As soon as we stopped laughing, somebody started again and then we were all off. By the time we managed to get a grip on ourselves my stomach ached.

Gemma checked her watch and then nudged Ian with her elbow. 'We should head off,' she said.

Nothing more was said but he seemed to understand what she meant. Amy didn't move and, instead, Ian and Gemma sauntered slowly up the street, in the vague direction of town.

When Amy and I kissed that time it was different.

Gentler.

Better.

I had a hand touching her hip and she had one on my upper arm. I felt alive and, although there was a wetness around my eyes, it wasn't a bad thing this time. It was as if everything had built to that moment. We separated and then sat on the wall holding hands.

'How was sports day?' I asked.

'Alcott girls officially finished last. Gemma's mob won.'

'*Mob?*'

She snorted. 'Whatever. Let's just forget this week and try again.' A pause. 'Are you coming in for visiting day tomorrow?'

'I don't know. Maybe.'

She squeezed my fingers into hers and both our hands were cold.

'I've been reading *Little Women* without you,' I said.

'What do you think?'

'I've got a bad feeling about it.'

She squished my fingers a second time and then released me. 'I've got to go,' she said. 'But I'll see you soon...?'

It sounded like a question.

'Of course.'

We kissed again, short and brief. Enough.

And then she was gone up the road, to join Ian and Gemma's shadows that were waiting on the corner.

As I watched her leave, I thought that I never wanted to let her down – which is why it was such a shame that I did.

31

MAP

Michelle slept over again that night. She said she was going back to her own place the next day and that I should go to camp, or cricket, or whatever I had on. Crucially, she also bought more bread at some point.

I cycled up to camp the next morning – and it was as busy as I'd known it. The parking area was rammed and cars had been left on the verge along both sides of the narrow lane at the front.

There was a buzz about the site itself – both literal and figurative. With all the five- and seven-dayers present, along with their parents, the conversations were like the hum below an electricity pylon. For some of the campers, the first three weeks of camp would have been the longest they'd gone without seeing their parents.

Sun had returned to greet the weekend and the various arts and crafts from the gallery were on display outside. Some campers were eagerly showing their parents what they'd done that week, while others were wearing medals from sports day.

As I walked across the site, I realised I'd never seen so many grown-ups sitting on the ground. Campers from various bunks had clustered into small groups and they'd drawn their parents in with them as they introduced friends to family.

I'd not quite got to the staff lounge when Luke appeared. He sounded hurried but concerned. 'Are you OK?' he asked. 'I heard it was something about your mum.'

'She's all right,' I replied. 'Or she should be.'

'You didn't have to rush back. I was on top of things...' He realised what he'd said and then added, 'It's good to have you back, though.'

'How was sports day?'

'Busy – but there was this one kid who fell over doing the egg and spoon race and it was the funniest thing I've ever seen. He stabbed himself in the ear with the spoon and—'

I wondered why he'd stopped but followed his stare to where George was standing a few paces away.

'It's good to see you,' George said.

Luke wilted a little, probably wondering if he'd been over-heard, though George didn't appear to mind either way.

'How's your mum?' George asked.

I went through that routine over and over across the following hour or so. There was Fiona and the other directors, then some of the counsellors. Even Neil from the kitchen, who barely did more than grunt, asked if Mum was OK.

I replied that she was OK so often that I started to wonder how those two letters were linked in the way they were. Why 'OK', instead of 'GV' or 'BX'?

I couldn't remember a time when so many people asked if I was all right. I didn't know the names of most of the counsellors but that didn't stop them asking. So many asked if there was anything they could do. There obviously wasn't but the fact they'd offered was enough.

I somehow spent twenty minutes with George as he swept through camp like an anchor through water. He knew every-one's names, whether camper, parent, brother, sister, uncle, counsellor – and everything in between. There were hand-shakes and backslaps, promises to catch up and call one another.

I had never seen anything like it and there didn't seem to be a single person who was anything other than delighted to see him.

And then Amy was at my side and we watched as George did his thing. He offered a high five to one of the younger campers and then pulled away – 'too slow!' – before accepting a gentle slap on the back of the hand for being naughty. The camper roared and the parents smiled.

'I have no idea how he remembers so many names,' Amy said.

'I can barely remember yours.'

She nudged me playfully with her elbow.

'How do you know him?' I asked.

'Friend of my dad. I think they might have gone to university together – although Dad says that about everyone he knows. Everyone either went with him, or they're friends of friends. Sometimes friends of friends of friends. This one big web of people.'

She sounded a little bitter but I didn't push – because Charlotte was tapping her on the back. Amy turned and broke into a beam as Charlotte bellowed a happy 'This is Amy!'

Charlotte's mum was in a dress too tight for a field. Her knees were squashed together, which meant she was struggling to balance on the uneven ground. Her heels probably didn't help.

'I've heard so much about you,' Charlotte's mum said.

'All the good stuff is true,' Amy replied. 'All the bad stuff is either exaggerated or outright lies.'

Charlotte's mum laughed and I wondered how people my age learned to talk to adults in such a way. Dan could do it – and Amy could as well. Except for my immediate family, I wasn't sure I'd ever been able to make an adult laugh like that.

'Did you see Charlotte's elephant?' Amy asked.

'An elephant...?' Charlotte's mum looked down to her daughter. 'She did say something about it.'

'It won gold,' Amy replied.

Charlotte's mum failed to hide how flustered she suddenly was. She looked up to Amy, down to her daughter, and then started fishing in her bag for something that she apparently couldn't find. The bag was roughly the same size as my backpack, though made of shiny light pink leather that I guess cost a lot more than anything I owned. 'I remember something like that from one of the letters,' she added. 'I've been a bit busy and Leo's in Geneva. It's all been a bit, um...' She tailed off and went back to searching in her bag.

I looked down to Charlotte and her face sank as she realised her mum had no idea what had been going on at camp, despite the daily letters. I wondered if the 'heard so much' about Amy was a front too. Perhaps all the interest was? Perhaps, deep down, even though she was eleven, Charlotte knew that too.

But Amy was there – and she was so good, so entrenched in that world, that she let the older woman off.

'Did Charlotte tell you about the gold star she got for making her bed properly every day for two weeks?'

Charlotte's mum stopped fiddling with her bag and took the olive branch she didn't deserve. 'Oh, yes. I read all about that. We're so proud.'

'She's read three books in three weeks, too.'

'Of course she has. She's always been so advanced for her age.'

'Nearly four!' Charlotte said.

They danced around the truth. Amy fed Charlotte's mum things she clearly didn't know – and she latched onto every one, throwing praise at her daughter with ever-increasing eagerness.

And poor little Charlotte's features broke from that stomach-curdling anguish until she was grinning and glowing with pride. She grabbed her mum's hand and said she wanted to show her the pictures above her bed in the bunk. Her mother was mumbling something about having to rush off home but she allowed herself to be hauled away.

That left Amy and me alone at the edge of the girls' field. I took her hand this time, squeezing her fingers in the way she'd done to me the night before. I didn't say anything because she needed those few seconds to gulp away the moment. I had never known that was what growing up involved for some people.

Charlotte's story was Amy's.

I don't think I'd ever felt closer to another person than I did right then. I'd looked into Charlotte's desperate face, and now Amy's, and I felt *their* hurt. They wanted to be appreciated and noticed... and, instead, they were afterthoughts and inconveniences. I wanted to say sorry, even though it wasn't her and it wasn't me.

I could have stayed in that moment with Amy all afternoon – but then work kicked in again. Parents started leaving as latecomers arrived. Luke and I ended up directing traffic in and out of the car park and then had to help push a couple more cars out of the mud.

Some of the parents who weren't in a rush headed down to the town on foot with their children. Others ate lunch in the mess hall, perched on chairs that were too small and made it look like they were at a giant's tea party.

Amy was busy, too, greeting the parents and brothers and sisters of her campers.

I was on my way back to the car park when I spotted the woman milling around the toilets towards the back of the boys' bunks. She was in a smart brown skirt-suit that was more

Monday morning at the office, as opposed to Saturday afternoon in a field.

She was squinting at a scrap of paper, bringing it closer to and further away from her face in quick succession, and then turning in a circle, clearly lost. I went across and asked if I could help and she held up the paper to show a map someone had drawn in biro on a lined sheet of paper. There was a series of large squares, plus arrows and the word 'HERE' in capital letters.

The woman's mistake was immediately obvious to me in that she had confused one car park with the other, entered from a different gate, and was in the boys' field when she was looking for the girls.

'Who are you looking for?' I asked.

'My daughter. She's a counsellor. I can't remember which tent she's in.'

The word 'tent' jarred as everyone seemingly went as far out of their way as possible to avoid it. There were the bunks, the staff lounge, the mess hall, the medical bay, the directors' quarters, and so on. The supply tent was the only exception.

I already knew the answer before I asked the question. The woman had long black hair, parted in the middle. 'Who's your daughter?' I asked.

'Amy Ashworth. Do you know her?'

I almost laughed as she looked to me with the sort of naivety I would usually associate with myself.

'This is the boys' field,' I said. 'I'll take you.'

She offered enthusiastic thanks and then I led her across camp to the girls' bunks. There was nobody around Alcott – but I quickly found Sarah and Amy close to the parking area, where they were waving off a car of parents.

When Amy turned, she honed in on her mum and me instantly. I expected some sort of horror in her face but, instead, a sense of bemused amusement flitted across her lips. She said something to Sarah and almost skipped across the field towards us.

I watched as they hugged and went through a string of almost rehearsed-sounding snippets. 'You look good,' 'Your hair's so long,' 'You've gone so brown,' 'How have you been?'

Then George appeared – and, instead of Amy giving Charlotte's mum an easy out, it was George doing the same. 'One of the best counsellors', 'So conscientious', 'Always wanting the best for her girls', 'Invaluable around here', 'An incredible addition', 'Welcome any time' – and more.

Amy's mum nodded along and she clapped her hands and gripped her daughter's shoulder as if she already knew it all. And I watched Amy watch her mum and I could see that same desperation that Charlotte had. Despite the talk of annoying her mum with Skunk Anansie, the colour black and wanting to be a mechanic, deep down, all Amy wanted was to be seen.

It was hard to say nothing.

I wanted to tell this stranger that her daughter was one of the most popular people at camp. As Gemma said at the café: 'everyone loves Amy.' And they did. I wanted to shout 'Look at her! Just look. *Look* at your daughter.'

I didn't, of course. This was all a dance and my feet were still planted to the floor in the way Amy had said. I stood and watched the lie unfold, wondering if that particular lie was better than the truth.

George asked about Amy's dad – but he was apparently working, so George laughed that they'd have to catch up on the golf course one day soon. Promises were made about dinner and drinks and golf and phone calls. I didn't know any of them but I knew none of it would happen.

Then George turned to me and I was still a gormless statue standing there.

'Have you met Joe?' he asked.

And then Amy, her mum and George himself all looked to

me. There was a nervousness I'm not sure I'd experienced before. I was never great at talking to adults but I didn't shy away from them – until that moment.

Perhaps Amy saw that in me, or perhaps she knew me well enough by then, because she stepped forward and turned between me and her mum. 'This is my friend, Joe, Mum.'

'He's a *really* valuable member of our team,' George added. 'This place wouldn't run without him.'

Amy's mum looked to me with the air of someone looking for a clock that was once on a wall but was no longer there. I don't think she actually saw me, even though she was looking right at me.

'Pleased to meet you,' she said. Before she could say anything more, if she was ever going to, she glanced off to the side and did that weird half wave people do as if they're royalty. 'Fancy seeing you here!'

Amy's mum bounded away from us at a far greater speed than she'd used when looking for her daughter. She started air-kissing one of the other parents and they were busy complimenting each other's outfits as George moved on to another family group further around the field.

It was Amy and me again – and, perhaps for the first time, it really did feel as if it was just us.

'We going out tonight?' Amy asked.

'Hell, yes.'

32

BITTERS

As camp returned to normal in the late afternoon, I cycled home. Technically I hadn't been working that day anyway. Mum was on the sofa when I got in – but the window and curtains were open and, for the first time in a while, she asked about my day. I told her about the mess of the car park and how busy everything had been – and she said that she'd done some weeding in the garden. I almost asked her to repeat what she'd said because I thought I'd misheard. When I went out to the back, there were piles of greeny stalks next to the bin.

Then I realised she'd actually asked about my day and listened to the reply. I thought of Charlotte, Amy and their mothers. How I doubted their mums ever actually *listened*.

Back inside, I asked if it was all right for me to go out that night and Mum laughed in a way that still felt surreal at the time. 'When did you ever ask?' she replied.

With her blessing and a definite shift in mood at the house, I was set for the night. There was no need to meet at camp that time, so I went straight to the café bar in time to catch Ian, Gemma and Amy on their way in. After their long day of heightened politeness, there was an eagerness and a bounce to the three of them as we headed inside.

I felt a familiarity this time about the low ceiling and the clammy walls. It helped that we were received as some sort of conquering heroes by Ian's friends. They'd ended up on the same sofa again and I went with it as everyone hugged and said how fantastic it was to be back in the café again. Owen tugged at the sleeve of my T-shirt, saying I should have worn the same one as the week before. It was weird but flattering as well. I couldn't remember ever being noticed in such a way.

Amy and I didn't sit together the whole time but that was fine. I talked to Ian and Gem, then some of Ian's friends. When Amy finally dropped next to me and took my hand in hers, Owen said we were a cute couple. 'Too cute,' he added. 'Makes me sick.' He faked vomiting under the table and then came up with a grin on his face.

We all drank the blue stuff as people read their poems and I banged the table in enthusiastic support of people I didn't know.

Then the tables were cleared and a different band from the previous week started playing. We were dancing again and Amy stuck close to me. Her hands were around my neck and I tried to move my feet, even though I was frequently met with Amy saying 'Those are my feet' every time I trod on her.

I trod on her a lot.

I'd never thought of myself as clumsy before but there were times when it seemed like she was some sort of octopus. Everywhere I put my feet, hers were already there.

The evening raced by as we drank, danced, laughed and drank some more. I'd never had an evening like it, where I could be myself and not have to worry what anyone else thought.

Amy and I didn't creep out to the grass bank at the back that night. By the time the band stopped playing, the room had emptied and I realised I had somehow not noticed. The servers were collecting glasses and someone was sweeping the corners as the final couple of dozen drinkers began to file out. Our group bundled our way onto the street but not before Ian hit his head on the low beam as we went up the stairs. He faked fainting when we were out on the street and one of his friends gave him the kiss of life on the floor before Ian leapt to his feet.

We were all tipsy, swaying in the shadows between street lights. I figured we'd all be going our separate ways but Owen was bouncing on his heels.

'It's early!' he announced, to an admittedly willing audience.

'Everywhere's closing,' Ian said.

'I know a place. I'll get you all in.'

I don't remember anyone questioning what or where this place might be. Instead, we cheered and followed as our drunken Pied Piper skipped and danced his way through the town. Amy and I held hands the entire way but it wasn't us I remember: it was the joy of the adventure. There were no silly games, no attempts to trip each other up, or make fun. We sang to songs I barely knew and tried to remember the poems that came from soberer times.

Owen led us out of town, heading up the same hill I'd cycled to get to George's house. There were only big houses there, no pubs or clubs – but still nobody questioned him.

There were very few lights on inside houses and even fewer places that had gates open. It was all high hedges or towering walls as residents either craved privacy from people who couldn't see them anyway or security against crime that didn't exist.

Beyond that, a low hum of noise clung to the breeze like a swarm of bees somewhere out of sight. We kept walking, up and up, deeper into the estate until we were almost at the woods, where we stopped outside a large pair of gates at the front of a long driveway. Faint lights glowed from the house beyond and the bees were louder there, although the hum still felt difficult to pin down.

There was a buzzer at the side of the gate and Owen thumbed it before standing to the side. 'Any minute,' he said.

We definitely waited for longer than a minute and then Owen tried again. This time he held his finger on the buzzer for a good ten seconds, before removing it and repeating himself.

Still no reply.

'We're going to have to get creative,' he said.

Nobody questioned this and we were a giggling huddle as we followed the high hedges towards the back of the property. We were almost in the woods when the hedge thinned at the corner. Owen spotted it first and stood in front of us, stretching high and touching his toes as if about to head out for a run. This was, of course, hilarious to all of us in our tipsy states.

Owen hurled himself into the narrower part of the hedge and pushed himself through to the house beyond, which was the signal for us all to do the same. The branches were spindly but clawing – although, by the time it was my turn to go through, they'd been bent and snapped by those before me. Amy went last and then we were all in the grounds of the biggest house I'd ever seen. It was two storeys high and I counted fourteen windows across the width. It was a scaled-down stately home and there were lights on in every room.

In front of us was a pool, lit from the bottom with neon green lights and surrounded by tiki torches. There were men and women in swimming costumes both in and out of the pool and, though I had no intention of joining them, the pool was between us and the house.

I thought we'd get a few curious looks, partly because of our ages, partly because of our casual outfits, partly because we'd appeared from nowhere, but – as we passed the pool – nobody gave us a second glance.

We were almost at the house when a boy barely older than

me stopped and stared. I figured he was the host and that we'd quickly be dispatched back outside but, instead, he came bounding towards us.

'Owen! My god! You made it!'

The boy's voice was posh and over-pronounced, like the lads at the private school against whom ours played cricket and rugby. He threw himself at Owen, who spun him around in a circle before putting him down.

'Who are your friends?' he asked.

Owen introduced us all and the apparent host welcomed us with tight, sweaty hugs as if we were old mates. I was probably told his name but it was the type of giddy, frantic introduction where, five minutes later, nobody remembered anybody else's name.

'There are canapés in the games room and an open bar in the lounge,' he said, holding his hands wide. 'Enjoy yourselves!'

Even tipsy, I knew I was out of my depth. The only time I'd ever heard of canapés in the past was at the wedding of one of my parents' friends a few years before. Those 'canapés' turned out to be sausage and pineapple on cocktail sticks – and I very much doubted that was what awaited us in the games room.

We started to separate at that point. Owen went off to talk to someone he knew near the pool, while a couple of Ian's other friends were already stripping down to their underwear to try the pool itself.

The inside of the house was like George's but grander, with high ceilings and chandeliers. There were men in suits carrying food on silver trays and, even though we were in shorts and T-shirts, it was as if the disparity was invisible to everyone else.

That's probably because there was so much more to see than us.

There were people kissing in corners and on sofas, although 'kissing' was an understatement. Hands were up skirts and down the fronts of trousers – and that's if people were wearing that much. I found myself laughing nervously, keeping close to Amy, who seemed to find it as curious as I did.

'Bit of a change from camp,' she said.

We splintered further as Ian recognised a boy a few years older than us whom I'd never seen before. Ian bounced across to him and neither of them said hello before they disappeared into the shadows, hands inside each other's tops, tongues entangled.

Gemma found that hilarious and then she was led away by Ian's friend to meet someone he knew.

It was unquestionably exciting but it felt dangerous, too. A world that wasn't ours and certainly wasn't mine. When Amy squeezed my fingers with hers, I could feel that nervousness in her as well – although she was determined not to show it.

'Let's get something to drink,' she said.

We found the lounge with a bit of help from one of the suited servers. I'd expected a messy table of cans – but there was an actual bar. Bottles of spirits lined three shelves and there was a glass bowl filled with lemons and limes. As we approached, someone passed us with a cocktail glass filled with something pink that had a sparkler flashing fire from the top.

'It's not quite bottle of Blue territory, is it?' I said.

A man in a suit was behind the bar. We asked what was available and he shrugged with a straight face and said he'd make anything we wanted. The only cocktail I knew was Sex On The Beach – because Mark had talked about it at some point. I doubted Mark knew what was in one – and I certainly didn't.

When Amy ordered an Old Fashioned, I said I'd have the same, which made her snort with laughter.

'Do you even know what's in it?' she asked, still laughing.

'Ice...?'

'What else?'

I looked across the bar, where the man in a suit had picked up a bottle of Jack Daniel's.

'Whisky.'

'Bourbon – but I'll give you it. What else?'

I glanced across to the barman, who was behind Amy's back. He tapped a pile of sugar cubes.

'Sugar?'

Her eyes narrowed. 'Hmm. I'm not convinced. What's the other thing?'

The barman pointed towards a brown bottle with a squeezy pipette at the side. 'Um... food dye?'

Even the barman laughed this time.

Amy turned and saw the sugar cubes and brown bottle.

'You're a cheat,' she said.

'You're one to talk after that rigged election.'

The barman squeezed a couple of drops into each of our drinks and then placed them in front of us.

'Bitters,' he said.

'What's a bitter?' I asked.

'I don't know really. It's sort of... bitter.'

Amy laughed as she picked up her drink and toasted the barman. We clinked glasses and then drank. I coughed and doubled over, head almost between my knees as my throat burned. The ice did little to help. Amy found this even funnier than the bitter talk.

'You'll have to excuse my friend,' she told the barman, 'he only usually drinks lager and cider.'

'It's true,' I said.

'Another?' the barman asked.

Amy and I looked to each other, grinned, 'Of course!'

We carried our second drinks through to the games room – although it was far from the games room in Dan's garage. There was a full-sized snooker table in the middle, on which a man was lying naked as another man ate olives from his nipples.

'I hope they have plates,' I said – and Amy snorted so loudly that I had to hold her up. I was still counting them that night. Still relishing every time I made her laugh.

It turned out there *weren't* plates – but only because everything was bite-sized and being served by men in suits on those silver platters who were standing around the edge of the games room.

The first one we approached had black soggy sand on some sort of cracker. Amy squealed, saying I had to try it.

'What is it?' I asked.

'Caviar!'

I nibbled at one of the crackers and, when I told her she was right and that it was like a salty fish finger, she was delighted.

We continued on around the house and grounds. A steady *thump-thump-thump* echoed from speakers, though it never felt loud enough to attract the attention of neighbours or, worse, the police. There were more people in the pool by then, kissing and groping and swaying with the music.

'Have you ever been anywhere like this?' I asked.

'Course not. You?'

The idea seemed ludicrous. 'The cricket club gets wild sometimes.'

She missed the joke. 'Really?'

I told her I was having her on and we continued past the pool, towards the back doors where we watched a girl kiss a guy and then lean across to kiss another girl.

Nothing would have surprised me that night. It was my first proper introduction to adulthood, although I later realised nights like this were once-in-a-lifetime affairs. It wasn't my thing anyway, not *our* thing, but perhaps everyone needs at least one night like that in their life?

Owen had reappeared and he was bouncing with excitement or, I suppose, with chemical enhancement. He asked if we were having fun and then smirked and put his finger to his lips before pulling a transparent baggie from his jeans pocket. It took him a few seconds to figure out his fingers but he reached into the bag and slipped out a white disc, which he passed to Amy.

'Half each,' he said. 'You won't need more than that. My gift to the happy couple.'

She held the pill in her palm.

'What is it?' I asked.

Owen smirked wider and returned the baggie to his pocket. He never answered, instead bobbing away towards the pool.

Amy and I kept walking, heading for the shadows towards the back of the house and what turned out to be a fenced tennis court. The lights were off and the gate open, so we pressed inside. Amy stopped almost immediately and took off her shoes – and then we continued into the darkest shade on the furthest side. We sat on the springy ground, leaning against the mesh of the fence, watching the distant green glow of the pool and the dancing, happy shapes of the partygoers.

Amy held out her palm and the white of the pill shone in the glimmering moonlight.

'Have you ever done this before?' she asked.

'I don't know what it is.'

'Probably E.'

We sat quietly for a few seconds, listening to the faint throb of the music.

'I've never done drugs,' I said. 'I tried smoking once but I coughed all the time. I didn't understand why anyone would bother.' A pause. 'You?'

There was a pause and I almost feared what was to come.

Amy's voice was slightly gravelly from the night and the drink. 'Rachel's parents are into weed,' she said. 'They bake cakes with it and have this oil stuff that they put on their tongues. I tried it once but it didn't do much for me.' She placed the pill on the court between us and it sat there, untouched. 'I don't think we need it,' she said quietly. 'Who wants to be a cliché?'

We held hands for a while and then we kissed lightly. It felt like we needed each other and was the opposite of those in the corners with wandering hands. She tasted of whisky and bitters – but then I did as well.

After that, we lay on the court and stared up at the sky, where the drifting clouds were blocking the stars. We held hands. Held each other. I listened to her breathe and my head swam from the alcohol.

'It's the halfway point,' Amy said quietly. 'Three weeks down, three to go.'

It was true, though it had somehow passed me by. Time had flown yet time had crawled. It was impossible not to think about what might happen afterwards, although I couldn't bear to say it. Amy was off to her performing arts college, while I was considering that job offer from Barry. Was there any way we could be together afterwards? I wanted to ask but didn't want to risk the answer.

After a while, Amy pushed herself up and then we stood and headed back towards the house. We ignored the pool, ordered four Old Fashioneds, downed the lot, and went into a room where black and white check tiles speckled the floor. Music was playing, the sort of thumping bass I hated, but people were dancing – and so we did too. I moved my feet but it was still impossible to avoid hers, so we gave up and kissed instead.

It wasn't gentle any longer. We were drunk and it was primal, forceful and desperate. We were on a sofa, her on top, and there were people around. Nobody cared and nobody was watching but, even through the alcoholic whirring haze, we knew it wasn't for us.

We stopped and lay together instead. Her head was on my

chest and the room spun one way then the other. My eyes closed and opened and still the room twisted and twirled.

'I can hear your heart beating,' she whispered at some point.

People drifted away and the music stopped abruptly. We must have slept like that because it was suddenly light and both our legs were dead. Nobody was in sight and there were hints of sunlight splaying from somewhere, with the gentlest reek of stale cigarette smoke.

When we tried to stand, we ended up crawling on the floor, laughing at one another, before groaning because of the headaches.

There were plastic cups and bottles scattered across the floor and a woman was snoring on the sofa across from us.

We sat on the floor then, Amy's head on my shoulder.

'I have to get back to camp,' she said.

I shrugged her off but only so I could look at her. Her hair had been tied back at some point but the tie was long gone. It was kinked and long, greasy from the night. A thick black line was smudged across the top of her eyelids – though that only made her eyes greener.

'I think I'm still drunk,' she said, partly through a hiccup.

'Me, too,' I replied.

We climbed up one another until we were standing and using the sofa to support us.

'Do you think Ian and Gem are all right?' I asked.

'Ian's the sort who's always all right,' Amy replied. 'I bet he took Gemma back to camp with him hours ago.'

'Shall we look for them?'

Amy groaned and reached for my hand. Missed. 'Will you give me a piggyback?' she asked.

'What if I drop you?'

'Ugh.'

We staggered towards the doors, where we each grunted at

the punishment being beaten into us by the sun that was definitely too bright.

'Where are the clouds when you need them?' Amy asked.

We looked back behind us to the shattered remains of the evening. There were cups and bottles everywhere, as if a bin lorry had tipped over. Out by the pool, there were people sleeping on the loungers.

'That was a good night,' Amy said.

She reached for my hand and got it that time.

'A really good night,' I said.

And then I jumped in the pool.

33

PLAY

I dripped my way across the area around the pool as a barefooted Amy found her shoes at the tennis court. She spent five minutes trying to tie them and then gave up, tucking the laces under her feet as we cut through the hedge and started the long walk across town. The streets were deserted and the only sounds were the birds going mad about something.

'Why did you jump in the pool?' she asked.

I was leaving a trail of water behind me. 'I don't know. It felt instinctive in the moment.'

'You don't seem like the instinctive sort.'

My head was muddled from the night before and I struggled to process what she'd said. 'Is that an insult?' I asked.

'The opposite,' she replied.

We walked in the middle of the road, mainly because we could. It was early and there was no traffic, no people. I felt free that morning.

'Imagine breakfast with this hangover,' I said.

Amy shuddered. 'Ugh. Don't. Apparently they get worse as you get older.'

'I guess we shouldn't get old then.'

Amy snorted. Another for the mental tally chart. 'I don't think it works like that.'

The sun was warm and I was drying with every step. We tried to remember the song that had been playing in the Night And Day the evening before but couldn't come up with the melody. Instead, Amy started to hum Savage Garden, and then we stumbled through the chorus. Everyone knew the bit about standing on a mountain and bathing in the sea. The 'lay like this forever' line felt appropriate, considering where we'd woken up and our respective headaches.

We didn't make it to the second verse. We petered out and went quiet. And then: 'That's the first time I've ever slept with someone,' Amy said. There was a momentary pause and then: '*Actual* sleep, I mean.'

It was probably because I was still drunk but the question came instantly. 'Have you ever…?'

There were no inhibitions that morning.

'Once. You?'

'No…'

We walked and I thought about that, wondering if I should care. I knew I shouldn't, but there was a part of me that hated whoever that one might be. It was childish but, at the time, I'd never hated anyone more.

'What was it like?' I asked, not sure if I wanted to know.

Amy didn't answer at first. She took my hand, squeezed, let me go – 'You're still wet' – and then we continued to walk along the middle of the road, a gap between us.

'Last summer,' she said. 'I was fifteen and he was in the year above me at school. Mum signed me up for this summer play workshop thing. It was six weeks of learning lines and rehearsing, that sort of thing. At the end we did two performances on the Saturday. A matinee and an evening.'

I added that to the list of things that felt like they came from an alternate world. I didn't remember ever being in a play, let alone rehearsing and learning lines. I'd certainly never heard the word 'matinee' before. There were always signs around town advertising various amateur dramatics but it was the sort of thing other people did.

'What was the play?' I asked. She wasn't answering my question of what it had been like, but I wasn't going to push.

'The director had adapted *Fahrenheit 451*. Do you know it?'

'No.'

'It's about censorship, book burnings, the media and reading. It was a bit heavy for a bunch of fifteen-, sixteen- and seventeen-year-olds. A bit worthy, too. It wasn't the sort of thing where you got up and thought you couldn't wait to get to rehearsals that day.'

She sighed elaborately and, though it might have been for show, it felt as if she had genuine regrets about the summer.

'There was this boy,' she said. 'Jonah, believe it or not.'

I had never met anyone called Jonah, though I knew I would hate anyone with that name until the end of time.

'We spent a lot of time together during rehearsals. We had a few scenes together and we'd practise lines with each other. One thing led to another and...'

There was no need to finish the sentence.

It took me a few seconds to reply. 'Spent a lot of time together... like we have...?'

Amy stopped and I was already a few paces past her when I realised. I turned and she stepped towards me and took both my hands in hers. We stood in the middle of the road, looking at one another. I was still dripping and her eye make-up had smudged even more. We were a mess but, in that moment, we weren't.

'It was nothing like the time *we've* spent together. Not even close. Jonah and I never talked like we do. He wasn't interested in me and I wasn't interested in him. We got together on that final Saturday, after the two shows. There was this big cast party and everyone was drinking... and I suppose it was a bit emotional. I didn't really enjoy the summer but he was the one person who had time for me that night.'

She paused and we let go of each other's hands and continued walking, a little slower.

'I've only seen him once since,' she said. 'That was from a distance. Just one of those things.'

A pause. Time to absorb it.

'This is better.'

We walked and I felt both better and worse for asking. It was none of my business and I knew that. I was jealous and hateful of Jonah, whoever he was, but I was aware enough to realise what Amy and I had. I had changed over those three weeks.

'What was it *actually* like?' I asked.

It took Amy a while to reply and I wasn't sure whether she would.

'It hurt a bit,' she said quietly. 'Then it was OK. It didn't last long. It just... happened.'

'Sorry for asking,' I said.

She laughed, though softly, more to herself than me. 'Don't be. If you'd said yes, I'd have wanted all the gory details.'

'Is it gory?'

Another laugh, louder that time. She wasn't sure whether I was joking – and I suppose I wasn't either. 'Of course not.'

Neither of us said out loud what the next step could be for us. I was afraid of what the answer might be, even though every part of me wanted to casually ask the question. I wondered if it was up to me to ask, or whether it should be her. Nothing like that was ever explained in a biology lesson... although our class would have nervously laughed our way through it even if it was.

The town was empty and we carried on walking in the road until a milk float hummed its way towards us and we shifted onto the pavement. We were almost at the camp gates when

Amy asked if I was working that day. I wasn't – though I said I'd hang around if she wanted company.

'Go check on your mum,' she said. 'And dry off. I'll see you tomorrow.'

I told her I would – and it was only as I turned that I realised I hadn't worried about Mum once the previous night.

34

WASHING

There was a shift at camp through the start of that fourth week. After missing their parents, the seven-dayers were back on a similar sort of high as at the start. Their energy was matched by the blazing weather. The eclipse had come early, because there were no clouds the week after and the sun shone every day as if it would never end.

According to the newsletter, it was democracy week at camp – which sounded bizarre for a group of ten- to twelve-year-olds. That wasn't to mention the fact that, from experience, camp elections were far from democratic.

Gemma was hanging out some clothes to dry in the sun when I caught up with her on the Monday. She clocked me with a smile and nodded me across to the space at the side of the girls' bunks.

'Did you have a good night Saturday?' she asked.

'Too good.'

'That house was a bit... *much.* I had such a hangover on Sunday.'

'Amy and I looked for you before we left,' I replied, which

was a half-truth. Our search involved eyeing all the people we passed on the way out.

Gemma picked a top out from her washing basket and pegged it to the rotary line. 'I walked back with Ian. We saw you and Amy sleeping on the sofa but you looked comfy and we didn't want to wake you.' She paused and then: 'Same again Saturday?'

I laughed. 'I don't think I could handle that every week.'

She wrung out a sock on the grass and then clipped it to the line. 'Me either. Ian was sick three times on the way back, so I'm not sure he's up for it.'

Gemma did the same to a second sock.

'What's going on with democracy week?' I asked.

She groaned to herself. 'It's to teach the kids about elections. It's brainstorm day today. Every bunk has to come up with a manifesto of policies.' She looked to me and rolled her eyes. 'Wanna swap jobs for a day?'

'No chance.'

'Shame.'

Gemma picked out a camp T-shirt and hung that.

'Tomorrow, each bunk has to vote for a candidate to represent that bunk's manifesto. Wednesday, we make posters and leaflets. Thursday is debate day and canvassing. Friday is election day.'

'What do you do with the manifestos? Do the policies actually happen?'

A shake of the head. 'They come up with stuff like "free milkshakes for everyone".'

'Won't everyone vote for the candidate in their own bunk?'

She turned to me: 'You're not rigging this one, are you?'

'Are you asking?'

She pouted her lips, pondering the question. 'I'll get back to you. Anyway, nobody can vote for someone from their own bunk, which means they're supposed to vote for whoever has the policies they most like.'

Gemma handed me a pair of wet jeans and two pegs, then asked me to put it on the high line that was strung above the rotary.

'That sounds very high-brow,' I said.

'There's still the usual badminton and everything. Just with added democracy.'

'Free cans of Coke for all?'

Gemma looked over her shoulder, off towards the bunks. Her voice was a whispering hiss: 'Don't say that too loud. We've still got brainstorm day yet – and it'll be hard enough trying to stop them offering free sweets for all.'

'How about a policy where counsellors have to do all laundry for campers?'

Gemma's eyes narrowed. 'You and I are going to fall out.'

Election week rolled into Tuesday and Luke and I ran the site with the precision of army drill sergeants. We were so ingrained in the timetable that we'd end up with free time with which we didn't know what to do. Luke joined in with the sports on the boys' field, while I either hung around the lounge or went to see if anything needed doing on the girls' side.

What I was really doing, of course, was trying to catch Amy's eye. We continued to spend reading hours in our spot under the tree in the adjacent field. The long grass had been rolled flat over the course of the time we'd been spending there. I'd read part of a chapter to her, in among the kisses. We were good at it by that point. Practice makes perfect and all that.

Monday had been a frustrating day for her, although I didn't hear much about it until reading hour on Tuesday.

'Unlimited Coke,' she said. 'That's one of our bunk's core policies.'

I wondered if one of her bunk members had overheard me. 'Is that a problem?' I asked.

'It's not equal pay for men and women, is it? Not quite the suffragette movement.'

'What else have you gone for?'

Amy shrugged. 'Different flavours of Monster Munch at the tuck shop.'

I laughed at that. 'If that's what the people want, that's what they want.'

She rocked herself back until she was laid in the shade of the tree, arms wide. I lay at her side and we held hands, as we did so often.

'What else?' I asked.

'We want a guarantee that girls can play touch rugby,' Amy said.

'Do you *want* to play touch rugby?'

'No – but that's not the point. At the moment only the boys can.'

'What are your other policies?'

'The usual. Later bedtime, longer free play time. Extra scoop of ice cream for pudding?'

I thought on that. 'I'm pretty sure that's one of Tony Blair's policies.'

Amy laughed, not a snort, so not a full point. 'What policies have *you* got?' she replied.

My eyes were closed and the sun prickled at my cheeks and eyelids. 'Counsellors should get more time off during the day,' I said.

She reached across and worked her fingers into the spot above my hip, where she knew I was ticklish. I wriggled away and batted aside her hand.

'What would a counsellor do with so much time off?' she asked.

I rolled back and pecked her on the lips. 'I reckon we could come up with something.'

Our eyes were open and she rolled hers. 'Something sensible,' she said.

'Hire an extra assistant counsellor?'

'Something that doesn't directly benefit you.'

Little Women was at my side and I thought of Michelle's name in the front and how she'd passed it to me. How each bunk was named after an author.

'How about a library?' I said. 'Campers can donate books they've finished and don't want to read again. There'll be new books for future years – and there will always be counsellors who have books they don't want from when they were younger. It'll grow and grow over time.'

Amy craned her neck back a fraction. 'Is that your idea?'

'I just came up with it.'

She hrmmed to herself. 'I wish we had you yesterday. That's so much better than the rubbish we came up with.' She wriggled and wafted her top in and out, trying to cool herself in the heat. 'You can be our clandestine campaign manager.'

'What does that involve?'

Amy had the same conspiratorial look as when she'd asked me to rig the gallery vote. 'There are going to be posters everywhere on Thursday,' she said. 'If you stand still for long enough, someone's going to tape a poster to you. All I'm saying is that you could do a bit of cleaning up for anything that's not Alcott girls.'

'What do you mean by "cleaning up"?'

'Chucking in the bin.'

I laughed at her directness. 'I'd be worried about you ever going into real politics. Rigging votes left, right and centre. You'd be a right dictator.'

'That's another one for the manifesto,' she said. 'It's about time we had a woman dictator.'

35

CUSTARD

Life at home had settled by that fourth week of camp. Mum opened the curtains every day in the living room and, from what I could tell, she was sleeping something close to regular hours in her own bed. She was either taking her pills, or clearing them out of each day's slot – and I chose to believe the former.

Michelle went from dropping in every night to every other. Then one in three. Mum even went food shopping one day, a proper old-school big shop that filled the cupboards and fridge. She also made me tea: not just beans on toast but a spag bol, created from scratch, with mince bought from the town butcher. Every evening, she asked about my day and, though I left out the parts about Amy, I told her about the work. She had follow-up questions and remembered names. It was like living with another person.

Meanwhile, at camp, I couldn't bring myself to perform any 'cleaning up' on the posters. Amy had been correct about them being everywhere, though. On the Thursday, Ian had two taped to his back and another to his front as he trudged into lunch, pretending none of it was his idea.

The slogans and chants had something of a similar theme,

though 'What do we want?' 'Vimto!' 'When do we want it?' 'Now!' felt a little lightweight as policies went.

Luke's black market was going as strong as ever and, from what I could tell, he had got at least three counsellors into smoking over the course of a month. It might not have been good for their lungs – but his wallet was doing terrifically. The biggest indicator was that the area at the back of the staff lounge, where I left my bike each day, suddenly had a bucket that was being used as a makeshift ashtray.

Amy and I stole away into the field next door every reading hour. Nobody ever bothered us, even though a few people had to know. We kissed a lot, though I read to her more. Those early days of frantic face chewing had been replaced by something a lot calmer. A lot more grown-up. If I wasn't reading, we were talking. She told me about the election and what she called 'my girls' – and a part of me loved the way they'd gone from 'campers', to 'the girls' to '*my* girls'.

Then, on Friday, it was election day – and, despite the silly policies and sillier chants, everyone was into it. Ian had found rosettes somewhere and all his boys were walking around with orange emblems on their chest, politely asking if they could rely on campers and adults for their votes. When I asked one lad what his main policy was, he wanted chips for tea a minimum four days a week, plus a daily Dairy Milk for evening snack.

Politics finally spoke to me!

Charlotte was the candidate for Alcott girls – and I voted for her out of loyalty to Amy.

It was late afternoon when George got on the stage and announced that all the votes had been counted and that the top two candidates were going to have a final debate, before a run-off re-vote. Tables were banged and names were cheered as George went through positions five, four and three.

He said the top two were 'in no particular order' – and, as the sound of claps and bangs crescendoed, he announced that a boy from Lewis and Charlotte were the most popular candidates.

There was a definite gender split as the boys cheered the boy and the girls cheered the girl.

I stood at the back of the mess hall and watched the debate as Charlotte picked apart the boy's policy of pick-your-own-bedtime as unsustainable because, if they stayed up too late, they'd be too tired to do much of anything in the morning. She said an extra thirty minutes would be a better idea.

I doubted I could argue with the same clarity at my age, let alone hers.

Charlotte said that the Alcott girls' policy of a lending library would work not only for their age groups – but for all future campers. She used the word 'legacy' and said that girls should be able to play touch rugby. 'It's not for me,' she said, 'it's for other girls who might.'

There were boys who booed, though they were quickly shushed by George, who was moderating. It was stupid but I struggled not to smile because it was *my* policy that was being pitched.

As Charlotte spoke, I watched across the hall as Sarah and Amy quietly whispered to each other, as if proud parents watching a child in their first nativity.

It was obvious who should win. Charlotte presented better policies in a clearer way – but, if the aim was to teach the campers about democracy, then that was certainly achieved.

The re-vote happened between the main course and the sponge and custard dessert at tea – and the results were announced immediately after.

Obviously, the kid from Lewis won. The boys' tables erupted, though Charlotte took it well enough. There was a polite handshake between her and the winner, who was trying to get the Vimto chant going.

George quietened the tent and said he was proud of the

way everyone had taken part that week. As a reward, he was going to follow through on one policy – which led to a couple of the kitchen lads emerging with boxes of Dairy Milk bars.

That got the biggest cheer of the entire time we were at camp. It was so loud, I'm sure I saw the tent flaps swish open.

Then the five-dayers were on their way home for the weekend and Amy was at my side as we waved some of them off.

'I hate democracy,' she said.

'Shall we stage a coup?'

'I want the full-on dictatorship you promised.'

'Just give all the campers chocolate and they'll do whatever you want. It'll be the most peaceful coup in history.'

She thought on that, possibly for a few seconds too long.

'Sarah's going to cover me tomorrow,' she said. 'I've got the whole day off as long as I do the lates every day next week.' She nudged me with her shoulder, which is what we did when things were a little too public. 'We've got the whole day together?'

'Let's spend it building our own military.'

36

GORGE II

The next morning, I met Amy at the gates of camp. I thought she would ask about what I had planned but she seemed happy for whatever the surprise might be. We walked down the hill towards town and it felt different in the day. We'd only made that journey at night before and there was still a part of me that thought she might want to separate when away from camp.

In reality, it was me who'd drifted a few steps from her as we reached the high street. She asked what was going on and then offered her hand, which I took in mine.

'You ashamed of me?' she asked.

'Of course not. I suppose I thought you wouldn't want to be seen with me...'

She gripped my fingers tighter and we continued through the centre at a crawl. She wanted to hear about the town itself, so I told her about the paper round I used to do at the newsagent we passed. My bike was broken at the time and Dad lent me the money to buy a new one on the proviso that I got a job to pay him back. I spent seven months across autumn and winter doing the paper round, only to end up with a slightly newer bike than the one with which I'd started. When I finished paying him off, it turned out Dad had been storing all those coins in a tub underneath his bed – and he'd given everything back to me, saying I'd earned it.

I realised towards the end of the story that I was going to struggle to finish it. Even though I rode that bike every day, I'd pushed away Dad's role in me buying it.

Amy couldn't have missed the way my voice cracked, or the way I'd slowed further, but she let it sit. Perhaps we both realised those silences were as important as our words.

I hadn't meant to end up outside Michelle's garage – and I hadn't known she was working that day – but I was lost in those thoughts of Dad and suddenly Amy and I were there.

Michelle was in the yard, overalls tied at her waist, the arms dangling towards her feet.

'Joe...?'

She would have known it was me – but the fact I was holding hands with a girl must have been enough to make her question her own eyes.

Amy and I stopped at the low wall that ringed the garage yard and Michelle came across. She looked between Amy and me, eyebrows raised.

'This is the part where you introduce us,' she said.

'Are you Michelle?' Amy asked.

My sister seemed delighted at the recognition. 'I am! And you must be... somebody that Joe has never mentioned...'

Amy looked to me slightly crookedly, though a smidge of a smile crept across her lips.

'I'm Amy,' she said, before looking to me. 'Why have you never mentioned me?'

I stumbled over a reply that never fully formed.

'I know why,' Michelle replied. 'He's not told you about his doll collection, has he?'

Amy snorted loudly. 'He's definitely kept that quiet.'

'He's got hundreds of dolls. His whole room's full of them. He loves his dolls, don't you, Joe?'

The situation had turned a lot faster than I could have thought. Amy and Michelle were both laughing.

'What else does he collect?' Amy asked.

I said, 'Don't you start' – but it was too late.

'My Little Ponies,' Michelle said. 'He's a huge fan. He's got them all and knows all the names. He sings them songs when he thinks nobody's listening.'

Amy was close to hyperventilating – and I started walking along the street, away from the garage.

'You coming?' I called.

'No way,' Amy replied. 'I'm finding out some serious truths.'

'And he loves sprouts!' Michelle said.

Amy had started to walk but much more slowly than me.

'Plus he can't tell his left from his right!'

I was on the furthest end of the yard as Amy called after me. 'Is that true?'

'It is,' Michelle answered for me. She was shouting now. Laughing. 'And he never learned to use a knife and fork. He carries a spoon around with him everywhere he goes. I call him Spoony.'

Amy was with me by that point, though she was covering her mouth to stop herself from giggling quite so loudly.

'And he can't tie his own shoelaces. He gets Mum to do them for him!'

Michelle was bellowing after us and I flicked her the Vs as she headed slowly back towards the garage, still laughing to herself.

Amy had to sit on the wall to regain some semblance of self-control.

'None of that's true,' I said – although I wasn't sure if I'd found the whole episode funny or annoying.

'Shame. I was looking forward to seeing your doll collection.' Amy waited a moment. 'Is it true you can't tell your right from your left?'

'Course not.'

'Prove it then.'

I held out my hands at arm's-length, extending my thumbs and forefingers to make and L and reverse L.

'L for left,' I said.

Her amusement was beginning to subside as she pushed herself off the wall and nudged me with her shoulder. 'Your sister seems nice.'

We walked a few steps away from the garage, on through town.

'Yeah...' A pause. 'She moved out a couple of weeks ago, into her own flat. I think she might be living with a boyfriend.'

'Is that a problem?'

'No... I mean... it's just she never said anything about a boyfriend.'

'You didn't tell her about me.'

'That's different.'

'Is it?'

I thought for a moment. 'Things have been so busy at home, with her moving out and Mum being ill, and...'

Those things were true but it was also the case that I'd deliberately chosen not to tell anyone about Amy.

'I didn't want to curse it,' I said.

'Curse what?'

'You and me. I figured if I told Michelle, or Mum, or anyone else, that it might all go away.'

Amy took my hand again and we walked a few paces more. 'Maybe that's what your sister thinks about her boyfriend...?'

As soon as she said it, I knew she was right – although it was hard to see how I'd missed that myself.

We kept walking, up and around the camp and then over the stile next to the green and white National Trust board at the bottom of the gorge. It was cool under the shade at the bottom and Amy walked a little quicker than me as we continued up and up.

It was still early, before the bulk of the day's tourists would arrive, so we had the trail mostly to ourselves. When we got to the top, the only people there were an older couple, with poles, bags, the lot. Amy and I were the complete contrast in shorts and T-shirts without even a bottle of water between us.

The couple were about to set off down and we all said hello to each other, then commented on the sun, the heat, the climb and the view. It was perhaps the first time I really thought of Amy and myself as a couple in anything other than the camp setting. She finished one of my sentences and the fact she hadn't realised she'd done it was the thing that really stuck from the day.

After those few minutes of small talk, the other couple headed back towards the trail – leaving Amy and I with the gorge to ourselves. We crept towards the edge but stopped as a small stone skittled into something hard from somewhere a little into the woods.

'What was that?' Amy asked.

'Rabbits? Squirrels?'

She suddenly seemed unsure. 'Is it safe up here?'

I moved to the edge and peered down, looking over the camp and the town. 'I guess so.'

The truth was, it had never occurred to me that it wasn't.

Amy crept forward in small quarter steps until she was close enough to crane a look over the edge. I held out an arm, hoping it would reassure her but she waved it away as she lowered herself down until she was sitting near to the edge of the overlook. I had been standing but moved to sit next to her.

'The famous gorge...' she said.

'What do you think?'

'It's high.'

We were a little too far back to see the camp properly but Amy edged forward and allowed herself a brief peek before moving back to me. I thought of the previous time I'd been there, the day after I'd fought Mark, and how gloomy everything had seemed then. I hadn't seen a way that things could be better... but then they were.

Amy rested her head on my shoulder and we listened to the rustle of nature and the distant sounds of the town. The silences were almost the best parts of us being together. There was nobody else I knew that I'd have felt comfortable sitting next to while not saying anything.

People came and went over the course of the next few hours. There were families and couples, or hikers having a brief look, before charging off into the woods to head for the next peak. Some were overdressed in heavy coats, others were in sandals. It felt like we said hello to the full breadth of humanity that morning. We ticked off the list of what a nice day it was, and how the view was lovely, and that the walk up was exhausting – plus the rest. Everyone accepted us a couple – and we happily went with it, holding hands and letting the other speak.

We were ready to go when Amy pointed into the distance. There was a field on the opposite side of town, a little past the green of the cricket club, filled with colourful dots.

'What's that?' she asked.

'The county fair,' I said. 'It's always the third full weekend in August.'

'Ian said something about it to Gem...' She mused on that for a moment. 'We should go.'

'We can – but it's a bit... intense.'

Her features crinkled and then she laughed. 'Too many dolls?'

She reached for my ticklish spot and I batted her away.

'Right,' I said, 'we're going. But don't say I didn't warn you.'

She was happy, excited for something new, but I was hit with a different feeling. I'd somehow forgotten the annual tradition my friends and I had of visiting the fair. Not just that, in the previous days, it was as if I'd forgotten them completely.

And after camp finished, without Amy, without my friends... what did I have left?

37

FAIR

Ian, Gemma, Amy and I walked in a tight line as we slid in and around the heaving mass that occupied the site of the fair. There were some families out together – but it also felt like everyone under the age of eighteen within a twenty-mile radius had descended upon a relatively small field on the edge of our town.

We were walking slowly, partly to take everything in – but mainly because it was the only option given the sheer number of people around us.

Amy leaned into me, calling into my ear so I could hear over the music and the screams. 'It's a bit... intense.'

I laughed at her. Coming to the county fair was something of a rite of passage for people who grew up in the town. We might come to the day version with our parents when we were younger – but that was a gentle trickle of water compared to the after-dark cyclone. There were lights spinning and twinkling from all directions, plus music from the rides blending with each other, along with the screams, shouts and overall din of thousands of people all trying to talk over everyone else. Each step brought a new smell, with the sweetness of candy floss and toffee clashing with the meaty sizzle of the multiple kebab vans.

It was those vans that proved our biggest problem.

'We're supposed to be meeting Owen and that lot near the kebab van,' Ian said.

'Which one?' Gemma asked, although she was speaking for all of us. From where we were standing, close to the dodgems, I could see three – plus there were at least another two we'd passed.

The four of us continued on a loop around the site, partially keeping an eye out for Ian's friends, though mainly taking everything in.

With no sign of them, it wasn't long before the four of us ended up on a ride with some sort of flying car that was cranked high into the air. We were dropped vertically, raised a little, and then dropped again. We were sharing a car, screaming with joy, though, at the end, Gemma very much wanted to get off. She rested on the metal barrier at the edge, doubled over, as Ian, Amy and I shared amused looks that we failed to keep to ourselves.

After that, we continued on through the fair, looking for the toilets. Ian and Gemma were at the front, with Amy and me behind. We were talking among ourselves, pointing out things we might want to try later, when I bumped into the back of Ian. He'd stopped and, when I looked around him, I realised why.

There was a slow-motion stand-off with us four on one side and, a short stretch away, coming from the other direction, Dan, Pete and Mark.

I had a strange sense of watching myself, even though I wasn't with them. Mark nudged Pete with his shoulder into a couple who were coming the other way. As Mark laughed, Pete was left apologising to the couple. A year ago, and it would have been the four of us elbowing and bouncing our way around this exact field.

They continued walking towards us as we carried on towards them. Dan saw me first and he missed a pace as Mark barged into the back of him. Mark was already halfway through a swear word when he noticed what Dan had. It was the first time I'd seen him since we'd been nose to nose, snarling in each other's faces.

We were all level and I was no longer holding Amy's hand, though I wasn't sure if I'd let go, or if she had.

For a couple of seconds, we all eyed one another and it felt as if anything might happen. Two tribes, meeting on neutral ground.

'Hi,' Dan said, talking to me.

'How was cricket?' I asked.

A shrug: 'Lost by loads and finished early.'

We were battling threads of static, our two groups repelling each other.

I glanced sideways towards Mark, who was eyeing Ian, his eyebrow twitching.

Ian wasn't shrinking away. He was taller than Mark, something I'd never noticed before.

'You all right?' Ian asked, talking to Mark.

It was nothing, a normal greeting that I'd hear over and over each and every day. But, in that moment, it felt like a challenge. A call to war.

Mark looked up to Ian and then turned and looked to me instead. I was more his level. He shrugged and the only reply was a dismissive 'Come on.' He continued walking, on past us as Pete quickly dashed to catch him. Dan mumbled a quick 'See ya' before he turned and hurried after the others.

I couldn't work out if I was relieved or sad. It was a crossroads where I'd chosen one direction that offered no route back to the other.

The four of us continued on but nobody spoke for a little while. We'd turned the corner and were close to the toilets when Amy asked if they were my friends. I said 'yes' and waited for a follow-up that never came. It was only later that I thought about Gemma telling me that actions were louder than words. My choice had been made – and it was Ian, Gemma and Amy.

We waited as Gemma went to the toilet and then, around the next corner, we finally ran into Owen and the rest of the gang from the Night And Day Café. They saw us first and whooped with happiness before we all hugged. It was a different world compared to with Dan and the rest. There were compliments about how everyone looked and how fantastic the fair was.

Because we'd all now found one another, they said were going to get some bottles from the offy and then head off to the canal bank. Owen had heard rumours of another party and we were all invited. Ian and Gem stepped forward but Amy took my hand and held me back.

Ian turned and looked to us curiously. 'You coming?'

Amy answered for us. 'Maybe later. We'll find you on the canal if you're still there.'

'What if we're not?'

'I'll see you back at camp, I guess.'

Ian exchanged a look with Gemma that was a little too knowing for my liking. It felt as if I'd missed a conversation somewhere along the line. He hugged Amy, then me. I guess I'd turned into a hugger at some point.

'Don't do anything I wouldn't do,' he whispered.

38

GENERATOR

Amy and I walked back through the fair, hand in hand. The lights blinked and the music played as I told her about the other times I'd been at the fair. Two years earlier, a week before Dad died, I'd been there with Dan, Mark and Pete. We'd drunk a good couple of litres of cider each before going on something called the 'Stomach Buster', which unquestionably lived up to its name. When we got off, my stomach busted and I vomited repeatedly into the nearest bin until I felt so empty that I could barely stand.

'What did you do then?' Amy asked.

'Ate a kebab and drank more cider.'

She didn't reply and I wasn't sure it was that funny given the time that had passed. It felt like something that had been done by somebody else. Something that happened, rather than something to boast about. How were we allowed to drink so much while so young? Why were we then released into a place such as the fair by ourselves? Some of the oldest campers were barely a year younger than we were at the time.

I pushed away those thoughts as Amy bought herself some

candy floss and picked at it while we continued ambling. We tried to buy beer but couldn't get served, so got hot dogs instead. I suppose the fair had tightened their drinking policy in the two years since the Stomach Buster incident.

We sat at a high plasticky table, carefully balancing on rickety stools as we ate. Amy managed to squirt ketchup onto her top and then made it worse by trying to get it out with her finger.

'No posh party for us tonight,' she said.

'I really don't think that lot from last week would notice a red sauce stain.'

'True.'

We talked about the best sauce (brown), then the best way potatoes could be cooked (roast), then Amy told me what was in a hot dog and I vowed to never eat one again.

It was so effortless. So real.

We got off the stools and continued in a loop. I asked Amy if she wanted to go on a ride but she pulled my arm instead, guiding me around a group of kids and into a gap at the side of the food vans. It was dark, a hidden passage between the main part of the fair and the hedges that ringed the site. The nearby generators hummed and we found a spot hidden in the shadows on top of some plastic matting that looked like it might have once belonged to a bouncy castle.

The sounds of the fair swirled around us, the lights flickering in the sky. We were kissing hard, pressing into one another, and there was a desperation, a hunger. I'd never felt that sort of intensity before as she moved my hand away from her hip, up and under her top. When I squeezed, she moved away a fraction, our breaths heavy on each other.

'Gently,' she said, smiling. 'Cup them like... I dunno, something you cup.'

'Like that?'

A bigger smile. 'Like that.'

She shivered as I skimmed my fingers along her side and then dug what little nails she had into my lower back. I pulled away a tiny bit and we grinned at each other, before she traced the line of my jaw with her fingers. We kissed and then she was inside my top, avoiding the tickly part above my hips and holding me instead.

Our lips were apart by then and she squeezed me before angling away slightly. She lifted her top and rearranged her bra before, letting her T-shirt drop again.

'We should probably stop,' she said quietly.

'Don't you want to?'

She smiled kindly. 'Yes... but it's not right, is it...?'

Amy nodded sideways, towards the overflowing bin and it was hard not to laugh. A massive part of me, maybe the biggest, wanted to say that it *was* right, except...

'You don't want this to be your first time, do you?' she said.

Amy helped smooth down my top and then she took my hand. That thought was still there, that I *did* want my first time to be here because every physical urge in my body was screaming at me to say so.

Except, deep down, I knew.

We kissed gently then and she rested her head on my shoulder as I held her.

It wasn't my first time that night but it was the first something else.

Something better.

She cricked her neck backwards so she could talk in my ear. It was only a whisper but it boomed above the whirring roller coaster and the screams of those on it. Those words dwarfed the hum of the generators and the endless babble of the people squashed onto the field. They were the clearest words I'd ever heard.

'I love you.'

She rested back on my shoulder and I wrapped an arm across her front, holding her to me. I've never meant four words more.

'I love you, too.'

39

TREE II

It was my Sunday at camp – but it was even quieter than my previous one. Amy and I spent at least half of it on the field at the back, underneath our tree. Our lips were sore and we needed a break – but I read to her and she told me that Gemma and Ian had ended up at another house party the night before.

'Were there naked people?' I asked.

'No but Gemma said there was some sort of drum circle.'

'That doesn't sound much like a party.'

Our conversations were a little more stunted that day because the spectre of only one more full weekend hung over us. There were twelve more days of camp and neither of us dared to talk about what might come then. We found all sorts of reasons to whisper those special three words to each other. She said she loved strawberries, then added: 'I love you, too.' I told her I loved the sun but that I loved her more.

It was never the same as the first time we said it. Almost a catchphrase, I suppose – even though that didn't really matter. I loved hearing it and I loved saying it.

That word again.

'What's next week's theme?' I asked after a while.

'For what?'

'There's been craft week, sport week, democracy week...'

'Talent show,' Amy replied. 'There's a full two-week build-up. People come in to do workshops on singing and dancing and comedy. Someone mentioned a magician. Everyone gets to have a go and then figure out what they like, or what they're good at. Then the final Friday is the big show in front of all the parents.'

'Do eleven-year-olds really do comedy?'

'I guess we'll find out. Anyway, aside from the usual, you're going to see a lot of people practising dance routines and hear a lot of singing in the next two weeks.'

We lay on what was left on the grass and I closed my eyes. Stars swam on the underside of my eyelids as the sun beamed from above.

'Ask me something,' Amy said.

It sounded as if she was on her back too.

'Like what?'

'That's the point. Ask me something you wouldn't usually.'

I rested in the heat, wriggling my bare toes in the warmth, trying to think of something. 'What did you think when you first saw me?' I asked.

Amy laughed gently and I felt her close by. 'I'm not sure. I thought the supply tent was empty and I was surprised at first. I thought...' She stopped herself and I breathed in the parched air, waiting. 'I thought you looked a bit lost,' she said.

Thing is, as she said it, I knew what she meant and knew she was right. I think I needed to hear it, though.

'How'd you mean?' I asked.

'Like you were somewhere you shouldn't be.'

There was the obvious point that the supply tent was precisely where I was supposed to be in that moment – except she didn't mean that. Camp Sycamore was a place I should never have been and it was chance that George had talked to Michelle after she worked on his car. If Fiona had come in, or if

Michelle had been on a break, or if I'd refused the interview for the job – or if a million other small things had been different, then I wouldn't have been in that tent when I had.

'What did you think of me?' Amy asked.

'Truth?'

'Of course.'

'I was surprised a girl was talking to me. I've not really had girlfriends… or friends who are girls.'

It wouldn't have been long before that I'd have been embarrassed to admit anything close to that – but, probably for the first time in my life, I felt comfortable to talk about anything.

Almost anything.

The future still felt off limits.

'I don't have many friends who are boys,' Amy said.

I kept my eyes closed, though I felt her breathe in and perhaps knew what was coming.

'Ian said you were a bit of a bully at school,' she said. 'He reckoned you were an angry kid.'

I didn't dare open my eyes, barely dared to breathe. My palms were damp and there was sweat oozing around my neck and ears.

'He said you weren't the worst,' Amy added. 'But Gemma said you made one of her friends cry one time.'

I breathed in but it didn't feel as if enough air would ever come. Amy was waiting for the reply that I knew she was owed.

'I didn't mean… I mean… I don't know what to say. I'm not proud of it.'

Her fingers nudged mine, although our hands didn't slip into one another's as they so often had. 'None of us are perfect,' she said. 'I'm not. I've said things I don't mean. Done things I wish I hadn't.'

I didn't know what to say to that either – but she wasn't done.

'There was this girl in year eight and she split her gym skirt in front of everyone. There was this moment where everyone stopped and looked, this second of silence, and we all laughed. All of us. *Everyone.* And there was this look on her face that I don't think I'll ever forget. Like she wanted to be invisible, to disappear.'

Her fingers twitched and I felt her take the same deep breath I had. It felt like she was excusing me for something when I didn't deserve it.

'Sometimes, I feel it in my stomach,' I said.

'What?'

'Anger. It builds and I don't know what to do with it.'

I felt her shifting and when I opened my eyes, she was leaning on her elbow, looking across to me, the light making the edges of her face fuzzy.

'I think we all start new here, don't we? That's the point. That's what places like this are for. We become the people we choose to be – and that's what matters. It's not who we are at the beginning, it's who we are at the end.'

We squeezed each other's hands.

'I love you,' I said – and it wasn't like the other times we'd slipped it into conversation that day. It was like the night before. It mattered.

There was a pause, a moment in which I thought she wasn't going to say it back, that the words we had spoken the night before were somehow misheard, or mistaken.

And then: 'I love you, too, Joe. I love you so much.'

40

HAIR

That fifth week continued in much the same way as the one before – and Amy was quickly proven correct. Groups of girls had carved out parts of their field to practise synchronised dance moves while walking around with imaginary microphones. It might have been a cliché – but there was none of that on the boys' side. For a few of them, their idea of an entry for the talent show was doing keepy-uppies for so long that counsellors had to intervene because it was time for lunch.

I sat in on the magician's workshop and watched as he made balls and coins disappear and reappear. There was a series of card tricks where he either guessed the correct one someone had picked – or pretended he'd got it wrong and then pulled the right one out from various places around the mess hall.

The campers were going crazy by the end, largely because they had no idea how he was doing any of it. The workshop finished with him showing them a few basic tricks that involved making sponge balls disappear, and removing a knot from a piece of rope. He had a few of them on stage to try their luck and, with a lot of his help, they all got enthusiastic Oooooooohs from the rest of the crowd. He finished by telling them to practise – and then spent the best part of forty minutes signing so many autographs that I was convinced some of the campers had gone up three or four times.

Amy and I spent every reading hour together. Sometimes, I'd read her another chapter of *Little Women*, other times we would talk or kiss.

I thought a lot about her saying that it was who we are at the end that mattered. It felt so important, so *right*... and yet our time was ticking away. I didn't know who I'd end up being.

It was the Tuesday when I asked if she could get the whole of Saturday off again.

'I have a plan,' I said.

'A plan for what?'

'You know...'

It didn't feel right to say it out loud – but we both knew what I meant. We both wanted it, or I hoped she did.

'I'll ask Sarah,' she said. 'But I can probably get it off if I cover all the evenings again.'

'Is she still seeing that lad from Lewis?'

'I think the bins is their official spot.'

'I prefer ours.'

She leaned in and pecked me gently on the lips. 'I agree.'

We talked about everything and nothing that week. About the time her uncle ate a blob of wasabi, thinking it was a pea, and then vomited on her aunt's new dress. I laughed, although I had no clue what wasabi was.

Her other uncle had been having an affair and had been kicked out by her aunt. He'd ended up living in their spare room for a few weeks – but Amy didn't like him because she could hear him hovering outside the bathroom door whenever she was in there. She'd been thirteen at the time.

We talked about my dad, though not really *about* him. I told her about how our family visited the coast every year and stayed in a caravan. How our first car once broke down on the side of a dual carriageway and that some bloke in an ice-cream van pulled over and gave us a jump-start.

There were so many of those small stories, things I'd forgotten, that suddenly burned bright. She brought it out of me. We laughed and we kissed and she said that my hair was getting long.

'I'll get it cut,' I replied, too quickly, too eager to please.

'Don't,' she replied. 'I like it like that.'

Every moment we had together was wonderful and new. We never ran out of things to talk about and I couldn't get enough of her. I felt more alive than I ever had.

And yet... that tiny voice never left. It whispered mischief in those quiet moments between jobs, in those seconds before I fell asleep. We only had eleven days left together. Then ten. Then we both agreed we'd stay on and work the final Saturday for clean-up day, which took us back to eleven. Except I blinked and it was ten again.

With nine days to go, George said I could have the whole day off because everyone's GCSE results were due. Ian and Gemma were in the same position, though they only had the morning off. They asked if I wanted to go to the school with them and, though I wanted to, I had to say no.

I'd already made a promise.

41
_____

JUKEBOX

I got to Dan's garage a few minutes before nine the next morning – and he, Mark and Pete were already outside, leaning on the wall. It was another warm day and we were all in T-shirts and shorts, as if we were settling down for a day of PlayStation and darts.

'We didn't know if you were coming,' Dan said – and it felt as if they might have spent the previous few minutes talking about me.

'Where else would I be?' I replied.

We waited there for a second or two – and then, unexpectedly, while looking at the floor, Mark apologised.

'Sorry, like...' he said.

The earth had shifted on its axis and there was a second where nobody spoke, until Dan threw himself to the ground, clutching his chest.

'Call an ambulance,' he said through a laugh. 'I can't believe what I've just heard.'

'Get lost,' Mark said, although a small smile creased his lips.

Dan picked himself up and brushed himself down – and, in that moment, it was as if the fight had never happened.

I think I said I was sorry, even though I wasn't – but that didn't matter. We really were a group to forget, though maybe not forgive.

We headed towards the town and it was like a crowd descending upon an arena. Our numbers swelled and I realised how much I missed actually seeing the faces who'd been my life for so long. There were people I'd seen almost every day since I was five years old and they seemed so different out of uniform, hair down, shorts on. People's skin had tanned over the summer. There was more than that, too. A lack of burden, perhaps.

Our walk to school had been almost like the old days. Mark had nudged Pete into a couple of bushes, though he hadn't tried it with me. There'd been talk of 'babes' he'd met over at the caravan park. He said they'd invited him back to their caravan but that he'd had to get home, so he was planning to catch up with them another night. It was nonsense but we went with it, as we always had. The idea of talking about Amy never occurred to me. She was one life, my friends were another.

The steps that led up to school would usually be filled with students having lunch, or occasionally sneaking a crafty smoke if there were no teachers around. Waiting for us that day were our familiar teachers – except they were also dressed down. Instead of suits and smart shirts, there were jeans and T-shirts. I'd never seen Mr Freeman in anything other than a suit – but he was wearing a Star Wars T-shirt and jeans that had holes in the knees.

There was a man with a long-lens camera at the bottom of the stairs. He was surrounded by a group of girls whom he was encouraging to jump in the air while holding their results aloft. As he finished with them, he ignored two groups of boys who were heading down the steps, results in hand. If he wasn't from the local newspaper, then I thought someone should probably phone the police.

A line stretched from the glass double doors at the top of the stairs, snaking along the path at the top and looping around to where we joined it midway down the steps.

There were nerves in that line. Mark's brags about 'babes' had descended into a silent long stare as we waited to see our future.

We were at the top of the steps when I spotted Ian and Gemma emerging from the doors. It wasn't that long before I'd have ignored them, or, perhaps – shamefully – helped Mark cycle through the list of nicknames.

Instead, I told Dan to hold my place and then walked across and cut them off as they were halfway down.

'What did you get?' I asked.

'As to Cs,' Ian replied. He thrust a sheet of paper at me, as if I wouldn't believe him otherwise.

'I failed French,' Gemma said, sounding gloomy.

'You passed everything else,' Ian said – and it sounded as if he'd already pointed that out to her a few times.

'Yeah but Mum's gonna be annoyed. We went to France the other year and she kept going on about how it was an investment in my future.'

'Wasn't it just a holiday?' Ian said.

'Try telling *her* that.'

They looked across to where Dan, Mark and Pete were watching us.

'Are you coming back to camp?' Ian asked. 'We can wait if you are.'

'George gave me the day off.'

'What about Saturday? Are you coming to the Night And Day?'

'I think me and Amy have plans.'

That got matching smirks from the pair of them.

'Good luck,' Ian said.

I must have frowned, thinking he meant with Saturday, but he held up his paper.

'With the results,' he added, laughing. 'I didn't know you had such a filthy mind.'

We said goodbye – and there were hugs, more congratulations, more good wishes. Then I was back in line, closer to the front, and none of my friends said anything. I suppose it wasn't only me who had changed.

It took fifteen minutes for us to get to the doors. There was little need to ask how people had done as they came out – because their faces said it all. Below us, the photographer had found a new group of girls to harass, while, at the doors, Mr Freeman was consoling a lad who was crying into a plant pot.

Then it was our turn.

The school hall felt the same but different. We'd sat on the floor for so many assemblies, through so many announcements, concerts and whatever else we could be dragged in there for. We'd eaten lunches inside when it rained, sat our exams as every chair-squeak echoed high to the heavens.

It had felt so huge, that enormous vast space – and yet it was so small in that moment. So quaint.

There were a handful of tables set up with teachers sitting behind, handing out brown envelopes that contained our results. We queued some more and then Mrs Platell handed me an envelope with 'MILLER, JOE' printed on the front.

'Good luck,' she said – and, although she was saying it to everyone, it sounded as if she meant it.

I thought we might open our results together but, by the time I found Mark in the corridor outside, his envelope had been torn into pieces.

'What did you get?' I said.

'Don't ask.'

Dan found us next and he struggled to conceal the wide smile. 'As and Bs,' he said as he tried to pretend it was no big deal. Pete passed everything but was annoyed at his D in religious studies.

And me? Not five passes – but six. A double-E in science, a C in maths and IT, a B in design tech and, best of all, most incredibly and unexpectedly of all, an A in English.

Dan asked if I was happy and I was. It was what I needed to take that job with Barry, or perhaps go to college if I wanted.

Meanwhile, Mark dumped the remains of his envelope in the bin and refused to say anything more about it.

We made that same journey down the stairs that we had hundreds of times before, probably thousands, and were ignored by the photographer.

As we headed for town, people were shouting a series of letters across the street to one another. 'Three Cs!' – 'All As!' 'A U in history!' There were thumbs ups and high fives. Oh, mates and Oh, wells.

By the time we reached the Red Lion, the only people there were underage drinkers clutching exam results, not even pretending to be eighteen.

The four of us ordered our ciders and lagers, then headed out to the beer garden, close to the fence that overlooked the canal.

We drank and we laughed about our school triumphs. Not the grade-related kind.

There was the time Mark persuaded the whole class to play along and pretend nobody could hear what our geography teacher was saying. It got to the point where he was shouting and we all still said 'what?' Or when we unplugged the video machine and Mrs Davidson couldn't work out why the tape wouldn't play. We wasted a whole lesson as she tried to figure out what was wrong. Or when we drew up bingo cards with a list of sayings which we tried to goad our design tech teacher into saying. Pete would have won but he was too afraid to call bingo in class, so Mark claimed the victory a few seconds later. Then he got detention.

We talked about cricket games and football matches, about

their runs and their goals. The dodgy referees and blind umpires.

And they were my friends – but 'were' was the important word.

We laughed so much that it hurt. So much that we needed a break. And it was funny because it was gone. It was the past, not the future.

I knew it was never going to be like that again and I suspect we all did.

Even Mark.

There was more cider, more lager. Then Mark went inside and, minutes later, the jukebox was playing the entirety of *Be Here Now*. I knew more words than I cared to admit and we sang loud and out of tune. Mark was on the table, swinging his top around his head, and then he was back down because the landlord told him to knock it off.

The rest of us howled. That final time of being told off and backing down. Then Pete had to go because his dad was driving him the forty minutes it took to get to KFC as a celebration. He staggered away tipsy, if not outright drunk, still singing Oasis, even though the jukebox had long finished playing it.

It never quite worked when there was no Pete. There was nobody for Mark to play off – and his restless energy was never fully tolerated by Dan and me.

He knew it, we all did, so there were handshakes and see yas and a big 'let's do this again soon', even though we knew we wouldn't.

Then it was just Dan and me. We sat and watched the canal ebb into the distance as the faint white of the moon doused us in a bluey glow.

We were sobering up by that point, the booze and heat of the day starting to thicken our heads and thoughts.

'It's been good, hasn't it?' Dan said quietly.

'What?' I replied.

'Everything.'

I agreed that it had – and perhaps it was true in one way. If it wasn't for them, I wouldn't be who I was.

We sat on those chairs, surrounded by empty glasses, our bare arms and legs chilled and freckled with goosebumps.

'How's your mum?' he asked.

'OK, I think.' I waited and then: 'Do you think you'll ever come back?'

He waited too. Thinking about the answer, even though we both knew it. 'Not properly. My sister's got a place out by where I'm going to college. I'm going to stay with her at first, see how it goes. She says there's a whole basement I can have.'

There was relish in his voice, like there was when he talked about cricket and the other things he loved. Perhaps he'd always known this town would only be his until it was time to go? He sounded so assured, as if he knew where his future would take him.

The beer garden had emptied but we sat there, just us, watching a canal boat drift across the black water, on towards the gates.

'I'm glad this is how it ended,' Dan said. 'All of us together one more time.'

'Me too.'

And it was true. Despite everything, I think we needed that one final day.

It wasn't quite over.

'You love her, don't you?'

Dan and Amy had never met, not properly. There was that fleeting moment at the fair where we hadn't even been holding hands – but he'd seen something and he knew. Perhaps everyone did.

'Yeah,' I said – and the word caught in my throat.

He let out a long breath. 'Good on you, mate. I'm glad.'

It was almost time to go but we watched as a set of spinning blue lights emerged from the distant dark. There were no sirens but the car zoomed over the bridge, slowed, and then took the bend that would take it up towards the big houses where George lived.

And that was it. No massive heart-to-heart, no outpouring of emotion. No crying. It was enough. It was us.

We stood, shook hands one more time, and then set off towards our homes.

I didn't think much more about the police car that night, how those blue lights had cut across the night. What I didn't know was that the next time I saw a police car, I'd be in the back of it.

42

PROFILE

My head was heavy, thoughts slow, on Friday morning as results day caught up to me. Barry had told me to get five passes and I had six. I supposed that would be my life before long. What else did I have to do?

Mum was happy enough with my results, especially the 'A'.

I tried not to think about the future too much.

It was a foggy cycle to camp – though there was a surprise waiting when I got there. Amy had left a message with, as far as I could tell, everybody on site, telling me to find her as soon as I got in.

She was near the bunks watching some of her girls practise a dance routine. As one stepped forwards confidently, another stepped backwards with equal assurance. A third tripped over her own feet and then scrambled to try to get back into formation.

'Are they meant to be doing that?' I asked.

Amy elbowed me gently. 'Oh, har-dee-har. Aren't you the funny one?' She turned, grinning. 'What did you get?'

'Six passes. An A in English.'

She pouted her lip, impressed or surprised. I wasn't sure which.

'You?'

'Mum phoned them in yesterday.' There was a pause as she turned back to her girls. 'Do you really want to know?'

'Of course.'

'All As, with an A-star in French.'

I mimed vomiting on the ground and she pretended to ignore me.

'Is that why you've been leaving messages for me?' I asked.

There was a wicked grin to her – and a sense that I wasn't going to like what was coming.

'My girls are in charge of the newsletter today and they—'

'No.'

'Need someone—'

'Absolutely not.'

'To—'

'No.'

'Interview—'

'No.'

She spoke quickly: 'So I told them you would *definitely* sit down and let them interview you for the staff profile bit.'

I'd known at the mention of the word 'newsletter' what was coming.

'No.'

Amy rested her head into my shoulder, which was about as public as we had ever got at camp in front of other people. Her voice was a sing-song: 'For me?'

'No.'

'Please?'

'I said no.'

'Pleeeeeeease?'

'Definitely not.'

Twenty-three minutes later, I was sitting on a low chair at

the edge of the Alcott girls' bunk. Amy's girls were in a funny, giggly mood: the sort of laughs from which nothing good ever came.

'When's your birthday?' one of them asked.

I told them – and then we were off with a rat-a-tat-tat of question after question. They wondered where I'd been born, and wanted to know my favourite colour, band and movie. Up until that point, I'd seen the answers to those same questions appear in other counsellors' profiles across the weeks.

But there was more. They asked my favourite food, drink and biscuit. My preferred chocolate bar, flavour of crisps and sandwich filling.

I asked if it was all for the profile – but the campers were particularly hysterical by that point and no answer came.

They wanted to know my favourite animal, my opinion on the best dinosaur – and, last of all, which Disney princess I liked the most.

I didn't answer that last one and turned to Amy instead, who was sitting next to Sarah. The pair of them were almost as giddy as their girls.

'I get the feeling they didn't come up with all these questions themselves,' I said.

'Dead wrong,' Sarah replied.

'This is vital information for the running of camp,' Amy added.

'We need to know your favourite Disney princess,' Sarah said. 'It's a crucially important matter of security.'

Every camper in the circle around me was trying their best not to laugh.

'I don't know any princesses,' I said.

Someone booed.

'Nobody believes that,' Amy replied.

'Not a single one of us,' Sarah said.

I made a point of looking at my watch. 'I've really got to—'

'Answer the question!'

It was Charlotte who'd shouted loudly enough to freeze me to the spot. She sounded more forceful than either Amy or Sarah.

'Fine!' I said, sitting back on the seat. 'It's Aurora.'

A girl other than Charlotte had been noting my answers, though they were past the point of pretending and she didn't bother to write anything. I think that was the greatest number of people who'd ever laughed *at* me – but it was infectious and impossible not to join in.

I started to stand but Charlotte tugged on my leg. 'We're not done,' she said.

There was a degree of reluctance as I lowered myself back into the circle again.

'*Almost* done,' Charlotte said.

'What else do you want to know?'

Charlotte's grin was as wicked as anything I had ever seen. She exchanged a titter with the girl who was writing the answers. 'Do you love Amy?'

I tried to laugh it off – though the girls weren't going to let it go.

'I can't—'

'It's a simple question,' Charlotte replied.

'Yes, but—'

'He said yes!'

They laughed and made a series of 'ugh' noises, then the chant started. 'A-my and Jo-ey sit-ting in a tree, K-I-S-S-I-N-G.'

I stood then, manoeuvring myself out of the circle and bending to peck Amy on the forehead as I left.

'Might as well give them something to chant about,' I told her.

I could still hear the mass 'urrrrrrgggggghhhhhh' from the campers on the furthest side of the field as I headed into the staff lounge with a grin on my face.

43

BED

I met Amy at the camp gates after breakfast on the Saturday morning. I'd left my bike at home and walked. There wasn't much point in bringing it, with Amy not having a bike of her own. We each had a bag on our backs and the two of us walked slowly down the hill towards town.

'Where are we going?' she asked.

'I don't think I should say yet.'

She hrmmed at that. 'It's not a sheet close to a bin, is it?'

'Why are we always talking about bins?'

'I don't know. But it's a fair point.'

'We're not touring the bins,' I said. 'It's somewhere much better.'

Amy grumbled quietly about not being a fan of surprises. 'It's not some hostage thing, is it?' she said. 'You made me pack more or less all the clean clothes I have left...'

'It's not a kidnapping.'

'I didn't say *kidnapping*, I said hostage!' A pause, then quieter: 'Now it feels like this might be a kidnapping.'

'It's really not a kidnapping.'

'That's what a kidnapper would say.'

We reached the base of the hill and Amy knew the route by then as we turned towards the high street.

'Are you doing anything Tuesday night?' she asked.

'I don't think so.'

'The main talent show is on Friday but not everyone gets to take part, or we'd be there all night. There's a dress rehearsal on Wednesday, and Thursday is supposed to be a time for everyone to fix whatever needs doing before Friday.'

'So what's Tuesday?'

'My girls are having their own mini talent show in our bunk that night. Everyone will get a go, even if they're not in the main show. Sarah and I were wondering if you'd be a judge.'

We were passing the Red Lion and it was impossible not to see how different the request was compared to the drunken days I would have spent there across the summer if it wasn't for camp.

'What does a judge do?'

'The clue's kind of in the name...'

'Do I say what I actually think?'

Amy stopped and tugged on my hand, so that I was facing her. 'God, no. Whatever you do, don't do that. Just say that everyone's great.'

'Even if they're bad?'

She twisted me around and we carried on walking. '*Especially* if they're bad. Say something like, "I'm not sure that's the best song for you but you gave it your best." It sounds like a compliment.'

I thought for a second: 'You know when you sang Savage Garden the other day? I'm not sure it was the best song for you – but you gave it your best.'

She whacked me playfully on the arm as I laughed.

'It'll mean more coming from someone outside the bunk,' she said, back on point. 'They expect Sarah and me to be nice about them. You're this mystery man who puts up the umbrellas. They'll want to know your opinion... especially now they know you've got posters of Aurora on your wall.'

She laughed at herself and I let it go.

'What time?' I asked.

'After tea.'

'I'll be there.'

We were across the canal and on our way towards the large expensive houses when Amy asked if it was round here where the party had happened. I told her it was – though there was no doubt it looked very different during the day. At night, on our way to the party, fuelled by alcohol, there had been an excitement that was difficult to square with what, in daylight, was a series of large but bland houses on a hill.

It was as if Amy was reading my mind as we walked. 'That night feels like a dream,' she said.

'The party?'

'All of it. The people, the food, the drink. It was all so... *weird.*'

'What about sleeping on the sofa?'

I felt her smile, even though I wasn't looking at her. 'That was the best bit.'

We continued on and up – and then our destination was in front of us. There were no cars in the drive and I walked confidently up to the front door, unlocked it, and ushered a bemused Amy inside.

I quickly closed the door behind us and then turned to see Amy staring up at the high ceiling and wide hall.

'Where are we?' she asked.

'George and Fiona's house. He gave me a key because I've been cycling up here to pick up parcels a few times a week.'

Amy turned in a full circle, looking up the whole time. She stretched and opened a door that led into the living room that contained the bookshelves. I waited in the hall as she took a step inside and then quickly moved out, as if she'd been stung.

'Do they know we're here?'

I didn't answer but she knew.

'When you said you had a place,' she said, 'I didn't think you meant breaking and entering.'

'I couldn't think of anywhere better. Mum's at home all the time – and where else is there? I thought—'

'*Did* you think?'

I couldn't tell whether Amy was annoyed. I'd thought my plan was perfect but now it seemed stupid. Thoughtless. She had every right to be angry.

'There was no breaking involved,' I said.

'Entering, then.'

'I don't think George would mind.'

Amy looked to me, eyebrows raised. 'Shall we ask him?'

We stood together in that vast hallway and it was impossible not to be deflated.

Amy edged across towards me and we stood shoulder to shoulder, the backs of our hands touching.

'It's such a nice house,' she said.

'Would you have come if I'd said this was the plan?'

She thought for a moment. More than that. Maybe a minute and then: 'Probably.'

'They won't be here tonight,' I said. 'All the counsellors are off and they're covering. George told me they always sleep at camp on weekends.'

A pause.

'What's it like upstairs?'

If there was doubt before, then it evaporated like an ice cube in a fire. We looked to each other and then a race was on. Amy sprinted for the stairs and I was a step behind as we bounded to the top. We stopped on the landing, out of breath.

I pointed towards the door that was opposite the stairs. 'I thought maybe in there. It's some sort of guest room.'

What had felt like a good idea suddenly felt seedy at best and criminal at worst.

'Perhaps we should go?' I said.

Amy looked to me curiously and then opened the door I'd indicated. She disappeared inside as I waited in the hall. A few seconds later, her face appeared around the door.

'Are you coming?'

I followed her inside and she closed the door behind me. 'It's the smallest room,' I said.

'Shush.'

She stepped forward and angled up to kiss me gently as my back was pressed against the door. It only lasted a second and then she stepped away as we took in the room together. Even though it was the smallest, there was the double bed that had been made with rigid corners and a large bedspread that stretched down to the floor. There were small tables on each side of the bed and a large dresser on the other side of the room. It was otherwise bare aside from cream walls and a cream carpet.

'It's a lot better than behind a hot dog van,' Amy said.

'Or the bins by the boys' bunk.'

Amy laughed a little at that but it was more nerves than anything else. I felt it too.

'I figured we could stay in here the whole time,' I said as I reached for my bag. 'I brought drinks and snacks and—'

'What have you got?'

I lifted my bag onto the pristine bed and Amy started to empty it. There were some crumpled packets of crisps, a bottle of wine that had been in one of the cupboards at home, plus some bottles of Blue.

'How'd you get those?' she asked.

'Waited outside the Spar and asked this older lad. He said OK, as long as I paid for his fags.'

Amy turned back to the bag and pulled out a giant bar of Dairy Milk. 'Nice varied diet,' she said.

'I didn't know what to bring. I wasn't really thinking.'

Amy swept the snacks back into the bag and arranged the bottles on the side table. She sat on the bed and then offered me her hand, which I took. We sat side by side for a moment, heads angled to look at each other.

'Hi,' she said.

A thread of hair had fallen across her face, so I pushed it behind her ear. 'Hi.'

Her eyes were so green that day. I know it's a cliché to bang on about meadows or fields and that sort of thing but I'd never seen anything like it.

'Is this OK?' I asked.

'Yeah.'

She kissed me so gently that our lips barely touched. Then she traced the line of my jaw with her finger, before pressing harder to kiss my top lip. She pulled away and leaned back, then stretched up to take off her T-shirt, under which she was wearing a plain black bra.

'I'll teach you to take it off one day,' she said – and then she arced her arms backwards and unclipped it, before dropping it onto the floor. I gawped and stared. Eyes on stalks and all that. Full heart attack territory. There were actual, real, boobs right there in front of me.

'Gently,' she said.

We kissed and I did my best but there were times when she had to pull away and smile patiently. 'Gently' was our catch-phrase that day, although mainly hers. 'Slowly' was the other one.

It wasn't long until we were only in our pants – and then not even that. She guided my hand, telling me where – and I listened, or tried, but there was a lot to remember. At times, it felt as if two hands weren't close to being enough.

When I opened the packet, all I could think about was the biology lesson where Mr Green put a condom on a banana and our whole class united in laughter. It was probably the only time we had all agreed on the same thing – that our teacher putting a condom on a banana was the funniest thing we'd ever seen. We were still making jokes about it years later and I don't think any of us ever looked at him in the same way again.

Amy asked what I found funny and, when I said, she told me that it had been a big test tube in their lesson – and that her class found that hilarious, too.

Laughing made it better.

I asked if she was OK and she told me to stop asking because she was. And then it was *really* OK. As OK as it had ever been. In the full range of OKs, that was as OK as it was possible to get. The most OK of them all.

One of the shortest OKs of them all, too.

I said sorry and she replied that it didn't matter because that was our practice run and we could try again soon. Which we did.

We drank the wine from the plastic cups I'd taken from camp – and we ate the crisps and the chocolate. I read to her and we would sleep and then wake and get some more practice.

Saturday day became Saturday night and we didn't dare put on the light, just in case a nosey neighbour was watching from somewhere we couldn't see. We lay in the dark, the digital clock on the dresser blinking down our time together. It was a little after one in the morning and, apart from trips to the bathroom, we'd been in that room for the best part of fourteen hours.

Amy was sleeping on my shoulder and there were around seven hours until she had to be back at camp. I stared at the ceiling as her breath danced across my chest.

It had been the best fourteen hours of my life.

And then the front door sounded.

44

SUPPER

I didn't breathe in those seconds after the front door sounded. There was silence for a moment and I hoped the noise was something else, perhaps the usual creaks of an unfamiliar house.

Then there was the unmistakeable rattle of keys being dropped on a table.

I gently nudged Amy awake and, as she drifted back to awareness, I whispered in her ear. 'Someone's downstairs.'

Her body tensed. 'Who?'

'I don't know.'

We lay there, my arm still around her as we didn't dare move for fear of making the bed creak.

Below us, footsteps clipped around the hard floor of the kitchen. A cupboard opened and closed, then something else that might have been a fridge. There was a clink of metal on ceramic and it sounded like someone was making themselves something to eat.

Amy carefully eased herself away from me until she was on her own pillow, leaning on her elbow. 'Do we hide?'

'Where?'

'Under the bed?'

'But we can't *make* the bed before we hide. If someone comes in, they'll notice it's messed up.'

I stared through the gloom towards the empty bottles that were on the floor, close to the door. Even if I could move silently, there was no chance of getting all that into my bag without making a noise.

'What do we do?' Amy's voice was a desperate hiss, a tone I'd never heard before.

'I don't know.'

My stomach was gurgling and Amy patted it lightly. 'Can't you keep it down?'

'If I could, I would.'

From nowhere, it felt as if someone was sitting on my bladder. Two minutes before and I hadn't needed a wee – and yet, in that moment, I'd never needed to go more.

We listened as someone continued to move around the kitchen. More cupboards opened and closed – then there was the sound of a microwave dinging.

Whoever was sitting on my bladder was getting heavier.

Then there was someone on the stairs. Neither of us risked breathing as the steady *squeak, squeak, squeak* got closer and closer.

Silence.

Then another *squeak*, from the landing this time. A sliver flooded under the door of the room, the golden light flashing across us. Amy was wearing only a T-shirt and I wasn't even wearing that.

We didn't move.

A door opened and then clicked back into its frame and the two of us finally let out long, silent breaths.

'We could run for it,' Amy whispered.

I didn't reply because I couldn't see any way we'd make it – plus every word we spoke felt like a risk.

Moments later, a toilet flushed. There were more footsteps

and the light from under the door disappeared, then more creaks, a silence, a door closing and then, hallelujah!, the sound of a car starting.

When Amy breathed out, the reprieve was like the first drops of an icy drink on the hottest day. 'Check they've gone,' she hissed.

'Why me?'

''Cos this was your idea!'

I did as I was told, carefully opening the bedroom door and then creeping onto the landing. I peered over the stairs, to the shadows and darkness, and then edged down to the ground floor, where all the lights were off.

After that, I ran up to the bathroom and had the greatest wee of my life. It was so good, I'd easily rank it in the top-ten things that have ever happened to me.

When I returned to the bedroom, Amy's T-shirt had gone. I'd been expecting her to be dressed and ready to go – but she pulled me towards her and was then on top. There was no light and everything was different compared to the previous day. We couldn't see each other for cues and everything happened through the rhythm of our breathing and soft whispers. Every time seemed better than the last but that's the one I really remember.

Afterwards, we lay with her head on my shoulder again, listening to the night. We were close enough to the woods that we could hear owls hooting to one another in the distance.

'Read to me,' she said.

'It's too dark.'

'Put the light on. Nobody's coming back a second time and everyone else is asleep.'

And so I read to her through the rest of those early morning hours – and it wasn't long until the sun came up and we didn't need the light anyway. Amy was on her back, eyes shut, and I was sure she was asleep, even as I continued to read. The book was almost finished but, when it got to talk of chocolate, she pursed her lips and whispered a gentle: 'Stop there.'

I closed the page, with only a chapter to go. 'For what?' I asked.

'For another day.'

45

ANNIVERSARY

It wasn't my day to work – but I spent Sunday at camp anyway. There wasn't a lot to do and, on a misty morning and cloudy afternoon, there was a general sense of everything winding down. When Amy and I had our hour in the adjacent field, we spent much of it resting in each other's arms, talking about the fun of the previous day.

Monday wasn't that different to Sunday in terms of workload – except George had already said I could have the afternoon off. I had something to do. We were sitting under our tree when I told Amy I was leaving early. She asked why and I felt that old pull of wanting to keep things to myself. Wanting to keep everything pressed down, where nobody could possibly know what I was feeling.

I'd changed though.

'It's the anniversary of when Dad died,' I said.

We had been sitting against different sides of the trunk but Amy shuffled around until we were facing each other.

'Are you visiting his grave?' she asked.

A shake of the head. 'He doesn't have one. We scattered his ashes in the sea at the end of the pier where he met Mum.

The idea was that, whenever we saw the ocean, we'd think of him.'

Amy stretched and took my hand. Squeezed it. 'That sounds nice.'

I nodded, although I'd never been quite sure that it was. As Michelle had emptied that box over the edge of the rail at the end of the pier, I'd watched that grey powder fall out of sight and wanted to tell her to stop.

It was too late by then – and it wasn't as if I had a better idea.

'There's something I didn't tell you about Dad,' I said.

'What?'

'I've never really told anyone before. I mean, they know. People *know* – but I've never told anyone what it was like for me.'

I thought she'd say it was fine for me to tell her but our silences were king and that was somehow better. She waited and I took those seconds, wondering if I could actually say that which had felt stuck within me for so long.

'Dad died on a Saturday,' I said. 'I found out at my friend's house in the evening and my sister picked me up. Then Diana died the next day. The next morning. I remember our neighbour came over and she was like, "Have you heard the news" – but she wasn't talking about Dad, she was talking about someone she'd never met.'

My head was bowed and I couldn't quite bring myself to look up. I'd gone two years back in time.

'Everyone just sort of… forgot,' I said. 'They were all focused on Diana – even people who knew dad. But he was a real person and they were… I mean, I know she was real too – but nobody actually *knew* her. No one we knew had *met* her. But they were all upset about her – and nobody talked about him.'

Amy didn't speak but I didn't want her to. She was so

good at listening – and perhaps I was too. Perhaps that was why we worked, because we each actually listened to each other.

I didn't want to say any more about it, so we sat for a while. When Amy did speak, her voice was croaky. 'It's the mini talent show tomorrow,' she said. It was as if she'd read my thoughts because I needed that change of subject.

'I'll be there,' I replied.

'Charlotte's written a poem for you?'

'Has she?'

'Well, for the man who puts up umbrellas, who I assume is you.'

'Is that poem one of the things I have to judge?'

'Yeah but just tell her it's great.'

'Even if she calls me, um... I dunno, a stinky poo head, or something?'

A snort: 'Why is "stinky poo head" your first choice of insult?'

'I dunno, isn't that how kids think?'

'Speak for yourself.'

When we went back to camp at the end of that reading hour, we hovered for a while longer in the space at the back of the staff lounge. Amy held both my hands and leaned in for me to kiss the top of her head.

'Look after yourself today,' she said.

'I'll try.'

After that, I headed across to the gates at the front of camp and waited for Michelle. When she pulled up, she popped the boot and I squeezed my bike inside, then got into the back seat. Mum was in the front and it was a sombre, silent journey as Michelle drove us out to the coast.

Weeks before, when Mum had disappeared to here, it had felt as if everything was ending – but things were different as Michelle parked. The three of us walked along the wooden boards, out above the ocean, as Mum told us about the time she and Dad had first met, even though we'd heard it before.

We sat on the bench at the end, closest to where we'd released his ashes, and we talked about the time he'd fallen off a stool when replacing a light bulb – and then proceeded to spend fifteen minutes blaming the stool. He even threw it out and bought a new one. Or there was the time he took us to the safari park in the car the day after he'd cleaned it. As we drove through the animal enclosure, one monkey ripped off his windscreen wipers as another flung what we hoped was mud across the paintwork.

We had visited the pier on his first anniversary – but we had barely spoken then and, when we got home, I felt worse than I had at the start of the day.

Not that day.

In the same way that final afternoon with Dan, Mark and Pete after we got our results felt like the end of something, the afternoon on the pier was similar. I wasn't forgetting Dad and I wasn't forgetting my friends – but it was time for something new. I didn't know what it would be but being ready was enough in the moment.

Michelle drove the long way around on the way back and we passed the caravan park in which we'd stayed year after year. The gates were open, so she parked in an empty spot and we walked around the lanes together, pointing to our memories. There was the time I'd been running back from the beach and tripped over a tyre that had been left at the side of the path. Michelle delighted in reminding me how much I'd cried – although she was less happy when I said that I'd seen her snogging some lad in the alley at the back of the arcade. Mum told a few stories, nothing we hadn't heard before, but she was able to bring up Dad without descending into a longing silence.

When we got home, Michelle came inside and we had a family meal of beans on fish fingers on toast. We ate off our laps and watched a repeat of *Catchphrase*, remembering the times we'd sat as a family and watched it first time around. There had been *Bullseye*, too – Dad's favourite. That had been our Sunday night for a while.

I ached for those days, though there was a silent relief among us. The second year after Dad's death had been harder than the first – but perhaps the third would be better? Perhaps they all would be from then on?

Michelle and I did the dishes, like the old days when we'd get pocket money at the end of the week for doing our jobs around the house. She had to vacuum, I had bin duty – and we shared washing- and drying-up.

When we were done, Michelle said she had to go and was looking for her bag when I asked if I could have a word. It sounded so much more formal than we were used to with one another. I don't know what came over me in that moment – but I think the elation of Saturday with Amy and then Monday with my family must have been what did it. It felt as if there was a future.

We were standing at the front door, Michelle wriggling an arm into her jacket when I told her that Barry had offered me a job. As soon as I said it, I saw a blankness flash across her. She finished fiddling with her coat and then stood taller. 'You're not working for him,' she said.

'Why? He said if I got five passes, he'd bring me in and train me up.'

'It's not about the passes.'

'So what is it?'

Michelle looked past me towards the wall that separated our hall from the living room. From beyond came the muffled voices of the TV.

'I can't say... but you can't work for him.'

'But it's a job. I can be good at it and he'll look after me.'

'You can't.'

I'd pushed it away and kept it down – but that old fury hadn't quite gone by then. I could feel it nurdling away.

'How come you can pick whatever job you want?' I said.

'It's not about that.'

'So what is it?'

'I can't... You don't want to know.'

We stared at one another and the release of the day had passed. 'If you don't tell me, I'm going to Barry's house tomorrow to say I'm taking the job.'

Michelle let out a long sigh and looked past me towards the wall again. I wonder if I knew already, or at least whether I'd guessed in that hallway.

And then she told me anyway.

'The reason Mum ran away on her first day with Barry is because he tried it on with her. Something about how he'd kept an eye on her the whole time Dad had been alive and that Dad was such a lucky man. But, with Dad gone, he thought there could be something between them. Said he was worth a fair bit and he could make her life as comfortable as she ever wished. He was... he was really pushy.' Michelle finished the sentence breathlessly and then reached for the door. 'You can't tell Mum you know. I promised. That's why we said you wouldn't understand. And maybe you *do* get it – but that's not the point. You shouldn't have to.'

I can't remember much more of what happened in the moments after that. I think I stared for a while. She said I could get whatever job I wanted – but not that one. She'd ask around. Have a word with her boss and see if he'd heard of anything going. Or I could go to college and see what it was like. Perhaps I'd enjoy it, after all? She asked about Amy, and whether I'd told Mum about her, which I hadn't.

Or perhaps none of that happened. It was all a blur of words and rage.

But mainly rage.

Contained rage.

Michelle left but I stayed in the hall, listening to Mum hum along to an advert theme through the wall. I thought about her on that bench at the pier when she'd ran out of Barry's office and got on a bus.

I wondered how long Barry had planned it. He'd been Dad's friend, supposedly – but had he secretly been lusting after Mum the whole time they'd known each other? Was he glad that Dad was dead? How had he decided that two years was long enough before making a move? And in August, of all months. The anniversary.

Then there were Dad's work vans that Barry had painted his own logo over the top. How he called me 'son' and said he wanted to help.

And the night when Michelle slept back at the house because Mum had been kept at the hospital for tests and questions.

Worse than that, worse than everything, I had apologised to him *for her*, even though he'd been the one who should have been saying sorry.

And, as I reran the conversation outside Barry's house, suddenly that rage was no longer contained.

46

ROCK

I was running through the streets, chest pounding, breath short, but I could have sprinted forever that evening. Night was dawning, the street lights almost ready to turn on and I was outside Barry's house. I was standing on the precise spot where I'd said sorry to him for Mum disappearing. He'd listened, accepted it, called me 'son' – and all the while he'd known what he'd done.

There was a gate that blocked his drive, though it wasn't locked with anything other than a simple bolt. The cold mechanism chilled as I clanked it out of the clasp and wrenched it open. The gate swung outwards and I shoved it hard, sending it clanging into the brick post.

Then I was on Barry's drive looking at his sparkling maroon Bentley, knowing how much he loved it – and precisely what I was going to do. I ran the few steps towards it, jumped, and aimed a kick at the wing mirror. I almost pulled out at the last second, half-expecting to bounce off – but it wasn't me that bounced. The wing mirror clattered to the ground and splinters of mirrored glass shattered across the tiled brickwork.

Still the blood thundered through me.

I picked up the shattered casing of the mirror and hurled it towards the house, screaming Barry's name as it hit the front window.

I aimed a kick at the double headlights and another at the fancy silver grille on the front, though neither did any damage to anything other than my toes.

Barry's house was too fancy for his own good, though. Along the length of the drive was a rock garden, made up of palm-sized pebbles, carefully arranged around smaller ones to create a series of swirls.

I flicked away some of the smaller stones and grabbed the biggest rock I could see. It was weighty, like a cricket ball – and, though I was no good at cricket, I knew how to throw a ball.

I thought of Mum in the days and weeks after Dad died. When she couldn't even have moments of grief to herself because the whole country had lost their collective minds. The nights she slept on the sofa. The days she didn't move. And, all that time, in the background, supposedly a friend of Dad's, was Barry waiting to pounce.

I've never thrown anything with as much precision and power as I hurled that rock. It went flat and fast through the air, hammering into the middle of Barry's windscreen, where it sent crinkling lines splintering into the corners of the glass.

An alarm started beeping and blaring as the indicator lights flashed on and off – but I wasn't done. I grabbed another rock and hurled it to the same place as the first. This time, the windscreen imploded, spraying shards of glass into the car and across those walnut features of which he was so proud.

Barry was out of the house now and the alarm stopped as we stared across the width of his driveway towards each other.

'What do you think you're doing?'

He was shocked and panicked – and I answered by picking up another rock and lobbing it at the side window of the car. It bounced off and snickered across the driveway back to me, where I picked it up again and hurled it into the front wing. It rebounded a second time, though not before leaving a satisfying, rounded dent.

Barry stormed across towards me, holding his arms wide and putting himself between me and the car as the alarm wailed on and then off.

He was shouting, a mix of confusion and anger. 'What's this all about?'

'I know what you did to Mum.'

Barry kept his arms out as a degree of recognition flickered across his face. We both knew in that moment.

'Look, I don't know what you're heard but—'

He didn't finish the sentence because I'd lunged for another rock. That one clattered into the wing at the back, leaving a matching dimple to the one at the front.

'I'm sure we can—'

BANG!

He ducked out the way of the next rock. It was either his head or the panel of the door – and it was the door that got it.

I kicked a shower of smaller stones in his direction. Some bounced harmlessly off him but others rained on the side of the car with a series of *tick-tick-ticks* as they rebounded of the paintwork.

I had another large rock in my hand as Barry lunged at me. I could see the whites of his eyes, that quivering lip, the blend of fear and fury.

I saw myself. That dread and panic when Dan's mum came into the garage to say that Michelle was going to pick me up. The same when I got home and Mum wasn't there. Worse when George said that something had happened to her.

But on that evening, I finally *knew* what had happened to her.

Barry had.

I stepped back and Barry slipped. He face-planted into his own driveway and craned his neck to look up to me as I stood over him, rock in hand. Blood was flowing out of his nose from where he'd hit the ground.

I screamed at him in a way I'd never screamed at anyone. 'COME ON THEN! COME ON!' and it was like he was begging me not to. My arm was back, fingers clenched around that rock – and maybe I was going to hit him with it. I think I wanted to.

By then, other people were there. Neighbours disturbed by the alarm and the shouting teenager. A man was on the driveway a little behind me, walking sideways like a crab, trying to edge around me without being seen.

'Look, son...'

Barry was talking – and perhaps he'd used that word instinctively, or maybe he knew what it would do to me. We stared into each other's eyes and I was clenching my teeth so hard that stinging shots of pain raced across my jaw.

But I thought of Amy and our last five weeks.

It's not who we are at the beginning, it's who we are at the end.

And I gripped that rock and squeezed it and felt soil caking my palm... and then I tossed the rock into the nearest bush and took a step backwards.

'Is everything all right...?'

The man who'd been creeping around the drive was a few paces away. Compared to the scene of such destruction, he was so polite that I almost laughed.

The anger was slipping, fists unclenched, jaw looser.

'I think you should go.'

It was that man again, the next-door neighbour as it turned out.

I took another step backwards and realised I was crying. Again. Perhaps I had been the entire time? My eyes were raw and my cheeks itched from streaky, drying tears.

'I don't want any trouble,' Barry said. 'If you want to be left alone, I'll leave you alone. All of you.'

I wanted to reply but the tears were too strong, the lump in my throat too big.

And so I turned and ran.

47

TEA

I barely slept that night. Each time it felt as if I might start to drift, a ridge of anger was back and I was on Barry's driveway, ready to slam that rock down into him. I must have drifted off between five and six and it wasn't long until the alarm went off. My palms were sore and, when I looked at them under the brighter lights of the bathroom, there were small red dimples across the middle from where I'd been clenching my fists through the night.

Mum was already up when I got downstairs. She asked if I wanted a cup of tea, as she always used to. In the years before, it had become a joke between us that she'd offer me a tea and I'd say no because I never drank it.

I said yes that morning and she looked to me curiously.

'Are you all right?' she asked. 'You look really tired.'

I shrugged it away and drank that tea – and then a second cup – before eating the toast she'd made.

It felt odd that I'd be going to camp again that day, as if the night before was too serious to put to one side. Except everything was normal. The sun was up, birds were chirping, life was as it had been.

When I got my bike from the back of the house, Mum again asked if I was all right. 'You look quite pale,' she said.

I told her I was fine – and was out the door when I stopped and let myself back in to tell Mum I was going to be late that night.

'What have you got on?' she asked.

'I'm judging a talent show.'

Even I could hear how ridiculous it sounded. She smiled, although there was a degree of bemusement there, perhaps even amusement. 'That doesn't sound like you,' she said – and she would have had a point if she'd said it a month before.

At camp, it was the final day of August and there were definite parallels to the final week of a school term. With the talent workshops from the week before finished, all that was left was for campers to practise their various skills and routines ahead of Wednesday's dress rehearsal and the main talent show on Friday. Some had already checked out and were using the time to play in mini football or badminton tournaments, or to work on various unfinished craft projects.

I refilled the tuck shop stock for the final time and there were no extras put to the side on that occasion. Even Luke's black market was running dry as he turned away one of the counsellors who was after a couple of cigarettes.

'I'm all out,' Luke told him.

I almost asked how much he'd made over the summer but a part of me didn't want to be involved any more than I was.

All through the morning, I thought about reading hour with Amy and whether I'd tell her about the night before at Barry's. I wanted to talk to someone, but she was simultaneously the only person I thought might understand – while also being the one I couldn't bear knowing about that moment of weakness and madness. About the rage I'd been unable to control. It wasn't me – and yet it apparently was.

I was putting out the umbrellas for reading hour when I saw

her for the first proper time that day. She came across and helped me lever one into place.

'See you out back in a bit,' she said. We were so casual around one another by then.

I said I was looking forward to it but she gazed up to me with confused eyes as if I'd said the opposite.

'What happened?' she asked.

There seemed little point in trying to act as if everything was fine. Clearly something in my voice, my way of being, was telling her it wasn't. 'It's complicated,' I said.

'What is?'

'I did something...'

I wondered in the moments after whether she thought I was telling her that because of what was about to happen. As if I was pre-empting it to try to excuse myself.

We turned together, looking across the field towards the staff lounge in the distance. George was walking across towards us, towards me. *Striding.*

Amy took a small step away from me and I felt the heat of her confusion. 'Joe...?'

She went unanswered and it felt as if everybody had stopped to watch. I saw Charlotte not far away, standing next to Sarah, both staring across the grass with interest and intrigue. The boys on the main field were no longer playing football, instead they had turned to watch George.

It was like the eclipse all over again. Everything was silent, everyone focused on the same thing – and still George marched, closer and closer until he was on the girls' field and then a few paces away from me.

Except it wasn't George that everyone was looking at. It wasn't me, either. Not at first. It was the police officers on either side of him.

48

LEATHER

In all the years since, I've never forgotten the confusion and shock on Amy's face. There was more, too. Disappointment, I think – and perhaps that was the worst of the lot. All those talks we had, all the words, the promises – and I broke the one that really mattered. The one that said we were at camp to start anew. That we were the people we chose to be.

I made my choice when I ran through the streets and kicked the wing mirror off Barry's car. When I threw those rocks and smashed his windscreen. When I stood over him, rock in hand, and screamed at him to come on.

When I lost control.

The police officers checked my name and asked if I'd go with them. There was no need to ask why they wanted me. If I'd been older there might have been handcuffs but George walked at my side, one police officer in front, the other behind. The walk across the field towards the staff lounge seemed to go on forever, as if the lounge kept glitching further into the distance. George asked if I was all right and it was one of those things that was simultaneously so kind and yet so misjudged. I'd never been less 'all right'.

There was a police car waiting in the back lane, close to the
directors' quarters and George got into the back seat next to me,
as if it had all been arranged without me knowing. It had, of
course. The officers had spoken to him before coming for me –
and they needed a guardian – but I wasn't thinking of that at the
time.

All I could think of was Amy and that look of crushed
regret. Despite everything Ian had to say about me, Gemma too,
she'd put her trust in me – but I'd turned out to be everything
they feared I was.

I sat silently in the back of that police car as it navigated the
country lanes, down through town and back out the other side.
There was no police station where we lived, so it took another
twenty minutes of narrow hedge-lined roads until we reached
the next big town and the police station.

Everything was a bit of a blur in the immediate aftermath of
arriving. Michelle was waiting for me, features stoic, as she
refused to let me see how she really felt. There was a handover
of sorts as she thanked George for coming. He said something
about getting back to camp and probably wished me well – but
it was hard to take in the words.

I was checked in and asked to confirm the same details of
my name, age and address over and over until Michelle and I
ended up in an interview room. I thought it would be bolted-
down table, rock-hard chairs and blank walls but we were in a
room with sofas and bright colours on the wall.

'You're too young,' Michelle said to me, explaining the
room, although I wanted that bolted-down table, those rock-
hard chairs and the blank walls. I wanted it to be grim and hard.

When the officers returned, they had a cup of tea for
Michelle and she sat sipping it as they ran through what they
knew about the night before. It seemed as if they'd spoken to the
neighbours and Barry himself before coming to camp for me.

They said I threw seven rocks and, although I didn't

remember that many, there wasn't much point in arguing. Even if it wasn't seven, it might as well have been. They asked what had happened and Michelle did some of the explaining, more or less all of it in fact, saying that Barry had tried it on with Mum in the office at his work and that she'd had to tell me because he'd offered me a job.

It was hard to judge what the officers thought of that. I think they probably realised there was more to it than a teenager smashing up someone's car for no reason.

That didn't mean I'd get away with it.

They showed me photos of the damage to Barry's car and it was a lot worse than I remembered. As well as the windscreen, a small triangular window that was part of the door had been smashed and so had the silver grille. There was the shattered mirror and the dents in the bodywork – plus a tyre had been cut somehow.

They asked if I'd threatened to hit him with a rock and I stared back to them blankly. 'If that's what he says,' was all I could manage. 'It feels like I dreamt it.'

The officers asked Michelle to step outside with them and I was left alone in the room, staring at the floor as the three of them talked about me for a few minutes.

I thought of Amy the entire time, wondering how I could possibly explain what had happened. How I could apologise for letting her down.

When the door reopened, Michelle said we could go.

I stared at her blankly for a second or two. 'I thought they'd lock me up,' I said.

'That's not how it works.'

'How *does* it work?'

'They don't know if there will be further action yet. They're going to go back and talk to Barry about everything. If he's intent on pushing his formal statement, then it goes to the CPS to decide. If that happens, you'll probably be charged with some sort of vandalism thing and it'll go to youth court.'

'What then?'

'That's up to the court.' I was still on the sofa and Michelle walked across towards me. I didn't feel strong enough to stand. 'It not might go that far.' She spoke a little more quietly that time, as if saying it out loud might stop it being true.

'Why not?' I asked.

'If it goes to court, your solicitor will tell everyone exactly why you went to Barry's house last night.' She nodded towards the corridor and the rest of the police station beyond. 'That's why they're going back to check with him. If he wants that to be reported, then it's up to him.'

'Oh...'

She put a hand on my shoulder and I stood as she pulled me into her. 'This is why we didn't tell you,' she whispered.

When she let me go, I couldn't look at her. A part of me hated it that she knew me so well. That she'd predicted what would happen, tried to avoid it, and yet it had happened anyway.

'You'll know in a day or two,' she said.

'Will I go to prison?'

She smiled sadly, almost laughed. 'No.'

That wasn't the worst question to ask. 'Will Mum find out?'

Michelle sighed and looked away, towards the corridor. 'Maybe. Things get around town so fast. If you're charged, she'll have to know. We don't have to tell her quite yet, though.'

'What if someone else does?'

A shrug. 'What's she going to do? Ground you? Besides, it was her idea not to tell you about Barry in the first place. She's not going to be surprised.'

My neck felt as if it had a permanent crick because I couldn't stop staring at the ground. The shame was too much.

'You get it from Dad,' she said.

I didn't know what she meant. 'What?'

'Mum tells us all the fun stories about how they met and all that – but he couldn't stand injustice either. There was a girl who used to pick on me at school and Mum kept it from him for months. When he found out, he was round her house, banging on the door, wanting to fight her dad. Then there was another time we were all going over the zebra crossing in town and a car didn't stop. You were in the pram and the driver almost ran over you and Mum. Dad sprinted up the road and caught the guy at the traffic lights. He was trying to drag the guy out of the driver's seat and it took a couple of blokes walking past to pull him away.'

She rubbed her forehead and scratched around her eyes, making her skin red.

'Look, I'm not saying any of that's right – and I'm definitely not saying *you* were. I'm just saying that you're not out there fighting because that's who you are. You just... you and Dad have too much in common.'

It felt like a double blow. Not only were these memories of Dad that I didn't have, things that portrayed him in a way I didn't like, they also didn't say a lot for me. Instead of being able to control myself, I was somehow a tinpot version of somebody else. I didn't want to be able to blame it away on genetics. It felt like a cop-out.

'Perhaps I *should* be charged?' I said.

'Maybe you will – and maybe you deserve it – but it's not up to either of us.'

Michelle motioned towards the door and I followed her out, to where a new officer was waiting. It was a man in a suit, not one of the two who'd interviewed me, and I wondered if he'd overheard everything Michelle and I had said. Whether it mattered.

We were led through a series of corridors, out to the waiting area of the police station, where George was sitting. I thought he'd gone back to camp but he rose from the chair that was too low for him and greeted the suited man with a handshake and a shoulder pat.

'How are the twins?' George asked – and then they were off with tales of sleeping through the night and comparing notes about when children were at the cutest. George said the man's kids should go to camp when they were old enough – and the other man said it was already in their long-term planner. They finished with George telling the man to ask his wife to call Fiona and then there were promises of dinner, drinks, or perhaps both.

The two of them then turned to look at me and I couldn't meet either of their eyes as the man in the suit told me to stay out of trouble.

'He will,' Michelle replied – and then it was only the three of us.

Until then, I'd never quite understood it when people said that things weighed on a person. I knew what Michelle had meant when she spoke about Mum and the rocks and her pills... but I'd never *felt* it until that time with just us three. There was such a crushing heft of disappointment in myself that, if I'd sat, I don't think I'd have been able to stand again.

Somehow it was worse that George was looking to me in that way.

'Thanks for coming,' Michelle said. 'You didn't have to wait.'

'He's part of the family,' George said – and that instantly filled my throat with a rock like the ones I'd thrown at Barry's car. I couldn't speak. 'Do you want me to drop him home?' George asked.

A silence passed between him and my sister and it felt as if more was being said than actually was. As if there was something they understood that I didn't.

'If you don't mind,' Michelle replied.

'Of course not.'

The evening was cool when George and I headed down the steps outside the police station. It wasn't quite night but the best part of the day had gone and clouds coated the sky. I shivered in my T-shirt and shorts and, when George closed the doors to his car, he turned on the heaters.

'Gets cold so quickly this time of year,' he said – and I mumbled an agreement.

The car smelled of leather, of newness and George reversed out of the space, then waved Michelle out of hers, letting her leave the car park first. At the end of the street, she'd gone through a green while we stopped at a red.

Tea time at camp would be close to finishing – and I was going to miss Amy's show. I was going to miss Charlotte's poem. Not that I'd be welcome in any case. I couldn't forget the haunted look on Amy's face as the police took me away. That look of betrayal as she saw I was everything I'd promised her I wasn't.

I couldn't think of anything to say as George drove through those narrow lanes as the sky darkened further. It wasn't quite sunset but there were dark clouds around and a sense that it might rain. It matched how I felt.

George pulled in a little along the street from where I lived and put the handbrake on. He unclipped his seat belt and then twisted to face me.

'Have you enjoyed camp?' he asked.

It wasn't hard to answer. 'More than anything.'

He licked his lips and I knew what was coming before it did. Perhaps I'd always known it would come. 'I went through the tuck shop stock numbers over the weekend...'

It was shame on shame. I wanted to slip through the floor of the car, through the road surface, down and down. I couldn't cope with the disappointed tone.

'I'm sorry.'

I could barely get the two words out. That lump in my throat seemed ever-present and bigger than ever.

'If you'd asked, it would have been fine. I know the twenty-five pounds a week is nothing. If it's any consolation, and there's no reason it should be, the camp makes no money. Everything paid by parents, churches, community groups and the like is fed back into supplies, permits, licences, and the various things we need. Fiona and I take no salary, neither do the other directors. Everyone is there voluntarily, which is why we cover expenses. But if money was a problem for you, you could've said something. We'd have found a way to sort it.'

I couldn't answer at first. He was right – except he wasn't.

'That's easy to say,' I replied. 'If you have money and never have to ask, it's easy to tell someone else that they should.'

Before Dad died, before his business had been sold to Barry, it had always been a struggle. If the electricity meter went down by too much in a day, there'd be a mini inquest into who'd left their light on. When Mum got home from the supermarket, the bags were always full of own-brand goods. We were never poor but the issue of money was always there. Mum and Dad never felt secure, so neither did I. I hated it even more that the only reason we'd stopped worrying about bills was because Dad had died. It never felt fair. It shouldn't have had to be one or the other.

In that moment, in George's car, I didn't know from where it had come but it was out there and I expected anger. I thought I'd be thrown out of the car – but George pressed back into the driver's seat, the leather squeaking under his weight, and he stayed quiet for a few moments.

'Y'know... maybe you're right on that.' There was a long pause but it wasn't awkward. It felt as if he was thinking on what I'd said. 'That had never occurred to me,' he added. 'Even though it's obvious now you've said it. It's *not* always easy to ask.

I've always had money in one way or another. I've never been on the other side.'

We sat for a while longer and the only noise was the creak of the leather as one or both of us shifted in the seats.

'How's your mum?' he asked.

'OK, I think. She's taking her pills. She seems better than she was.'

'That's good, Joe. That's really good. You shouldn't have to deal with everything you've gone through.'

He spoke as if he knew more than I'd ever told him and I wondered if he'd been keeping a closer eye on me through camp than I'd thought.

'Are you going to tell the police about the tuck shop?'

George breathed in. It was less than a second, but I could see myself being arrested a second time. Having to admit to what I'd done to the police, to Michelle, to Mum. To Amy.

'I shouldn't have thought so,' he said. 'We have stock issues every year, if you want to call it that. I thought it was something worth mentioning to you. A lesson for later life, perhaps...?'

There was relief but it still felt as if I didn't deserve the forgiveness.

'I don't think I should come back,' I said, that lump still catching in my throat.

'Because of a few cans of Coke?'

'Because everyone saw the police and...' I tailed off and then added: 'How can I explain that? They'll all think I'm some thug, or criminal, or whatever.'

George laughed very gently at that. A tickled amusement as opposed to anything more. 'Everyone loves a bit of gossip,' he said. 'Something happens every year we've run the camp. Last time, the mother of one child accused the mother of another of having an affair with her husband. That was day one, in the car park, in front of everyone. They were shouting at each other, using words I'm sure you can imagine, pointing fingers. All the while, campers and counsellors watched on until I could inter-vene.' A pause. 'They were secretly *thrilled* of course. It was the highlight of the six weeks. At the dress rehearsal of the talent show, a group of campers had turned it into a mini play. There were these eleven-year-olds wagging fingers at each other and using words they probably shouldn't know. I had to forbid them from doing it at the main show – but I will say it gave the directors and I the biggest laugh of the summer.'

He made his seat squeak once more as he rotated further to face me. 'There's always one thing. Now, admittedly, we're never had an outright *arrest* on site – but it's the dress rehearsal tomorrow and the final talent show on Friday. That's it. Three days. It'd be a shame if you missed it.'

He was right – but I still couldn't quite commit to going back. I didn't know how I could look Amy in the face again.

'Can I ask you something?' I said.

'Of course.'

I thought back to that first night out of camp, when Ian, Amy, Gemma and I had walked down the hill into town and I'd listened to them talk. I'd barely joined in because they spent all their time talking about the hour-to-hour mechanics of looking after a group of children.

'It all seems a bit... *crazy*,' I said.

'What does?'

'You have us looking after kids who are only a bit younger than we are. There's no training in how to look after the campers. All the counsellors just have to make it up as they go along and hope for the best...'

He waited and then: 'Is there a question in there?'

'I suppose... why not have adults doing everything? Wouldn't they know better?'

George laughed gently to himself. 'I think perhaps you're giving us adults a little *too* much credit about knowing what we're doing. But, that said, you're probably right if you're thinking about things only from the perspective of the campers.'

'How do you mean?'

'It's about you, too. About the counsellors. About taking responsibility and learning how to cope when things don't go right. Think about the rainy days when all plans go out the window. We have campers here from all across the area. Some whose parents pay for them to come, some who get funding from churches, or charities. All our counsellors learn how to get on with people from totally different backgrounds to their own. They figure out how to talk to others with different ideas about life. They learn how other people live and think. So you're right that we could have adults do everything – but, if we did, I don't think it would be a place where anyone would want to come.'

I squeaked my way back and forth in the seat and finally unclipped the seat belt. It sounded so simple and obvious when put like that.

'Like you,' George added.

I'd been reaching for the door handle but stopped. 'Huh?'

'You're a different young man than you were six weeks ago, Joe. On your first day, you'd barely talk – or you'd have conversations with your feet. Now look at you. Everyone on site knows who you are, they *value* you.' He took a breath. '*I* value you.'

I'd been close the whole time we'd been sitting together in his car but it was that which finally made me choke. I tried to blink back the tears but they were lapping the corners of my eyes.

'Thank you,' I managed.

'I'll see you tomorrow,' he said.

49

HAIKU

I tried to keep my head down at camp the next day, deliberately cycling along the lane at the back of camp instead of walking my bike across the main field. Luke's legacy was in full effect there, as a couple of counsellors puffed their way through cigarettes alongside Luke himself.

'Blimey, mate,' Luke said when he saw me. 'I thought I was pushing *my* luck. I didn't realise you were so hardcore.'

He sounded impressed at the previous day's events, though I shrugged it away. I wanted to try to have a normal day, though there was little chance of that. Everywhere I went across the morning, I could feel the stares of campers and counsellors alike.

I was busy re-fixing a guy rope for one of the bunks when a boy came up to me and stared. He waited until I turned to take him in.

'Are you on the run?' he asked.

'I'm not on the run,' I replied.

He looked backwards to a small group of boys who had assembled close to the football pitch and then turned back to me.

'We heard you were on the run,' he said.

'I'm really not.'

'But if you *were* on the run, you'd say you *weren't* on the run.'

I glanced past him, towards the boys who were anxiously awaiting the report back and then called out, so they could all hear, 'I'm not on the run!'

The boy who'd come across was unconvinced. 'We heard you are.'

'I can't win in that case. If I say I'm *not* on the run, you think I am. If I say I am, then I'm confirming I am, even though I'm not.'

He stared at me, nose wrinkled, trying to absorb what I'd just said. 'Does that mean you're on the run?'

I rolled my eyes. 'Yeah, I'm on the run.'

The boy turned and cupped his hands to his mouth, shouting so everyone within earshot heard, 'HE'S ON THE RUN!'

There was a cheer from the boys – and then they all raced off towards the football pitches to make sure everyone knew.

Apart from that and the endless stares, the morning happened as it usually did. The mess hall was cleaned, cleared and reset – plus the badminton nets went up and down. The sun was out but had lost its fire of the previous weeks and the breeze that had been cooling in the weeks before was chilled. The end of summer was close in more ways than one.

Lunch passed and I was putting out the umbrellas for reading hour when I sensed Amy. She was standing by the Alcott bunk, leaning in the door frame, watching. I didn't know if I should say sorry to her, or if there was anything to say at all. I should have found her earlier but was scared of what she might say. Scared of seeing the disappointment in her eyes. Or, worse, scared that she wouldn't want to talk to me at all.

After I finished wrestling the umbrella into place, I turned and she had gone.

It was during reading hour itself that I saw her sitting off to the side, in the spot where I'd first started reading to her weeks before. Sarah was sitting with the campers and Amy was by herself, a book open on her lap, as I settled down next to her.

She looked up, perhaps expecting me, and there was a sadness to her smile that I'd never seen when she was looking at me directly.

'I'm really sorry,' I said.

She closed the pages of her book. 'What are you sorry for?'

'Missing your night. Breaking promises.'

'Which promises?'

It felt so hard to say, because the words were more than simply words. They were truth and that was all I had left. 'I promised I was different. That camp had made me different. That *you* had.'

Amy bit her bottom lip and took a breath as she stared into the distance. 'What happened?'

I told her everything. About Mum and how bad things had been in the months since she lost her job. About Barry buying Dad's business and how he'd offered her a job. How she walked out, and why. How he offered me a job and that I'd apologised *for her*, even though I didn't understand what had happened at the time. I told her about his car and the rocks and the police.

It sounded like one big excuse but there was no other way of putting it. It had happened.

Amy listened without interrupting. She barely moved, except to manoeuvre herself away from the creeping shade, into the eroding sun. I couldn't bring myself to watch her as I spoke. The shame, the shame.

'What's happening with the police?' she asked when I was done.

'They said a day or two. Today or tomorrow. I might be

charged and it'll go to court.' I was trying to keep cool, as if I wasn't picturing myself in a dock somewhere.

'What then?'

'I don't know.'

She sighed and so did I. Whatever happened was out of either of our control.

When I risked a glance up, she was still staring into the distance – but I knew something in that moment that I hadn't when I'd woken up. Those final wisps of fury were gone. Talking about it had done that. The same as it had when I'd told Ian, Gemma and Amy about Mum being ill. Talking worked – but I had somehow forgotten. And, this time, it had taken me a day and a half too long to remember.

We sat listening to the stillness of the day, the serenity of what Luke had been right about. That reading hour was the best hour of the day.

And then, it came. Deadpan and quiet. 'I heard you were on the run.'

I laughed, not because I meant to but because it was her.

'Who told you that?'

'Everyone. It's all around camp. I heard you leapt from a moving police van – and some kid over on the boys' side reckons you fought off a policeman with an umbrella.'

It shouldn't be funny, it wasn't, except... it was.

'Both those things are true,' I said.

She snorted – and I didn't deserve it – but it was beautiful. When she finally turned to me, her eyes were wet.

'George tapped on the bunk door last night,' she said. 'He asked for me.'

'Why?'

'I was in my pyjamas but I put on my wellies and we sat by the fire near the lounge. He said I shouldn't be too hard on you. That six weeks is a long time but sometimes it's not.'

My eyes were wet then too. It was a click of the fingers, a

blink, and I was in that supply tent trying to lift the parachute. And yet the same period of time had also been my whole life. It was the impossibility of time travel that both things were true.

I hadn't meant to whisper but it was all I could manage. 'I love you.'

Amy leant forward and rubbed the back of my hand with her fingers. 'I love you, too.'

We sat there for a while, both swallowed by the shade, neither quite able to talk. A second chance I didn't deserve.

'You need to say sorry,' Amy said.

'I really am.'

'Not to me. You were supposed to be watching my girls last night. They *wanted* you there but you weren't. You have to say sorry to them.'

She nodded and I followed the direction towards the bunks, where Sarah and the rest of Alcott were sitting with their books. As soon as I looked up, those who had been watching us glanced down, pretending they hadn't been keeping an eye.

I stood and walked around the umbrellas until I reached Sarah and the girls. When I sat on the floor, they arranged themselves without prompting, so I was in the centre of the circle, with Sarah and Amy taking their own spots.

That was the first time that I realised I knew all their names. I'd never set out to learn them and yet it had happened. I turned to Maisy and said sorry. Then Georgina, Bethany, Enid, Rosa, Harriet, Sophie, Tessa, Charlotte – and lastly Sarah, then Amy.

There was a moment of quiet and then Charlotte spoke. 'Can I read you my haiku?' she asked.

I panicked momentarily and Amy got me out of trouble. 'It's a Japanese poem,' she said. 'Three lines of five, seven and five syllables.' She rubbed at the stain above the logo of her camp T-shirt. 'Never let it be said that Alcott girls are not highbrow.'

Charlotte hadn't moved.

'You can go get it,' Sarah said.

'I know it off by heart.'

'What's it about?' I asked.

Charlotte grinned. 'You.'

'Nobody's ever written a poem about me before.' The me of six weeks before couldn't have conceived of such a thing.

'It's a haiku.'

I laughed at the pretentious confidence. Admired it, really. 'Let's hear it then.'

Charlotte coughed to settle her throat and then spoke so clearly that I can remember every word, every intonation, all these years later.

'Umbrellas and shade: Two souls a summer longing: Their blossoming hearts.'

I wasn't sure what to expect. My idea of poems were things that rhymed, dirty limericks about a woman from Devizes, and it wasn't that. I wasn't even sure Charlotte was finished until she looked sideways to a smiling Amy.

'Do you like it?' Charlotte asked.

'It's the best haiku I've ever heard.'

Amy was sucking in her cheeks and I wasn't sure if it was to stop herself laughing or chastising. It was certainly the truth.

'It's all Charlotte's work,' Amy said – except Charlotte wasn't accepting that.

'You gave me "blossoming",' she said.

Amy bowed her head a fraction, acknowledging the point.

Nobody seemed to know what to say after that – until Tessa broke the silence.

'Are you on the run?' she asked.

Everybody laughed, including me, and it felt as if this was the only thing in which they were interested. The apologies and the poem could be taken or left.

'Yes, I'm on the run.'

There was a collective *oooooh*.

'Did you jump out of a moving police van?'

'Yes, and I landed on my feet. I did a forward roll and then a massive star jump.'

Oooooh.

'Did you fight off two policemen with an umbrella?'

I looked across to Amy, who was shaking her head.

'It was three.'

Oooooh.

'Do you love Amy?'

I waited for her to look up and catch my eye. 'Yes.'

There was no *oooooh* that time, just a few stifled giggles.

'I've got to get back to work,' I said.

I was already standing when Sarah cleared her throat loudly. She was looking to Amy but then turned up to face me. 'We can't let it go there, can we?'

'Absolutely not,' Amy replied.

'What do you mean?' I said.

'You broke a promise to the girls,' Amy said. 'And we can't let that slide without punishment.'

50

NAILS

'I knew it!' Luke said as he looked at my hands. 'I told you they'd paint your nails!'

I held up the newly acquired set of black nails for the somewhat bemused kitchen staff to see and then dropped my hands again.

'It could've been worse,' I said.

'How?' Luke replied.

'At least they painted them black. It could've been red or pink.'

Luke thought on that for a second, before turning back to the kitchen staff. 'I told him they'd try to paint his nails. He didn't believe me!'

Luke was still talking about my nails as we cleared the tables after the early tea. We laid out the rows of chairs and then the campers filed back in and filled the space ahead of the talent show dress rehearsal.

I watched from the back and everything went relatively well. A makeshift magician from Ian's bunk tried to make an egg disappear but it slipped out of his enormous sleeves and dropped on his shoe. Someone in Gemma's bunk was singing a song from *Aladdin* but forgot the words halfway through and ran off stage in tears. There was a boy who did keepy-uppies for so long that George had to usher him off the stage while applauding. He then announced talent slots would be kept to a strict time limit for Friday.

Girls from Milne and Blyton combined to put on a short play about camp, which mainly involved the girl playing George putting on a pompous voice and falling over various things with increasing degrees of slapstick. George had never seemed the clumsy type but that didn't matter as he laughed along. The campers couldn't get enough of it and had barely stopped laughing when it was time for someone from the boys' bunks to do his stand-up routine. The tone was set almost instantly as he gave a punchline about farting. Of his seven or eight jokes, none were funny – but he mentioned the word 'fart' so many times that the wave of campers' laughter could barely be constrained. George called for an intermission and it gave everyone ten minutes for the hysteria to pass.

After the break, Charlotte read her haiku, which got something of a mixed, confused reaction from the campers, though enthusiastic support from the directors. She knew her audience.

Following that, there was another song, someone dancing to Savage Garden, a mini skit about bedtimes – and that was it. George said it was the best year of talent yet and that he couldn't wait for Friday, then everyone spilled out of the mess hall and back to their bunks for the final two days.

Amy hung around by the exit as the campers headed out, waiting for the quiet.

'Did you enjoy your haiku second time around?' she asked.

'I understood it better,' I replied. 'I think it was *our* haiku, not mine.'

'Very observant,' she said and then: 'Love the nails, by the way.'

Three days had become two.

Two days would become one.

And then... I couldn't bring myself to think about it.

51

LOVE

I was about to leave for camp the next morning when Michelle pulled up outside the house. I opened the front door but she waved me across to her car, rather than coming inside.

'Get in,' she said as she reached across to unlock the passenger door.

'What about my bike?'

'Put it in the back.'

She popped the boot and I lifted my bike inside, then got into the passenger seat. It was another cool morning, the murky grey clouds sitting low and a breezy wind whipping through the wide streets. Except for the rainy days, I was wearing trousers for the first day since I started at camp. My heart was thumping. I was expecting to hear that I was being charged.

Michelle set off, driving slowly through the estate. 'When's your last day?' she asked.

'I'm helping clean up on Saturday.'

She pulled into a gap between cars and flashed her lights to tell the driver coming in the opposite direction that he could have right of way.

'They've said you're not going to be charged,' Michelle said.

'The police?'

'Who else?'

A rock had lifted. 'How'd you know?'

The car passed and the driver flicked his own lights in thanks as Michelle pulled back onto the road. 'It was decided last night but you were out and I wanted to tell you in person.'

She drove to the T-junction and waited, indicator ticking as cars passed ahead of us. It was only after she'd taken the turn that I realised she hadn't answered the question.

'Why didn't *they* tell me?'

'Someone probably will at some point – or you might get a letter. You might get the whole stay-out-of-trouble-thing, so you should probably listen to that.'

'But why do *you* know?'

It was a short journey to camp in the car and Michelle had already taken the turn that would lead up the hill when she glanced up to her mirror, then indicated to pull over. We bumped onto the verge and she left the engine running as she turned to face me.

'I need you to make me a promise,' she said.

'What?'

'That when I tell you, that's the end of it.'

'End of what?'

She shuffled in her seat and then switched off the engine, before unclipping her seat belt. It was so similar to what George had done in his car that goosebumps tingled up my arms.

'Promise first.'

'I don't know what I'm promising.'

'Just say it: "I promise this is the end".'

'End of what?!'

I was almost laughing by that point, though not because I found it funny. I was confused at the mystery.

Michelle continued staring, waiting wordlessly until:

'I promise this is the end.'

The windows were beginning to steam and Michelle wound hers down to create a slim gap across the top.

'I paid Barry for the damage,' she said. 'It's enough to buy the parts he needs and I'm going to do the work for free. I can't panel-beat the bodywork myself but I know someone who can. Barry agreed and that's the end of it. He spoke to the police yesterday and then I talked to them as well. They could have carried on but there wasn't a lot of point if he wasn't willing to go to court.'

It took me a short while to take it all in. 'You... *paid* him?'

'What do you expect? You threw rocks at his car and you kicked off the wing mirror.'

'But—'

'It doesn't matter what *he* did. There was still damage that someone has to pay for.'

'But he—'

'Joe.'

She waited for me to turn to face her. I fought against the seat belt instead of unclipping it because I wanted to fight against something. I could sense that rumble building within me again.

'I know it's not fair,' she said.

'How come he gets away with everything?'

She shrugged weakly. 'Because justice is complicated. Because two wrongs don't make a right.'

'But he gets to carry on as if nothing happened.'

'So do you.'

I turned away and rested my head against the misting window, dampening my hair.

'Joe.'

'What?'

'You're acting as if he's won.'

'He has.'

'Has he? Look at him. He's a sad little man so desperate for attention that he has to try to leech off a grieving woman. The only thing in his life is that stupid car. Is that winning?' She left a gap but I didn't fill it. 'There's justice in that, even if it's hard to see. If you want to win, if you can even call it that, it's not about these little moments here and there. It's about the bigger picture. The longer game. It's about living a good life.'

It was getting to the point where I felt as if tears were never quite that far away – and they were certainly near in her car.

'You're going to leave him alone, aren't you?' Michelle said.

'Yes.'

'Tell me you promise.'

'I promise.'

Michelle started the engine again and clipped her seat belt back into place. There was a moment in which it felt as if she wanted to add something but, in the end, she reached for the handbrake and guided us away from the verge. When we got to the camp gates, she waited for me to get my bike from the boot and then called me around to her side, where she had wound down the window.

'How did Amy take it?' she asked.

'OK, I think.' I held up my nails for her to see. 'Punishment from her bunk for missing their show on Tuesday.'

'I thought you might be turning goth.'

'Maybe after camp.'

She turned back towards the front of the car but I reached inside and put my hand on top of hers. That day was the first time in my life that I properly looked at my sister. We had lived together for a long time, we'd grown up together, but I don't think I'd ever really seen her until that moment.

'Thank you,' I said.

'I hope you remember this if I'm ever in trouble with the police.'

'*When* you're in trouble with the police,' I replied, hoping she'd laugh.

She didn't and I watched her do a three-point turn and there was a moment when it looked as if her back wheel might stick in the mud. The wheel span and spat, then gripped as the car lurched forward. Then she was gone.

Camp was busy that day, with lots of final, final practices and refinement to dance and song routines happening on every spare patch of grass. I heard the Savage Garden song so many times that I caught myself humming it in the staff lounge and had to assure Luke more than once that I wasn't secretly into that sort of thing.

That final-week-of-term feel persisted, with campers signing each other's clothes and workbooks. Dan, Mark, Pete and I had burned our old school shirts with half a can of lighter fluid. It had gone up so fast that we feared it would set fire to the tree in Mark's garden. We ended up filling a washing-up bowl with water to put it out.

It had happened weeks before but felt like a lifetime.

I drifted around camp, doing the small jobs that needed doing. According to George, anything major that needed fixing wasn't worth doing – so Luke and I ended up writing a lot of things into a logbook, rather than actually doing them. I cleared some more paper jams and sorted the mail for almost the final time.

I spent some time with Ian and the boys from his bunk, many of whom still seemed to believe I was some sort of fugitive. I taught a couple of them how to tie different types of knot, which was a skill I hadn't had myself six weeks before – one I'd learned from Luke.

After that, I helped a girl from Gemma's bunk, who was struggling to pack everything into her bag. I showed her the roll not fold technique that Dad had taught me back when we'd been making those trips to the seaside.

Then there was my time with Amy, though not only her. I spent time with Sarah and the rest of the Alcott crew. They had realised that Charlotte and Alcott more or less rhymed, so were trying to put together a chant for that, even though it was at least a month too late.

It's strange but that afternoon with Amy and her girls was how I remember her best from that summer. It wasn't being in bed with her, or in a field, or at a party, or those sofas in the Night And Day. It wasn't holding hands, or kissing. It was simply being around her. Being in her orbit. And I wondered years later if that's what love actually is. To appreciate the simplicity of being around someone.

The day was gone in a blink. One more down, one proper to go and then one to tidy up. We didn't know what came after that. We'd avoided talking about it.

I sat with the Alcott girls at tea that day and I wondered why I hadn't done it weeks before. I think I'd been worried about embarrassing Amy, or perhaps being too public and making the directors think that she wasn't concentrating. Except none of that was true. It wasn't about me and her, it was about us and those girls.

I stole a scone from Tessa's plate and put it on Sarah's when neither were looking, then pretended I knew nothing about it. Enid grinned at me and said nothing. Our little secret. I filled Amy's glass all the way to the top with water, so that it couldn't be moved without spilling. Then, when she spilled it in my lap and told the girls I'd wet myself, I had to admit that I'd been defeated by the more devious mind.

When I got home that night, Mum wasn't in the living room and she wasn't upstairs. I figured she had gone for a walk around the neighbourhood and was upstairs in my room when I saw her sitting in the garden, on a deckchair, with a blanket tucked under her chin.

I headed outside and the sun had gone, leaving a greeny-yellow haze around the horizon and a crisp chill on the air.

'What are you doing?' I asked.

'Just watching.'

I followed her stare up towards the sky, where white dots were starting to blink. She took my hand, her fingers icy, and she gripped mine, pulling it under the blanket to the warmth.

'I think it might be all right,' she said.

I crouched next to her, knowing that 'might' was a big word in that sentence. Except, in the moment I chose to believe her.

'I think it might be all right, too,' I replied.

52

HEADLIGHT

The final Friday of camp was busy but it wasn't. Campers were already packed, with their bags and suitcases waiting at the front of their bunks ready to be shuttled into their parents' cars after the talent show. The sky was grey all day and rain felt ever near, even though it never quite arrived.

The previous day had felt like the final day of term but that *actual* final day was far more meandering and mournful. There were nerves about the talent show, coupled with despondent realisation that the end had actually arrived. There was crying from campers and counsellors; numbers and addresses swapped, promises to keep in contact that everybody knew would never be kept.

George was in the office fighting with the photocopier when I offered him back his key. He seemed surprised, as if he'd forgotten about it, even though that was unlikely.

'Did you get good use of it?' he asked – and it was a week later when I realised what an odd question it was. I can't even remember how I replied, although it was probably a nervy 'yes'.

He waited as I fixed that final paper jam and then I waited as his pages spewed out.

'You're more than welcome to come back next year,' he said. 'Counsellors can always do two years, so it's up to you.'

'We'll see.'

It was what Mum used to say all the time when I asked for something she had no intention of giving. A way of saying 'no' without actually doing it. I think I knew that I would be doing something else the following year, even if I didn't know what.

George knew, too. 'If you need a reference for college, or a job, or anything else, give them my name.' He reached across to the desk and picked up a business card, then turned it over and scribbled on the back. 'That's my mobile number. If you ever need me, make sure you call.'

I remember thinking that mobile phones would never take off. Shows what I knew. 'Thank you,' I said.

The photocopier had finished humming and I had taken a few steps away when he called me back.

'There's one other thing,' George said. 'We're bringing in the lending library from next year. Actually, *this* year. We've told the campers they can leave any books they no longer want and that we'll store everything for next year's intake. We're hoping passing books from one year to the next will be a bit of a tradition.'

He waited and, when I didn't say anything, he added: 'I heard it might have been your idea...?'

'Something like that.'

I wondered how much George really knew about what happened around camp. Whether Luke's black market was as black as he thought and whether the tuck shop stock manipulation was something he'd known about and accepted forever. It felt as if very little got past George unless he was happy to let it go.

'It's one of the best suggestions we've ever had,' he said. 'And I wanted to say "thank you" to you personally. So... thank you.'

He stretched out his hand and I shook it – and then it was back to work. Cars arrived and Luke and I helped campers and parents carry their luggage across to boots and back seats. There were more tears and hugs and then it was the talent show – except, this time, the mess hall was heaving with parents and brothers and sisters.

I was standing at the back, in my usual spot – but it was genuinely standing room only as George thanked everyone for coming. I scanned the room, spotting Amy sitting proudly with her girls – but it wasn't only her I saw. Somehow, Owen and the rest of Ian's friends had got themselves in – and they were busy clapping and cheering as loudly as anyone.

The show was everything it had been at the dress rehearsal but it was sharper and better, with a more balanced running order. Nobody forgot their words and Ian's lad didn't drop his egg. The campers still roared at the fart jokes they'd heard over and over – and even I laughed because of the bemused reaction of the parents, wondering if their children had spent six weeks learning fart jokes. The dancers worked in unison and cameras flashed to capture the moment. There were more tears and hugs and cheer after cheer.

Then it was Charlotte's turn and she got on stage to read her haiku. I listened properly that time – and I still wasn't completely sure what a haiku was but it was perfect and beautiful.

Umbrellas and shade
Two souls a summer longing
Their blossoming hearts

It lasted seconds and got another somewhat bemused response, though none of that mattered because Charlotte hadn't written it for anybody else. She pointed to a sobbing Amy, who touched a single finger to her heart and bowed her head.

On and on and then it was that final Savage Garden song –

which Truly, Madly And Deeply got into everybody's head, not just mine.

Then it was the end.

The real end.

I was looking around for Amy but it wasn't her I spotted. The flap of the mess hall had been left open because it was so hot with all the people – and on their way outside, darting across the field towards the car park, was Charlotte's mum dragging her daughter behind.

'Amy!'

She somehow heard me over the clamouring, building din and we dashed around the burgeoning crowd, through the flap, out into the cold.

'What?' she called.

'Charlotte.'

Even from the furthest side of the field, I could see Charlotte crying as her mum bundled her into the passenger seat of their Range Rover. I didn't think in that moment, I just ran. The ground was soggy by then, the weeks of use leaving the grass bare and the dewy mornings leaving it wet. My trainers slurped across the surface but I wasn't about to fail.

Charlotte's mum was halfway out of the parking space when I jumped in front of her car. She slammed on the brakes, the top of the mini tank coming up to my chest as the headlights blazed around me into the distance.

'What are you doing?' she mouthed, barely visible through the glass.

When I didn't reply or move, she buzzed her window down and craned her head out. 'What are you doing? Leo's back from Switzerland in the morning and I need to get home.'

It was more anger than confusion by that point – but my work was done. Charlotte's mum twisted with confusion as the door across from her opened. Charlotte wasn't bothering to wait as she unclipped her seat belt and allowed Amy to help her out onto the sodden grass.

Tears poured down their faces as Amy knelt in the dirt and wrapped her arms around the smaller girl.

'You've got my address safe, haven't you?' Amy asked.

'Yes.'

'I've got yours and I promise I'll write.'

A lot of promises had been made in the previous couple of days but, as I watched them squeeze one another, I felt sure this one would be kept.

I stepped away from the front and Amy helped Charlotte back up into the car before rounding the vehicle and standing at my side. There was too much glare from the windows to know for sure but, as Charlotte's mum pulled away, I felt sure I'd seen Charlotte waving at us.

As we headed back across the main field, campers, counsellors and parents continued to pour out of the mess hall and head towards the car park. George was in the centre of everything, handshaking, cheek-kissing and wishing everyone well.

Amy and I disappeared through the staff lounge, out and around to our spot under the tree. The ground was bare and wet but there was a blanket sitting there, waiting for us.

'I planned ahead,' Amy said.

We sat together, pressed close, clinging for warmth but comfort as well.

'One more day,' Amy said.

'One more day.'

53

END

The final, final day was different again. All the campers had gone and almost all the counsellors. Luke was there and so was Ian and Gemma – and we had breakfast with George, Fiona and the handful of remaining counsellors. The kitchen was closed, so George picked up a McDonald's feast and we ate the terrible food and drank the coffee and juice.

The sun had returned warm and strong, one final flourish as we helped lower the tents and clear the remaining rubbish. When that was done, there were more people with whom to say our goodbyes. More promises to write and offers to come and stay. It was well-intentioned but everyone knew the truth, that those letters would never be written and no one would be coming to stay. Some would be back the following year but, for many, it was the end. The real end.

We all met Sarah's parents for the first time and they were as wonderful and funny as she was. Amy was in tears once more as they said goodbye to one another. 'Best friends,' they said – and when Sarah's dad said it was time to go, they slowly released one another.

'See you soon,' Sarah said – and maybe they would but maybe they wouldn't.

Then it was the four of us. Ian, Gem, Amy and me in the Night And Day, drinking that horribly wonderful blue stuff for one more Saturday night. Poems were read, people were cheered, tables were banged. The band came on and we danced and laughed. I even managed to move my feet a bit without standing on everyone else's toes.

Amy was staying at Gem's house that night, before being picked up the next day – but they said goodbye and then Ian, Gem and Ian's friends headed up the hill to adventure beyond.

'It's not the end,' was the last thing Gem said to me – and maybe it wasn't.

And then the summer was done.

The dark had dawned and the cold had arrived. It was only Amy and me on the bank overlooking the canal, with a blanket borrowed from the café.

I hadn't forgotten, and neither had she, because under the light of the moon, I read her that final chapter of *Little Women*. The first book I'd voluntarily finished myself in years. That 'A' in English didn't make sense and yet, as I got to the end, maybe it did.

Amy listened, her eyes closed, and when I was done, we lay there, holding hands, wrapped in the blanket.

'I love you,' I said.

'I love you, too,' she replied.

'Forever,' I said.

'Forever.'

54

TIME

Town was the same but different. All the buildings were in all the same places but there were new signs and faces I didn't know. It had been twenty-one years since I spent that summer at Camp Sycamore and a day hadn't passed when I hadn't thought about something from those six weeks.

On that bank, Amy and I had promised we'd love each other forever, that we'd give it a go – and we did. She lived two counties away and we caught buses and trains to see each other. Michelle sometimes gave me lifts at weekends and Amy's parents would drop her somewhere for the day if it meant she was off their hands.

We met in the middle a lot, which ended up being the resort where Mum and Dad met, although that's probably why it never quite felt like *our* place. It felt like theirs. We liked being back in this town, with the Night And Day and the gorge. With our memories.

Her parents let me stay over sometimes – and she met Mum and had a few nights at ours. They were nervous hours, with Mum on the other side of that too-thin wall.

And we did try, we really did, but when Amy started

college properly, I think we both knew. It just took us a while to accept. Not only did we live two counties apart – but her college was almost an hour further from that. We thought we'd see each other at weekends but she had college work and I was doing various jobs around town. I did a few months at a garden centre but they needed me to do Sundays. Then I had a few months more at a place that installed fireplaces. It was money. It was work.

Amy and I had our moments.

We spent her birthday together, which meant Christmas as well. She was given the money for driving lessons from her parents and a thin white-gold necklace from me. It was all I could afford and she said it was too much. That my money should be mine.

We saw in the new year together, the new millennium in fact. There were fireworks in a field near her parents' house – but those highs became the exception.

She'd get stuck at college, miss a bus, and then we'd miss each other completely. She failed her driving test and I failed mine and I'd be stuck, fighting away the anger at our missed hours because she had college but all I had was her. Then we'd finally have time together but it was hard to live in those moments and forget the ones we'd missed.

Not long after those fireworks and the new millennium, that was it. She cried. I cried – and they weren't fun tears any longer. We had one final weekend and it was over. Mobile phones were just coming in and we swapped numbers and traded a few texts. Sometimes we replied to each other, some-times we didn't.

A while later, I heard she went to New York to study at university – and I wanted to get in contact to say how happy I was for her. And maybe I was... but I didn't call, text or email – and neither did she.

Meanwhile, I drifted from job to job. I ran into Mark a few

times and we pretended the old days were still with us. Dan and Pete both went to university and we had one Christmas with the four of us poring over the imagined glory days. We even revisited Dan's garage, by then filled with old furniture from his parents' renovation. It was almost too full to move – but we had one final game of darts, which Mark won.

As for Michelle, she'd been seeing Connor for six months when I first met him. She hadn't wanted to upset Mum too much by making it seem like she was moving on from us, though, in the end, that wasn't a problem.

Mum kept taking her pills and then she applied for a job doing the books for a lighting company in town. She had never used her qualifications but she did such a good job with those accounts that she ended up doing more as a full-time freelancer.

Michelle and Connor got married and moved to a place in Dorset – and I was best man for him, even though we didn't really know each other and it was more best man for her.

I stayed in town and went through the motions. I had a couple of girlfriends as I turned twenty and twenty-one but I'd been spoiled too young and nothing ever quite worked.

It was me, not them.

And then, one day, I was visiting Dan in his poky London flat. Dan was doing a late shift in the restaurant where he worked and I was at a pub around the corner, feeding pound coins I couldn't afford into a quiz machine that was too smart for me.

As I want to press the wrong answer, someone else's finger got to the correct one first.

'You'll never know more about Eurovision than me,' Ian said. He was leaner and taller. A stunning picture of self-assurance and confidence. He'd shaved his head and had his spare arm looped into his boyfriend's jeans pocket.

Unbelievably, in the same bar, at the same moment, miles from where we grew up, we were in the same space.

Ian turned to his boyfriend and nodded at me. 'This is Joe. He used to bully me at school.'

It was hard to describe the look that spread across his boyfriend's face. Definite horror but it felt as if he knew who I was. As if they'd talked about me.

We ended up sitting in a corner of that bar, music blaring around us, glasses clinking, and we shouted to one another about our lives. So we headed outside, onto the street, and found a table where it was quieter – and we didn't talk about the now. We talked about the then. About camp and Gemma and the Night And Day and the talent show.

'And the police! Oh, God, you were on the run. I forgot you were on the run!'

Ian's boyfriend seemed even more confused by that – but I told him I wasn't on the run, though Ian told me never to repeat that because it was much funnier to think I was.

'And I escaped from a moving police van,' I said. 'I did three forward rolls and then a star jump.'

Ian howled with drunken laughter.

His boyfriend, Antonio – although I later found out it was really 'Anthony' – was wonderful and kind. He'd stroke Ian's hand for minutes at a time and they'd rest their heads on each other's shoulders and gently touch one another's faces.

Because I couldn't stop myself, I said sorry again for everything that happened. I didn't try to justify it with saying it wasn't me – but Ian said it was forgiven, not forgotten, which was as good as it was ever going to be. The opposite of how my friends and I used to be. Then Antonio called him an old grump and a drama queen. They laughed but I couldn't quite join in.

But Ian wasn't done. 'My god! You and Amy! What happened?! I heard she's married! To an American! Some sort of whirlwind thing!' He looked to his boyfriend then back to me. 'No offence but she probably did it for the money. I hope it's for the money. God! I'd love to marry for money.'

Antonio slapped his hands gently and chidingly.

'Don't *you* start,' Ian added. '*We'd* still be together. I'd be *marrying* for the money.'

But it hit so hard that it was like Charlotte's mum had simply ploughed into me with her Range Rover all those years before. I hadn't heard anything more about Amy, other than that she'd gone to New York. And then... she was married.

Ian must have seen it in me because he changed the subject. Someone we went to school with was living in Thailand. 'Dirty sod,' Ian said, before quickly adding: 'I'd love to live in Thailand. Let's move to Thailand and marry for money.'

We were drinking but it was no longer that horrible blue stuff. Antonio ordered me an Old Fashioned – my request – and I was six deep before I realised how much alcohol was in me. I texted Dan to say I was safe – and then Ian and Antonio dragged me back to theirs, where I spent a large part of the night puking in their toilet.

They found it hilarious.

I stayed the night with them... and then another. And another. And, before I knew it, we were housemates. They needed someone to share the bills and rent – not to mention Ian's filthy humour – and it was like the decision had been taken.

I'd finally left home.

I got a job behind a bar a couple of tube stops away and thought about finally going to college, mainly because Ian and Antonio seemed so keen for me to do so. I even tried it for a few weeks but I was too much older than the others and I never quite had the head for academia, despite that solitary A in English.

I did accidentally start a data management company with a younger classmate I met in that month. It was one of those things I could just do – and we borrowed some money and did OK. We bid for a council contract which we didn't get – but the person handling the bids had a friend who needed a company like ours – and we were up and running.

Ian and Antonio got a civil partnership because they were finally allowed – and I was somehow best man again. I had more precise instructions second time around. 'Be funny at the evening do,' Ian told me. 'Make everyone laugh.'

So I told the story of camp and rigging an election against Ian's candidate – and, even though it wasn't completely about him nobody seemed to notice or care. Least of all Ian, who stood on the table and demanded a recount. He bellowed that he was going to report me to the Electoral Commission, which must have been the only time that government body had been brought up at an evening do.

We ended up living twenty minutes from each other and, if anything, I was better friends with Antonio than I was Ian. We certainly saw more of each other. We did pub quizzes every Thursday, the three of us plus my business partner, because he was the only one young enough to know about music after the year 2000.

Somehow, 2000 was 2010 and then 2020.

The world got madder and madder than any of us could have imagined. We locked down and did Zoom quizzes, where nobody really cared who won.

And then, when it was over but not, when we could see each other again but not, there was a time when my phone buzzed with a message from Ian.

Have you heard?!!!!!!!!

I hadn't even typed a message back when he called – which is when I knew it was serious. Ian never made phone calls. He delighted in all the missed calls his phone counted.

'What happened?' I asked.

'It's George,' Ian replied.

I had met other people with that name since camp, men and women – but there was only ever one George.

He was a statistic of 2020. A number among thousands – except he wasn't, not to us. Not to our town. We couldn't go to the funeral because there were only thirty people allowed – but he was so loved, so special, that no amount of restrictions could stop people lining the streets.

And that's why town was the same but different. People in black lined up and down the high street, metres between us all, masks over our faces.

Antonio had never met George but he cried his eyes out as he and Ian tried to console each other.

The hearse eased slowly, slower, slower again along the street, almost stopping. People didn't know whether to clap, or cheer, or cry. George ran Camp Sycamore for almost thirty years. Generations of children had spent their formative years with him and so many of us returned home to say goodbye.

We left but he never did.

Michelle and Connor were there – and so was Mum with her second husband. We hugged because we could and because we hadn't in such a long while.

The hearse continued, through to the end of the high street and off to George's final resting place. Someone said they were going to name a road after him in the town – but I wasn't listening. Not properly.

Because over the street, she was there.

She was in black, a purple mask covering nose and mouth – but the eyes hadn't changed. I had stared into them for so long that I'd know them anywhere.

She didn't see me at first, she was watching the back of the hearse, but then she blinked around – and suddenly, among all those hundreds of people, it was only us.

Amy and me.

55

AMY

People were heading back to their houses or back to the pubs to sit in their bubbles and safe sixes. I don't think anyone quite knew the rules in those moments. Ian and Antonio were off for a drink, while Mum, her husband, Michelle and Connor were going back to her house.

But Amy and I had nowhere in particular to be that day. We walked away from the high street, up towards the shuttered Night And Day and ducked through the fence to end up on the bank overlooking the canal. The water flowed below us as the sun shone. We each took off our masks and sat a few paces apart.

She looked a little like her mum – though not too much. Her cheeks were softer, eyes kinder. Her hair was as black as her clothes, though still long. There was a lot of my Amy within her.

For those first few minutes, all we did was look at one another. Those few months together versus the twenty years apart.

'Did you hear about Charlotte?' she asked – and it was impossible to miss the crack in her voice.

I knew the name, of course, but it still took a few seconds for the context to arrive. 'What happened?'

'She's at the RSC in Stratford,' Amy added. 'Has been for about five years now. They're supposed to be doing something for the BBC but everything's on hold because...' She tailed off and held her hands up. So many lives had been paused.

'Did you stay in contact?' I asked.

She nodded slightly. Held up her phone. 'We message more or less every day.'

I pictured those two sobbing girls next to the Range Rover in that sodden car park. It was a world away and yet it was right where we were.

'I heard you got married,' I said.

A nod. 'Victor. I met him in New York. We graduated and did this off-Broadway thing and...' She sighed long and loud. 'Just one of those things. It felt right at the time and then, after, you're never quite sure why you did it.'

We looked down to the canal together, where the water crept along.

'We divorced after a couple of years,' she said. 'But we were only together about nine months.' She waited. 'Me not him.' A pause and then: 'You?'

I shook my head. 'I never got married.'

'Girlfriends?'

'On and off. Not recently.'

Amy stood and offered her hand to me. 'Shall we go?'

'Where?'

She grinned and it sent me spinning through time again, back to that supply tent, with the parachute and the girl who changed my life.

'Where do you think?'

There was mischief in her voice. I had no idea if we were supposed to be touching but neither of us cared. We held hands and we walked through the town as if two decades had never passed. We talked about our parents and my sister. About Gemma – who had done a few years on cruise ships and was living in New Zealand with a guy she'd met. About Sarah, who was a teacher on the Isle of Wight. Amy had kept in contact with them all.

'I heard you live near Ian,' she said.

'We lived together for a while – me, him and his boyfriend.'

Amy didn't reply at first but then there was a gentle: 'I know.'

I'd never been one for Facebook or anything like that but I wondered how much else she knew.

And then we were at the camp gates and there was a big banner across the Camp Sycamore sign, saying they'd be back in 2021. A wide blanket of flowers was on the verge, along with a series of small cards that had gone soggy from the rain.

The gate was locked but I helped Amy up and over. I remembered Ian telling me he'd spent fifteen minutes trying to get my bike over the top, then Gemma bickering back to say it had been open. It was the first time I'd thought about that since it happened.

Amy and I walked across the field, where the ghosts of bunks and lounges and quarters hung invisibly in the air. I could picture the guy ropes that once had to be avoided. The football pitch and the badminton courts. The umbrellas and the space where once everyone had stopped for an hour to read.

We passed through the back of the field and around the hedge, following the line until we were at our tree once again. It was still there, though the roots had bulged through the ground in the years since we'd last used it for shelter. The grass was up to our waists and we trampled a small circle before sitting cross-legged a step apart from each other.

I winced as I went down. 'Too old for sitting on the floor,' I said.

She laughed. 'We can go somewhere else...?'

'I like it here.'

Amy reached across and tugged on a strand of my hair that was curling in front of my ear.

'I guess I never forgot that you liked it longer,' I said.

'You've had long hair for twenty years because a sixteen-year-old said she liked it?'

'It does sound a bit silly when you put it like that.'

Her lips crinkled upwards. 'I *still* like it.

We looked into each other's eyes and I could see all those memories in hers, as I was sure she could see the same in mine.

'I think you saved me,' I said and, from nowhere, my throat was tight.

'When?'

'Here.' A croak. 'When we were kids. If you hadn't walked into the supply tent that day, I don't know where I'd have ended up. I don't know *who* I would have been.'

'You'd have still been you?'

I shook my head. 'You changed me. You made me better. Ian, too – and Michelle. I don't think I'd have coped with the anger otherwise. It was too much.'

'I didn't do a lot.'

'You taught me that it was good to talk about things. About myself. I learned how to listen.'

Amy inclined her head a little. So many years on, and she was still that person I could speak to.

'You did the same for me,' she said, quieter.

I wasn't sure I'd heard her at first. 'No I didn't.'

'That's what you never realised. Mum and Dad couldn't really stand each other – but the last thing they wanted was me in the way. They sent me to something new every summer and I'd have been at boarding school if they had the money. That summer, with you, I think...'

She tailed off and squeezed my hand like she used to.

'I think I started to value myself. You were so happy to see me – and I'd never had that before.'

We sat for a while, listening to the whispers of the wind and the spectres of our summer.

'I know it didn't work with us,' she said, 'but I'd have never passed college if it wasn't for the way I managed to feel about myself. Wouldn't have gone to university. To New York by myself. I got married because I was trying to find someone who looked at me the way you used to.'

I couldn't speak. The lump that barely left my throat the last time I'd been on the campsite was suddenly there again. Bigger now.

'Did you keep your promise?' she whispered.

'Which one?'

'About loving each other forever?'

She broke me in that moment.

So many people had made so many promises in those final few days and nobody expected them to be kept. It was the same dance Amy had played when feeding Charlotte's mum information about what her daughter had done at camp. The same dance George had played when he'd told Amy's mother about how valued she was. Those little lies covering up the bigger ones we concealed by making promises that would never be kept.

Except there was a promise I'd never broken. I took her hand and our fingers wrapped into one another's as if those years had never passed.

'Umbrellas and shade,' I whispered.

'Two souls a summer longing,' she said.

'Their blossoming hearts.'

AUTHOR'S NOTE

Writing this has been the most extraordinary experience of my life. On 4 November 2020, I turned 40. Where I live, this happened during the most severe pandemic restrictions of the year. I was lucky enough to spend the day with my wife and our dog and, though it wasn't how I imagined that particular day, it was with those I care most about.

Although the world had been dealing with the pandemic through 2020, the year wasn't only about that for me. I suffered a head injury in March, which left me with a serious concussion. I couldn't work, couldn't write, sometimes couldn't think properly. I did close to nothing for eight months.

On 6 November, I went to bed as usual. Nothing strange. Nothing weird. I woke up about seven hours later and my head was full of everything you've just read.

Sometimes books come in bursts. An author might have a hook for a beginning, or a twist for the end, that sort of thing – but the other parts figure themselves out through the writing process.

With this, I woke up and knew everything. There's not a

character or side-plot in the story that wasn't already in my head on that morning.

A part of that might be because I went to a similar(ish) camp to this in 1992, when I was eleven. It was roughly the time of the Barcelona Olympics and I remember cross-stitching the Olympic rings. I also worked at a different camp in 1999 – the year this is mainly set – and experienced some of the same things as Joe. Not all. This isn't an autobiography. I'll let you guess what's real and what's invented, or exaggerated. I promise, if you think anything sounds unlikely in the story, those are almost certainly the things that actually happened to me.

When I finished writing this, I was left with the oddest sense of melancholy. Sometimes, when finishing writing a book, it is cleansing to clear characters from your mind. Very occasionally, like this, you're bereft.

The moment I wrote those final lines, I started to miss Joe and Amy. I didn't really want them to leave my head. The day after I finished writing, when I woke up, they were the first people I thought of. It's hard to guess what readers will think of something you've created but, if Joe and Amy have meant anything to you while reading, then know they mean something to me as well.

Thank you for reading,

Kerry Wilkinson

PS: If you are not from the UK, I realise these tales of underage drinking might seem like something that would never happen. But, um, I don't know how to break this to you… I doubt there's a single British teenager who hasn't experienced at least some of the stuff in this book. Of all the things that *did* happen to me which are included in these pages, going to the pub after getting our exam results is one of them.

KERRY WILKINSON PUBLISHING TEAM

Editorial
Ellen Gleeson

Line edits and copyeditor
Jade Craddock

Proofreader
Loma Halden

Production
Alexandra Holmes
Natalie Edwards

Design
Leah Jacobs-Gordon

Marketing
Alex Crow
Melanie Price
Occy Carr
Ciara Rosney

Publicity
Noelle Holten
Kim Nash
Sarah Hardy
Jess Readett

Distribution
Chris Lucraft
Marina Valles

Audio
Alba Proko
Nina Winters
Joe Jameson
Carmelite Studios

Rights and contracts
Peta Nightingale
Richard King
Saidah Graham

Printed in Great Britain
by Amazon

35448191R00199